GHOST
MOON
NIGHT

GHOST MOON NIGHT

To the Nelsons,
Be brave!
:) Jewel

JEWEL ALLEN

Editor: Jonene Ficklin
Cover Design: Mikey Brooks
Formatting: E.M. Tippetts Book Designs
Back cover blurb: Julie Bellon

Tricycle and water buffalo photo credit: Jewel Allen

Jewel Allen
Visit my website: www.JewelAllen.com

First Printing: October 2014
Treasured Stories

ISBN - 978-0-9908479-0-8
10 9 8 7 6 5 4 3 2 1

To my parents, Carmelo & Celestina Punzalan,
for my wonder-filled Philippine childhood
&
my daughter Sierra, for believing.

PHILIPPINE TRICYCLE

WATER BUFFALO, OR CARABAO

PROLOGUE

Ghost Moon Night, 1881

THE BOY WAITED on the steps of a hut, slapping lazily at mosquitoes. His water buffalo, tethered by its nose ring to a coconut tree trunk, made a rhythmic swishing noise with its tail. The warm evening breeze smelled of the sea and of salted fish hung to dry.

Inside the hut, the voices of grown-ups were animated, punctuated by a booming laugh. Sometimes they broke out in song, accompanied by the boy's father on the guitar.

There was no moon. Ghost Moon Night, they called it. Beyond the lamplight spilling on the ground from the hut's open windows and door, the ocean was the blackest of blacks. The boy couldn't see the water, but he could hear it.

It lapped at the fishing boats that were pulled in for the night. It hissed as it fanned out on the sand. It gurgled as it got sucked back into the depths of the sea.

As the night wore on, the boy fell asleep, leaning against the door's bamboo frame. A scraping noise woke him. He rubbed the sleep from his eyes and squinted.

Scrape. There it was again.

Could it be some sort of animal? He looked long and hard into the darkness, but could see nothing. Getting off the steps, he moved closer to the water.

Fear seized his throat.

Four men crouched beside a boat, putting it out to sea. They appeared to be carrying bundles. The boy thought he heard a chicken squawking. A piglet squealing.

Maybe he should just pretend he couldn't see this. But his father would want to know.

The boy crept up the hut steps, entered the tiny *salas* and faced a roomful of adults. Their brows came together at the intrusion. His father's hand paused mid-strum on his guitar.

"*Piratas,*" the boy said. Pirates.

One of the villagers said the moonless night was so dark, the pirates saw nothing in the open water – not the four boats or the guns turned upon them – until it was too late. A pirate even tried to swim away, but someone caught him in a fishnet like a *tilapia.*

The boy squeezed his way through the crowd lining the main road and joined his father. Villagers tied the pirates' wrists with thick rope and prodded them with bamboo poles. In the torch light, their skin looked oily and had colorful marks on them.

"They're tribal tattoos," the boy's father said. "They don't worship our god, I can tell you that."

"Who do they worship?" someone asked.

"The devil."

The boy shuddered.

The *guardia civil* took the pirates to the jail while the village chief and his councilmen, who included the boy's father, decided their fate in a little thatched-roof hut on stilts over the water.

Just under the back window, the boy eavesdropped.

"This is the fourth time they've sent raiders," one man said. "I think we need to do something more permanent than just lashing them and sending them back out to sea."

"They're stealing only animals now," agreed another. "What if, next time, they steal our women? Or our children?"

The boy imagined an island of devil-worshippers huddled around a bonfire, holding him and his mother captive. He pressed closer to the side of the hut, thinking the night seemed even darker.

"There will be no next time," the chief said.

There was silence, then the boy's father said, "What? Shall we execute them?"

"We won't *exactly* execute them," came the chief's reply. "We'll just leave them to drown."

The boy's heart pounded. What had he done? He wanted the pirates to be punished – like Manuel Cruz, who they lashed to a boulder for three days for beating up another man – not *killed*.

"I've been to their island," someone said. "A typhoon destroyed their harvest. They're starving."

"So would we if we don't curb their attacks," the chief said.

The boy watched as villagers dragged the four men to the beach. One of the men begged, "*Maawa na po kayo sa amin!*" Have mercy on us!

A kerosene lamp on a bamboo pole cast a yellow glow over a cavernous hole. Someone chained the pirates' hands behind them and attached those chains to a huge rock. Then the villagers buried the men in the sand to their necks.

Through all this, the leader didn't say anything. The boy expected him to be angry, but he just looked around. His glance lit upon the boy. "I have a son your age," he said.

The boy shrank back. Was the pirate really talking to him? Thankfully, his father stood between them and said, "Be quiet."

I have a son your age. The words rattled in the boy's brain.

He felt his father's hand on his shoulder. "Come," the father said, "it's high time we went home."

As they walked away, the boy asked his father, "Are we really going to let them drown?"

"Yes, son."

The boy shivered.

They paid one last visit at the village chief's house and another hour passed. Two. Restless, the boy slipped out and

3

went to the beach. He hid himself behind a coconut tree trunk.

A lone *guardia civil*, smoking a little stub of a *cigarillo*, sat on a bench facing the sea. Water swirled around his boots. He tossed the stub into the rising water, and looked over his shoulder, patting his shirt pocket.

"No more cigarettes?" one of the pirates said.

"I have one, but you'll have to dig for it," said another.

"Hush," the leader told the others. To the guard, he said, "If you let us go, I'll tell you where there's treasure."

"I don't want your treasure," the guard said. He patted his pocket once again, glanced at the prisoners, and walked away.

"Where do you think he's going?" a pirate said.

"To get more cigarettes, most likely. Quick, pull on the chains."

The boy decided he'd eavesdropped enough. His father would be looking for him. He moved away from the tree and tripped over a coconut, falling face-first. He lay on his stomach, trembling.

Please, don't let them hear me. Please, don't....

But the leader said, "I'm so glad you've come."

The boy raised himself to a kneeling position.

The leader said, "Are you that boy I talked to earlier?"

Getting up, the boy walked to the tree and barely peeked around it.

"I hoped you'd come," the leader said, smiling. "You look just like my son. How old are you?"

"Eight," the boy said.

"Ah, yes. Like the son I left behind with his mother." He paused. "His mother is sick. She probably won't survive the night if I don't return soon. And then my boy will be left all alone."

The pirate's voice was soft, pleasant. Not the voice of someone who would take women and children away from their families.

"Help me save my son," the leader whispered. "Please."

The boy found a foot-long plank of wood and dragged it to

the beach. Surf rolled to the boy's ankles. To the pirates' necks.

He started digging, shoving the plank into the sand and scooping what he could. Two scoops. Three. And then the waves returned, washing off traces of his work. The boy tried digging again, but this time, the waves didn't only erase the hole, it knocked the plank out of his hands. He scrambled and caught it before it could float out to sea.

By now, water reached the pirates' ears. Slopped over their mouths. "Dig faster," one pirate said, but the leader told him to be quiet. "The guard might hear," the leader said.

The boy dug faster, making a bigger hole, before a wave came crashing. It ripped the plank from the boy's hands and sent him stumbling face first into the water. He sputtered to the surface. The water reached to about his waist.

At first, he couldn't see the pirates. Then the sea sucked the water back, revealing their heads. Gagging, coughing. Moving their heads about wildly. Twisting their shoulders.

Without the plank, the boy could only use his hands to dig. He scooped out as much as he could until a wave came, cutting off a pirate in mid-scream. The boy tumbled and slammed against a tree trunk, bumping into coconuts that swirled around his body.

He gasped as he broke the water's surface and wiped the water from his eyes. For several seconds, he couldn't see the pirates. Maybe they were already drowning. The boy heard them thrashing, like fish in a net, until the wave drained back into the sea.

Two of the pirates' heads lolled back. One pirate quivered like a beached fish. A violent coughing and desperate gasps racked the leader's body. His glance flickered over the boy.

"I'm sorry," the boy said.

"You tried. And for that, I thank you."

Suddenly, the pirate flung his head back, his eyes glimmering with hatred. Frightened, the boy sat back on his haunches. The man spoke words in another tongue. Low and rhythmic, like the beating of a drum. Then he said, in Tagalog, the boy's dialect, "I curse this village. Once a month, on Ghost Moon Night, evil spirits will rise again."

The boy looked at the sky, but nothing happened.

"Come here," the pirate told the boy, his voice soft once

more. "Now, before it's too late!"

The boy knelt close. His heart hammered as he listened to things that made his eyes grow wide. He nodded and listened some more until a giant wave, taller than twice the boy's height, devoured the beach like a starving beast.

The guard found the boy, curled up and crying, on the little strand of sand that sloped up to the nearest huts. One of the *baranggay* councilmen ran to join them. "This is my son," the councilman said. "What happened?"

"I just got back myself," the guard said, "to check on the prisoners." He looked at the knee-high water that had been a beach earlier. And now, a pirate graveyard.

The boy's eyes looked bleak. "One had a son."

The father reached for the boy's arm, but the boy stopped crying and stared at the sky.

"So it's true," the boy whispered. "What the pirate said was true." Scrambling to his feet, he shouted, "Run!" and headed for the huts.

The guard followed the boy's gaze. At first, he saw nothing but a dark night sky dusted with pinpricks of stars. Some stars twinkled. Several flapped their wings.

Wings?

There were dozens of them. Winged creatures with decaying skin, long black tongues, claws and unblinking eyes. The pirates led the contingent.

What were these creatures?

The father ran, and the guard tried, too, but tripped over a washed-up log. He scrambled to his feet only to be surrounded by the pirates. Their wings flapped slowly.

How could this be, por Dios Santo? They had drowned! And those wings!

Fingernails rasped against the guard's pants pocket as one of the pirates took out his cigarette sticks. "Here," the pirate said, stuffing one cigarette after another into the guard's mouth, until some fell out of his trembling lips. Then the pirate touched the guard's face.

Sharp claws nicked the guard's skin, scraped his stubble. He felt a cold, stinging sensation, colder than anything he'd ever experienced. Like ice from when the *gobernador* hosted that *fiesta* in the capital. Even colder than that. The guard tried to back away, but the pirates pressed against him on all sides. A hand gripped his jaw like a vise.

The cold seeped from the pirate's hand to the guard's face, down to his tongue which felt thick and useless, and down his neck to his chest, where his heart contracted painfully. He heard laughter, as though it were coming from a long tunnel.

The cigarettes fell out of his lips as he slumped onto the sand.

1

Seventy-five years later

WITH TWO LURCHES and a loud squeal of brakes, a Pantranco bus shuddered to a stop in Dasalin on a scorching April afternoon in 1956.

The sign "Manila to Ilocos" hung crookedly on a hook behind the windshield. Its folding door opened like a stiff accordion, prompting the driver to pound it fully open with his fist. Then he got out of the way as passengers streamed down the rickety steps, grimacing as they walked into the sticky, muggy air.

Many of them ambled over to the noodle shop across the street and filled their bellies with hot *mami* soup, held their breath while using the toilets at the station, then turned right back to their seats for the remainder of their bus ride. Dasalin was a mere pit stop, just one small village of about two hundred families along the coast to the northern province of Ilocos. It bordered a bigger city, where tricycles could draw passengers from, but Dasalin wasn't even on the Philippine map.

But to one of the passengers, who took his tidy little suitcase off the rack above him, this *was* his destination. Father Dionisio Sebastian cleaned his glasses with the white handkerchief

9

he kept in his pocket at all times, brushed the yellow *mamon* crumbs off his priest's robe, and made his way out of the bus.

A young man in his late teens approached the priest. He had an alert posture, a friendly smile, and a shock of black hair that fell over one eye. "Father Sebastian?" he asked.

"Yes," the priest said, smiling back.

"Welcome to Dasalin," the boy said, bending over the priest's hand in a sign of respect, or *mano*. "My name is Antonio Pulido. I'm one of the altar boys at the church, sent to pick you up. May I take your luggage?"

"I can manage, thank you," the priest said, holding up his suitcase. "This is all I have."

"Then we'll have plenty of room for you in my cart." Antonio paused. "That is, if you want to just go straight to the parish."

"Where else would I go?" Father Sebastian asked.

"Are you hungry? You could eat at Aling Dona's."

"Actually, I'm famished. I've only had a *mamon* cake since dawn."

Antonio grinned. "That's settled then."

As the teen led the priest across the road, a motorcyclist roared up, and would have clipped Father Sebastian had Antonio not pushed him to safety. One of the tires left a dusty tread print on the hem of the Father Sebastian's cassock. The driver laughed and sped away.

"Are you alright, Father?" Antonio asked.

"Yes," Father Sebastian said, mustering up a smile.

Antonio sighed. "That was Timo Sandoval. See that store right there?" He pointed at a two-story building with a white sign that said, *Sandoval's Store*. "His family owns it."

Father Sebastian followed Antonio up a small flight of steps to a building whose sign said, in slightly faded red lettering, *La Panciteria*. There was a weathered bench on the front porch and the door was open. As Father Sebastian reached the threshold, music and the delicious smell of chicken and *pansit mami* noodle seasoning – garlic, salt, green onions and the citrusy aroma of *calamansi* – filled the air.

A plump woman with her hair escaping in tendrils greeted him. "Welcome, welcome, Father," she said, smiling broadly. "Are you our new parish priest?"

"I am," Father Sebastian said.

This revelation unleashed hospitable overtures: an announcement to all the other patrons, who murmured their welcome; a seat at the best table by the window; a steaming bowl of *mami*, on the house. The priest thanked everyone for their hospitality.

Father Sebastian leaned over the bowl and savored the aroma of the soup, then took Antonio in one glance: a face sculpted by a lean diet, a politely averted gaze, yet still, that pleasant, winning smile. "How about you," the priest asked, "would you like some soup?"

"Oh, no, thank you," came Antonio's quick reply. "I can eat when I get home, Father."

Aling Dona walked over and stood by Antonio, a tray of dirty bowls in her arms. "This young man doesn't come here to eat," she said. "Go on, Antonio. Tell Father what you spend your money on."

Antonio smiled. "I can do better. I'll *show* him." He stood up and walked over to a large contraption that Father Sebastian recognized as a music jukebox. It had a list of song titles at the top as well as a rack of vinyl records and a record turntable visible through a glass window. Antonio pulled a coin out of his pocket, deposited it into a slot, and turned to the priest.

"Do you have a song request, Father?"

"Me?" Father Sebastian said, standing up and walking over. Surveying the titles, his enthusiasm soon turned into dismay. "These songs...they are all so *modern*."

Antonio's smile faltered. "Do you not like any of them?"

Father Sebastian felt his cheeks grow warm. "I know they play music like this in the capital, though. Unfortunately, the music's had a profound effect on the young people, too. Many think music is just pure entertainment, but I think it shapes someone's character."

"I'm sorry," Antonio said. "I didn't mean to offend you, Father."

"Oh, but I haven't taken any offense. Maybe I'm being unreasonable, but I thought your little town would be more sheltered."

"I have a cousin in Manila," Aling Dona said. "He supplies me with the latest in music. You prefer the old music, do you,

Father?" She slipped her finger slowly through the song titles. "How about this one?"

Father Sebastian said, "I would love that," as the strains of Doris Day's "Sentimental Journey" filled the restaurant.

"I love her music, too," Antonio said softly, the jukebox light reflecting in his eyes.

When the music stopped, Antonio continued to gaze at the song titles. Father Sebastian cleared his throat.

Antonio turned and smiled sheepishly. "Would you like to see the parish now?"

"If you're ready."

"Of course!"

Father Sebastian thanked Aling Dona for the delicious soup and good music, then followed Antonio to a parked cart attached to a handsome water buffalo. The priest looked around, taking note of his new surroundings.

The bus station consisted of a little shelter where passengers could stay out of the sun. Nearby, there were lines of tricycles for hire: colorful, roofed passenger sidecars attached to motorcycles, their exhaust lingering in the air.

"No jeepneys?" the priest asked, referring to the vehicles fashioned after American jeeps from World War II.

"A jeepney business went bankrupt several years ago," Antonio said. "Mr. Mijares – he owns the tricycles – could have bought it, but he chose to do only tricycles."

Beside the noodle shop stood a variety store, and a single gas pump. Beyond the little plaza, through a screen of trees on one side, the priest glimpsed a sliver of blue sea. The other side rose up to a lush mountain that jutted out into a series of cliffs.

Father Sebastian smiled at his good fortune. For ten years, he had been assigned to Manila. After the war, the Americans came and changed everything – music, dance, and mores. How he looked forward to tending His simpler flock in this peaceful little village by the sea.

As he climbed onto the bench at the front of the cart, he noticed a little sign just to their right, on one of the bus station's posts. Written on it, with half-erased smudges of chalk, were the following words:

Ghost Moon Night
Date:

GHOST MOON NIGHT

Sunset time:

"Ghost Moon Night," the priest read. "What does that mean?"

The teen looked at him strangely. "Do you not know?"

"Know what?" the priest said.

FATHER SEBASTIAN WAITED for an answer as Antonio flicked the reins on his water buffalo.

"That sign shows what time the sun sets on Ghost Moon Night," Antonio said. "It's the one night of the month when there's no visible moon."

"Why do you need to know the time of sunset?" Father Sebastian said.

"That way, we can go home in plenty of time, bolt our doors and windows securely, and stay indoors for the night."

Still, the priest stared. Uncomprehending.

Then he noticed that the huts they passed had heavy shutters in addition to *capiz* windows that could be slid shut. Thick doors gaped open. A feeling of dread settled in his stomach.

Antonio gave him a sidelong glance. Barely above a whisper, he said, "Our village is cursed. On Ghost Moon Night, evil spirits rise again."

The priest blinked. "You aren't serious!"

Antonio nodded.

"You mean they walk about?" Father Sebastian asked.

"They fly."

"Like the *manananggal*?" the priest said, referring to the vampiric creature who leaves the lower half of her body and flies off to prey on babies. He shook his head, thinking of a priest he'd spoken to just last year, who swore, in whispers, that he'd truly seen one. That priest officiated on a southern island.

"Except they have a full body," Antonio said. "We call these winged creatures *langbuan*. They appear when there's *walang buwan*, the one night of the month without a moon."

"And what do these evil spirits do, when they come upon one of your villagers?"

"They cling to you and draw all the warmth from your body...until you die."

Despite the sun bearing down on them in the cart, the priest felt a chill. "How many have been killed?"

"About a dozen every year."

Father Sebastian shivered. He believed in God and His powers on earth. And he believed, too, that there were evil spirits wanting to interfere in His master plan.

But this Ghost Moon Night curse; this was unheard of.

"Are you alright?" Antonio said, peering at his face.

"Yes, I think so." Father Sebastian took out a handkerchief and dabbed at his temple. His hand shook.

A villager stepped out of their yard and waved. Father Sebastian waved back. "What are you doing to fight back against them?"

Antonio flicked the reins. "Some have tried. Fathers, in their grief. Mothers mourning their children. Many died trying. These past few years, our village has done nothing."

"Nothing!" echoed the priest.

"What can we do? No one dares battle them, for fear of losing their lives. Anyway, as long as we stay within doors and our houses are secure, we're safe. It's considered the lot of the imprudent, to be attacked." Antonio looked at the priest. "I'm surprised no one told you about Ghost Moon Night."

"The Archbishop simply asked if I would be willing to go anywhere with any situation, in the service of the Lord. How pleased he had been when I said yes."

"If you'd known, would you have come?" Antonio asked.

Father Sebastian hesitated. "I don't see why I wouldn't have.

Just because something like that happens once a month doesn't mean the rest of the time couldn't be pleasant. But maybe I'd have come better prepared. Brought some things."

"Like what?"

"Oh, I don't know. More crucifixes? Garlic?"

"That's been tried before. It doesn't work. Nothing works."

"Surely something must!"

"Well, alright," Antonio conceded. "Two things do work. Bolting the doors and windows shut. Light wards them off until dawn. But nothing seems to destroy them permanently." He smiled. "It was probably best you didn't know about our curse. We've been needing a new priest."

"What happened to the last parish priest?"

"After he delivered his sermon a month ago, he took a nap and died in his sleep. He was very old."

"And it had nothing to do with your evil spirits?"

"No," Antonio assured him.

The priest relaxed. For a moment, he thought the last priest had been attacked by *langbuan*. "When is the next Ghost Moon Night?"

"In three weeks."

Father Sebastian squared his shoulders. Three more weeks to learn about this, and get his bearings.

"Here she is," Antonio announced. "The Lady of Miracles Church."

Father Sebastian studied its crooked, uneven foundation but decided it looked pretty, with its sun-bleached stone walls and delicate spires. As Antonio parked, the priest noted beautiful stained glass windows flanked by heavy shutters.

"It's a lovely church," Father Sebastian said.

"And that," Antonio said, pointing behind the church, "is the graveyard."

The graveyard seemed to extend at least three church lengths. Tombstones and vaults gleamed like a whitewashed city. "You have such a large graveyard, for such a small town," Father Sebastian noted.

"We've added a lot over the past 75 years."

The priest gripped the handle of his suitcase tightly. "From Ghost Moon Night?"

Antonio nodded. "From Ghost Moon Night."

16

GHOST MOON NIGHT

After a moment's silence, Father Sebastian made the sign of the cross.

Antonio helped the priest out of the cart and gave him an anxious look. "Will you be alright?"

"Of course."

"There's a caretaker here, Henry. He'll see to your needs."

"I'm sure he will."

"See you on Sunday!" And off clattered the teen and his water buffalo.

Standing in the doorway of the chapel, Father Sebastian watched him drive off. Clouds scuttled across the sun, turning the sky a muddy gray.

He gasped when he felt something touch his shoulder.

Turning, he faced a thin man whose face was cast in shadow. Stepping aside to let the natural light fall on his face, the priest noted the man's eyes. They were peculiarly translucent, a light shade of brown that stood out against his leathery brown complexion. He looked like he wasn't that much younger, maybe in his 60s.

"Sorry to scare you," the man said in a raspy voice, like he was gasping for breath. "My name is Henry. I'm the parish caretaker."

"Pardon me," the priest said. "Usually, I'm not this jumpy. I just found out about Ghost Moon Night."

Henry raised an eyebrow. "Ghost Moon Night makes everyone jumpy, but there isn't anything to worry about, not the rest of the time anyway."

The priest forced himself to smile. "That's what I thought."

"Would you like me to show you to your quarters?" Henry offered.

"Yes, please."

As the caretaker walked on, Father Sebastian took one last look outside. It was still gray, cloudy. Nothing like how sunny it had been when the bus was pulling into the station. He made the sign of the cross, then scurried after Henry, up the circular stairs.

3

As Antonio maneuvered Cupid to the road, he felt sorry for the new parish priest. It *would* be unsettling to come all the way from Manila to your new parish only to discover that it was cursed with flying undead once a month. It would all be outlandish to Antonio, too, had he not grown up living with the curse.

He sighed and focused on the road.

When he came to a fork in the road, he took the one on the right. Here, the huts were fewer and farther between, each one backing into rice paddies. Each yard had at least one handsome rooster, tethered to a knee-high lean-to shelter and scratching in the dirt. As he passed his neighbors, Antonio waved at them: at a woman sweeping her yard with a *walis tingting*, at a man burning a pile of garbage, and at children who were playing *patintero* across the road.

In one yard, a man sat under the shade of a mango tree. He was old as the sea and bent over like a prune left too long under the sun, ruminating on whatever it was old people ruminate about. His legs were crossed, his hands palm up on his legs, eyes glazed. His mouth, stained red, chewed the betel nut. He didn't wave back even though Antonio was sure he could see him. Antonio was used to that. As the oldest resident of Dasalin, Tandang Lino was entitled to his eccentricities.

Cupid slowed and veered as a basketball rolled in front of him. A tall boy sprinted to catch the ball, then dribbled it in front of the cart.

"One of these days you're going to get flattened like a tray of *bibingka*," Antonio said. "It's a good thing Cupid pays attention."

Antonio's best friend, Jose Pineda, twirled the ball on his long finger. Everything about Jose was long: his chin, his torso, his legs. Even his hair was getting long and starting to curl at the edges. He wore basketball shorts, a sleeveless *sando* shirt, and a pair of rubber shoes he paid for by cleaning urinals at the hospital.

"I've been dying to tell you my good news," Jose said.

"You quit your job?"

"No, not yet." He leaned forward. "I got a full scholarship to LaSalle University in Manila!"

"What about Ateneo University?"

"Even if they pay, I'll still pick LaSalle. They have a better basketball program."

Deep inside, Antonio's gut twisted. After high school, Jose would get to go to Manila, while Antonio was stuck working on the farm with his father. "That's really great," he said, trying to sound enthusiastic but failing miserably.

Jose was too happy to notice. "I'll live with roommates in a house with a real bathtub – a fancy one with clawed feet – and a flushing toilet. Across the school, there's a gym for workouts and practice. No more coconut basketball for me."

They both looked towards Jose's basketball "hoop," a wire ring upon which a woman's stocking was stretched over. The contraption was attached to a coconut trunk. Antonio helped him build that three summers ago, the summer when Jose started to shoot up like bamboo did in the rainy monsoon season.

"Did you ever apply to college, like I told you?" Jose asked.

"Whatever for?" Antonio said. "I wouldn't be able to pay for it anyway."

JEWEL ALLEN

Jose shook his head. "You're so thick-headed. It wouldn't have hurt to try."

"Besides, Papa won't let me go." Antonio picked up Cupid's reins. "Speaking of whom, I'd better go do my chores or I won't hear the end of it."

As Antonio drove Cupid and the cart homeward, he thought about college. If he had gotten a scholarship, would his father have let him go to Manila? Somehow, he couldn't picture his father saying yes. "I need you on the farm," Papa would point out. And what was the use anyway? Antonio wasn't as smart nor as athletic as Jose.

As he pulled up to their hut, he noticed an emaciated horse and cart waiting under the shed of their narra tree. Beside the little shed where they kept their grain, a man and a woman were talking to Antonio's father.

"Whatever you do," his father said, "don't do anything rash."

"I don't know how much longer I can do it, Romy, without extra help," the man replied.

Antonio unhitched Cupid and led him past casually, trying to not attract attention.

"There he is, right now," Romy Pulido, Antonio's father, told his visitors.

The man was Mang Fermin, Romy Pulido's perpetually moody friend, whom Romy had known from birth, almost. His arms were muscular, probably from chopping wood at his seaside mabolo orchard. A scowl cut ridges into his forehead.

The woman turned towards Antonio, flashing him a grin full of rotting teeth, her bulbous eyes gleaming intensely. A thick tangled mane formed a dark cloud around her face.

Mad Juana was crazy. It used to be that she just sang little unintelligible songs and danced while hiking up her skirts scandalously. But nowadays, she wandered off their orchard and snuck into town, stealing butcher knives at the market. So Mang Fermin resorted to locking her up in his hut. In public, she wore a rubber collar attached to a chain held by her brother. Like some animal.

"Yes, here I am," Antonio said cheerfully. "And in a few seconds, I'll be in the rice paddy."

"Why is it that when I usually ask you to help plant, you're not this eager?" his father asked. "Fermin needs your help clearing some dead wood. I told him I could spare you for a little while."

Antonio looked from his father to the rice paddy. "It'll be dark soon," he told his father. "If I cut down trees, I won't be able to help you on the farm."

"The farm will still be here tomorrow," his father said.

"That it will," Antonio muttered. "Let me put Cupid away and say hello to Grandfather."

Mang Fermin gathered his sister's chain in his hand, the sound of rattling metal grating on Antonio's ears. "We'll wait for you in the cart."

A NTONIO KNEW HE should hurry, but he let his feet drag taking Cupid back to his pen and entered the house through the back door. In the outside kitchen, or *batalan*, their servant Trining was frying some *litson kawali*. Before she could swat his hand away, he grabbed a piece of fatty pork, hot grease dripping between his fingers. He popped the meat in his mouth.

"Ah, ah, ah!" he said, spitting it out and fanning his scorched tongue.

"*Hala!*" Trining brandished her wooden spoon and cackled. "Serves you right."

Antonio licked his fingers. "Can I *please* have another one?"

"What, and ruin your appetite?"

"I have to go and help cut down trees at Mang Fermin's. Father volunteered me. I won't be home till late."

Trining eyed him suspiciously.

"It's true," he said.

"Hmmph, alright. But don't wipe your hands on your shirt!"

Then off she sent Antonio with three fatty pieces of pork.

GHOST MOON NIGHT

The skin was crunchy and the meat juicy and tender. Delicious. Inside the house, he wiped his greasy hand on his pants.

Two sounds greeted him as he stepped in the hallway: a sewing machine going at top speed, and music.

The sewing machine stopped. "Antonio, is that you?" his mother asked.

Antonio poked his head in the room where his mother sewed. Several dresses in different stages lined the wall. Fabric covered the floor, a table, and chairs. A tape measure was hanging around his mother's neck.

Mama looked tired around her eyes. She'd probably been up half the night finishing a dress.

"How was school?" she tucked a gray-streaked lock of hair behind one ear.

"About what you'd expect from the day before graduation. A little pointless."

"I'm sorry."

"But I met the new parish priest," Antonio said, brightening. "He seems really nice."

"Oh, that's right. You were going to pick him up." She bit her lip. "Are you up for another errand? I was wondering if you could make a delivery for me."

"After I cut trees for Mang Fermin and help Papa on the farm, I'm sure I'll have *plenty* of time left over."

Mother blinked and said nothing.

Antonio knelt beside her. "Sorry, Mama," he said. "I'm only one person here and it seems everyone needs me today. But if you need me, I can make time."

"It's alright," Mama said, patting his head. "That's a lot for one afternoon."

"Are you sure? If you still need help delivering tomorrow…"

"On graduation day? No, it'll be alright. Go then." She went back to her sewing. "Go!"

Antonio did as she asked, feeling terrible. Guitar music from the radio greeted him as he entered the living room. Immediately, his shoulders loosened and his pressing worries fell away.

His father's father, Lolo Sonny, sat on the scuffed wood *sala* set, a smile playing on his lips. Lolo Sonny's few remaining tufts of hair stuck straight up and his shirt, stained at the collar, had been buttoned incorrectly. Faded blue slacks he'd worn from his younger days hung loosely around his waist.

As Antonio approached him, Lolo Sonny raised a shaking hand and Antonio lifted it to his forehead, in a *mano*.

Most afternoons, before Antonio went outside to help his father in earnest, he stopped in for a few minutes to listen to music with Lolo Sonny. The radio revived the old man. Before they got the radio, a castoff from a neighbor's rich relative in Manila, Lolo Sonny used to shamble around the house looking lost, but now he had something he could get dressed for and enjoy.

Antonio knew that Mang Fermin waited outside, but he couldn't resist sitting in one of the chairs. Just for one moment. As he listened, his glance fell onto the portrait of Lolo Sonny and Lola Enteng, taken before she died a few years ago. Beside it was a framed medal of Lolo Sonny's from his service in World War I.

A *kundiman* tune played on a transistor radio by the window. A sweet, lilting song. Lolo Sonny smiled, his lips mouthing the lyrics. Antonio knew the melody, where it dipped and rose. He hummed along and closed his eyes. For a moment, he could forget that Mang Fermin and his crazy sister waited outside for him, that Papa needed him to plow the paddies, and that he let Mama down once again.

When the radio cut out and emitted a static noise, Antonio's eyes flew open. Lolo Sonny's smile faltered.

"Don't worry, Lolo Sonny," Antonio said, getting up and pounding on the machine. "We'll get this fixed." Two hard whacks and the radio leapt back to life. As he moved away, Antonio accidentally bumped a knob. Elvis Presley's new song flooded the room.

Lolo Sonny shook his head. "Off...off..."

Antonio quickly turned it back to Lolo Sonny's favorite *kundiman* channel. A man sang about his sweetheart under the light of the moon.

This time, Lolo Sonny's brow relaxed.

"Not a big fan of Elvis, are you, Lolo?" Antonio said, smiling. He kissed his grandfather's soft, slack cheek, which smelled of

Vicks and *arroz caldo* soup.

"Thank...you."

"You're welcome," Antonio said. Then he went out to the cart where Mang Fermin and his sister waited.

5

MANG FERMIN'S PROPERTY abutted the sea, the only length of coast that was kept off limits to beachcombers and fishermen. Over the years, he reinforced a fence as far as he could into open water, with coiled barbed wire, big chunks of wood salvaged from construction projects, and rusty odds and ends. People of the village said that the sun set darkly and extinguished itself quicker over that part of the beach, and Antonio believed it.

With a lash from the whip, Mang Fermin's little nag flew into a bouncy trot across a bridge over the Dasalin River, pulling the cartload of brother and sister in front, Antonio on the floor in the back. Soon after, they entered a canopy of trees. It was dark, dense and reeked of overripe mabolos, round fruits that had fallen off twisted boughs, their purplish pulp looking like open wounds on the ground. Once in a while a shaft of light came through a gap in the foliage, where determined little plants pushed their way out of the dirt. Otherwise, there was nothing but the trees and their dropped fruit, and a winding little path that got narrower and narrower until the cart brushed against overhanging branches.

Inside the mabolo jungle, the trees seemed to shiver, shaking the leaves on their boughs. Antonio raised his eyes as he sat, huddled, in the cart. And then bats flew low overhead, hundreds and hundreds, emitting tiny shrieks as they whistled past. They brushed against his hair, his face, his arms, his knees.

Mang Fermin laughed. He sounded like a donkey braying. Mad Juana laughed too, in a deep, man-like voice. Antonio kept his face to his lap, covering his ears with his hands until both the bats and the aggravating laughter subsided.

The horse and cart came to an abrupt stop. Raising his head, Antonio heard the sea, hissing and crashing against rocks. He could vaguely make out the water past the screen of trees and tall piles of chopped wood.

"I need the rest of this cleared," Mang Fermin said, gesturing with his arm over the area that, if cut into lengths, probably spanned the entire width of the village. "I'll leave the horse and cart. Take the wood to my house and add it to the stack leaning against the outside wall. Mind you, don't eat the mabolos. Each one is accounted for."

"I'll do what I can in an hour," Antonio said.

"Your father said you can stay the entire night if you have to."

Antonio bristled at his father's presumption. He gestured towards the dense canopy. "I can keep working while there's still some light."

"You're wasting time, arguing about this." Mang Fermin tugged at his sister's chain and got off the cart. "Come, Juana, let's go to the house."

Antonio felt quite alone in the middle of this dark, dreary clump of trees, with only the horse and the bats for company. Thankfully, the bats tired of their sport and returned to their decaying perches.

He started loading pieces of wood into the cart, making a dull thudding noise each time that echoed throughout the orchard. A cluster of bats seemed to watch him from gnarled branches, their little eyes blinking.

Soon, he was ready to bring in his first haul. He prodded the horse to move forward but it balked under the weight. A few lashes of the whip finally got the nag to move.

Antonio had been to Mang Fermin's house before, but it had been a while. And now as he maneuvered his way through the trees, he was becoming increasingly lost. After a while, he threw his hands up in disgust, shaking his fist at the horse, which he thought would lead him to the house.

The horse hung its gaunt head, looking beaten, but unrepentant. Then Antonio heard the wailing of a baby. *A baby, here?*

Antonio turned on the carriage bench and listened. The baby's cry seemed to come from the densest part of the forest to his left.

There, there it was again.

He got out of the carriage and walked towards the sound. Bats flew off as he parted some branches. And there, at the foot of a tree, in a sliver of light, lay a baby in a blanket. Alone. Antonio looked around, and, not seeing anyone, he went up to it. Its eyes grew round when he knelt by its side.

"Where's your mother?" Antonio asked, picking up the baby. He felt a little awkward picking it up, but the little thing fit right in his arms. He tried rocking it like he'd seen his mother rock babies at church socials. The baby gurgled and sucked on its fist.

"How'd you end up here?" he asked. "We better get you somewhere safe."

As he moved, the baby's coo changed into a deep sound. Antonio looked down and gasped. The baby's eyes were red and its gums sprouted sharp monster teeth. Its tiny fingers turned into black-nailed fists.

A *tiyanak*! A creature that disguises itself as a baby. It lured unsuspecting travelers and mislead them until they're lost.

Antonio tried to fling the *tiyanak* to the ground, but it clung to him with those sharp nails, digging painfully into his chest. It licked its lips and bared yellowish fangs, lunging for Antonio's neck. Antonio shoved it away by the forehead.

His mother's voice words of advice came to him.

If you see a tiyanak, turn your shirt inside out. It will find it entertaining, and leave you alone.

28

Bending at the waist, he tried to shake off the creature. It grabbed his hair and nipped at his ear. Antonio swatted the mouth away with his hand, and it jerked its head back. Antonio bent again. His shirt slipped off his body, sending the *tiyanak* tumbling backwards. This little baby with a monstrous face stood upright and marched towards him on bowed legs. Antonio plucked his shirt from the ground and put it on backwards.

The *tiyanak* laughed, flashing a malicious grin. In a twinkling of an eye, it disappeared.

Nothing like this had happened to Antonio before, but then, he'd never been on Mang Fermin's land alone. Antonio knew everyone steered clear of it. He'd thought it was because of Mang Fermin. But perhaps, he'd stumbled on the real reason. And it explained a lot about the eccentric pair. Antonio flicked the whip harder, shuddering as he peered this way and that through the trees, seeing nothing but shadows.

Through a gap in the forest, he saw Mang Fermin's hut. Relief washed over him. However, as he approached, Antonio heard the tinkling of a piano. Was his mind playing tricks on him?

The air smelled stale and musty, like leaves rotting. Above, only a small space in the forest canopy allowed for natural light. Antonio parked the cart. Before getting out, he scanned the trees, jumping at every little rustling noise. Watching for more danger.

Satisfied, he carried wood to a pile beside the window. Flies swarmed around droppings of cats and chickens. Mosquitoes buzzed over standing puddles. Torn woven baskets and crates littered the ground.

The music continued to play. It was a sad song, the kind that was played in melodramas at the movie theater. Antonio tiptoed toward the open window. Its sill came to a good three feet above his head. Looking around for something to step on, he found a waterlogged crate. It had been on the ground for so long that when Antonio picked it up, little white worms wriggled in its grooves. He set the crate on the ground under the window, then tested it with his foot. It bowed to his weight, but held.

He stepped up fully and peeked over the sill. Darkness shrouded the room, but he made out a few things: oddly enough

29

– a newspaper photo of American actress Princess Grace and her new prince husband from Monaco, books, and baskets.

Hiss.

Antonio flinched at the sound. It was quiet, but distinct. A snake?

Hiss.

As his eyes adjusted to the darkness, he saw something glinting in the corner, something that moved in a circular fashion.

A record player! It was a square box, with a circular turntable and an arm with a stylus that was positioned over a long-playing record. A marvel of technology. He'd seen one before, in an ad in a magazine at the doctor's. Antonio leaned forward so he could see better.

Something popped up, blocking his view. Over the window sill, Mad Juana's face appeared. He could smell her foul breath and could hear its ragged rhythm.

Gasping, he lost his footing and fell on his back onto the hard ground.

Standing over him, Mang Fermin's eyes blazing with anger. "What are you doing?"

Antonio scrambled to his feet. "I was just looking at your record player."

"Get back to work!"

Antonio drove the horse and cart as fast as he could back into the forest. He wondered why his father liked Mang Fermin so much. They had similar gruff personalities. Mang Fermin sometimes invited Romy over for drinks. But he had never been friendly towards Antonio nor his mother.

And then that record player! How did he get it? How Lolo Sonny would love one of those. He could play any song he liked. Antonio wouldn't have to take Lolo Sonny to Aling Dona's just to hear his favorite *kundiman* tunes.

As the darkness deepened, Antonio finished a few more loads. Antonio was only guessing at where to put his hands so he could grab some wood pieces. But it was so dark he missed the cart twice. He didn't care what his father promised, or what Mang Fermin expected; he was done for the day.

A mabolo fell off a tree limb with a little snap and rolled to Antonio's feet.

GHOST MOON NIGHT

Antonio bit his lip. He had been so busy he hadn't realized how hungry he was. He ate his last meal hours ago. Surely, Mang Fermin wouldn't *really* notice if Antonio ate one, would he?

Antonio picked up the round purple fruit the size of a man's fist. It was just the right amount of ripeness – fragrant and soft but not mushy. Squeezing it open, he inhaled its sweetness then took a bite of the firm pulp. It rolled in his mouth, making him crave for more. He spit out the seed, took one bite, another and another, until all that was left was its peel.

He threw the peel on the ground and found himself face to face with Mang Fermin, holding a shotgun.

ANTONIO SMELLED MANG Fermin's sour body odor, tobacco breath, and the metal of his gun.

"Did I give you permission to eat a mabolo?" Mang Fermin asked.

Antonio's voice shook. "It was just one."

"You are like other pesky kids. You come through my orchard and think," Mang Fermin mimicked in a high-pitched voice. "'It's just *one* mabolo.' But they never stop at one. They do it again, over and over. I'm not making any money as it is."

Mang Fermin pumped the shotgun, making Antonio jump.

"Tell you what," Mang Fermin said, "I'll be easy on you, since you helped me with two cartloads of wood. I'll count to two, then shoot two shells. Two is the magic number of the day. That'll give you a chance to run on home."

"You're crazy!" Antonio said. "Like your sister!"

"Leave Juana out of this!" Mang Fermin barked. "One…"

Antonio took off as fast as he could, towards what he hoped was the general direction of town. He couldn't see farther than his arm, stretched out. He kept running into mabolo trees and shaking the bats into a frenzy. But he kept running. Desperately.

32

GHOST MOON NIGHT

Especially as the first shot hit a tree somewhere to his left.

It seemed like he would never get out of the orchard. And then finally, *finally!* He saw a glimmer of light up ahead.

But it was not the direction of town. The exact opposite, in fact, in the direction of the sea. He had not been on this side for years and he discovered that Mang Fermin had added something to thwart intruders. Not only was the water dammed up so no one could enter the bay, he had put up a ten-foot tall rock wall along his property line. It had a locked gate.

When the shotgun boomed, Antonio scaled the fence quickly. On the top, broken shards of gin bottles stuck out like spearheads. Past this, the rising moon revealed a stretch of beach and the crazy line of junk obstacles, as well as a dozen sandy mounds. Not anthills but *nuno sa punso,* enchanted mounds that harbored spirits of the earth.

With a grunt, he avoided the shards by heaving himself over the fence, landing on all fours on the other side.

Mang Fermin cocked his shotgun again. This time closer. Scrambling up the beach, uncaring if what he stepped on was sand or *nuno,* Antonio ran up and over to his freedom.

Antonio would have put his best friend Jose to shame, running that fast home. As he neared his yard, relief at his narrow escape gave way to worry.

I demolished a nuno sa punso.

Well, it wasn't like he had deliberately tried to destroy one. He was trying to get away from a madman. Antonio didn't care if Mang Fermin was his father's friend. The crazy, old man should be committed to a mental hospital with his sister!

Antonio rounded the bend at the narra tree in his front yard, then hid himself behind its trunk. Mang Fermin stood in the doorway, talking to Antonio's mother. Mad Juana sat in their horse cart.

What did the man want now? Antonio wondered. His heart pounded in his chest.

Fortunately, Mang Fermin and his sister didn't stay for long. They said their goodbyes, then clattered on down the

33

road. When he was sure they were out of sight, Antonio went inside. He thought about just going straight to his bedroom, but decided he should at least say hello to Mama.

Her back was turned to the door. She was pinning a dress on a mannequin. "I'm home," he said.

"Mang Fermin was here," Mama said, not turning.

"What did he say?"

"That you stole fruit from him."

"One mabolo!"

"So you *did* do it." She shook her head. "Oh, son!"

"Mama, he has fruit *rotting* on the ground!"

"One or more, it doesn't make a difference," Mama said. "Stealing is stealing. He also said you tried to steal his record player."

"Now *that* is an outright lie!"

"He said you went to his window and was eyeing it."

"I did, but I wasn't going to steal it. Not with that madwoman standing guard."

Antonio realized what he'd said and stammered. "I mean, of course I wasn't going to steal it. And I wasn't thinking of myself, anyway. I thought perhaps Lolo could enjoy it." He paused. "Mama, surely you don't think that I would do that."

Him, a thief! Mang Fermin was the criminal, wanting to murder him over one stupid mabolo.

Mama sighed. "Go eat your supper, Antonio. I asked Trining to leave you out a plate." This was Margarita Pulido at her finest. She didn't raise her voice but somehow she managed to make him feel like he should join the legion of penitents at Lenten season.

She stepped back to survey her handiwork and turned. Her eyes went wide as she staggered backwards, hitting the mannequin with her arm. "My God, Antonio! Where have you been? What have you done?"

"What?" he asked, his heart racing. "What's the matter?"

"Your arms," she pointed. "Your face. Did you disturb a *nuno sa punso?*"

He was almost afraid to look. And when he did, he cried out. Thick hair covered his arms, like some beast.

7

ANTONIO SAT ON their dining table bench, his plate of rice and *pinakbet* – okra, squash, green beans and onion sautéed with his favorite cuts of *litson kawali* – growing cold in front of him. His one consolation was that their servant Trining had gone home for the day and couldn't harp on his misfortune. Papa was out playing mah-jongg, a gambling game involving little porcelain tiles. Mama sent the neighbor's son to fetch him. Once in a while, she paused at the window.

"Go ahead and help your grandfather get ready for bed," Mama told Antonio. "Knowing your papa, he'll be a while."

Lolo Sonny sat in his usual spot in the *salas*, nodding along to the music.

"Lolo," Antonio said, walking over to the radio and turning it off. "Time for bed, *po*." He turned to help Lolo Sonny up. His grandfather's eyes widened, then he raised his hand to his mouth. "*Halimaw!*" he said. Monster.

Antonio tried to explain, but Lolo wouldn't listen. He crossed his arms in front of him while making strangled noises.

Mama rushed in. "Oh my," she said. "I wasn't thinking. Antonio, go to the kitchen and stay there. Please."

35

Antonio stood rooted to the floor. Lolo Sonny twisted in his seat, anxious. Mama tried to hold his arm, but he pulled away from her.

"He'll hurt himself!" Antonio murmured. He crossed the room and turned on the radio. As soon as the music came on, Lolo Sonny stopped struggling. He still looked at Antonio askance, but at least he calmed down.

"There, there," Mama said. She gestured for Antonio to go out. Several minutes later, Mama returned to the kitchen without Lolo.

"Is he alright?" Antonio asked.

"Yes. Good thinking on the music. That really helps to calm him."

At the sound of their cart's wheels outside, she gave Antonio a sharp glance, then went to the front door.

In an irritated voice, Papa said, "I was doing well with my tiles. This had better be important."

"Something bad happened to your son," Mama said.

Antonio noticed her choice of wording. *Your son.* Like she didn't want to claim him.

"What now?" Papa asked.

"He's inside."

Papa walked in and stared, then said, "*Ay, por Dios!*"

Antonio shifted in his seat and caught his reflection in a small mirror attached to the wall. Coarse black hair covered his entire face except for his eyes. He looked like a gorilla.

"I stepped on a *nuno*," Antonio said. "Mang Fermin was chasing me out of his orchard."

Papa's brows came together. "Why was he chasing you?"

"Antonio stole a mabolo," Mama explained. "You know how Fermin is about his fruit."

"Do we not feed you enough?" Papa said. "And then on top of that, destroying a *nuno*!"

Mama said, "I meant to ask you earlier, Antonio. What happened to your shirt?"

"A *tiyanak* tricked me," Antonio said. "It attacked me, but I did as you said. I turned my shirt inside out and it left me alone."

"*Susmaryosep!* An eventful night," Mama said. Then she asked Papa, "Can you fetch Tandang Lino?"

"The old man hasn't cured anyone successfully in a while," Papa said. "Some say he's losing his touch."

"*Ay,*" Mama said, "how can you be so disrespectful?"

"I'm just saying maybe he's getting too old. He cured Aling Dona's boy, but not the brother." Papa looked at Antonio. "I think we should let Antonio march at his graduation looking like this."

Mama frowned.

Antonio tried to not react. Sometimes, Papa said things to bait him into getting mad. "That would certainly reflect well on you," Antonio said, "having your son look like a dog. Just think, the only Pulido in the family to finish high school, and I would embarrass you."

Papa's scowl deepened.

"Please, Romy," Mama said. "Fetch Tandang Lino."

"This time of night?"

"When else? When our son turns fully into a dog?"

Papa grumbled but did as Mama asked.

What if I do turn into a dog? Antonio amused himself with the thought that he'd always wanted to have a dog, then sobered quickly. He imagined Papa taunting him with people food while throwing scraps his way. That, to Antonio, would be hell.

Papa seemed to be gone for a long time. Eventually, he returned with Tandang Lino.

"Where is the boy?" the old man asked.

From where he stood, Antonio could see the door being opened more fully by Mama, revealing a man no taller than his mother at the shoulder. Tandang Lino shuffled in, dragging his flip-flops, a gnarled hand grasping a wooden cane that made a hollow knocking sound across the bamboo floor. His lips, stained from chewing the red betel nut, curled up into his toothless mouth.

Papa was right. Many in the village thought Tandang Lino was wise. But that night, Antonio only saw cloudy, vacuous eyes. Tandang Lino healed Antonio once, applying an herbal poultice to fix a broken arm, but that was a long time ago.

"There is nothing I can do for the boy," Tandang Lino said.

"Come here," Mama told Antonio. To the old man, she said, "May I ask why?"

Tandang Lino pointed at Antonio. "Look at his face. He thinks he knows it all. Let him solve his own problem."

Antonio joined his parents and let them wrangle for him.

"Please don't leave, Tandang Lino," Papa begged. "I have a chicken or two I can spare." To Antonio, he said, "*Rearrange* your face."

Antonio did his best.

"I don't need any chickens," Tandang Lino said. "I have enough for my larder. What I need is your son's cooperation."

Turning to Antonio, Papa barked. "Tell him!"

"I will cooperate." Antonio felt Tandang Lino's glance assessing him. More meekly, he said, "I'm sorry, Tandang Lino. I will do what it takes."

"That's better." He looked at Papa. "Hitch your water buffalo, Romy. We're going for a little ride."

THE CART RATTLED along the shoulder of the expressway, an occasional truck rumbling past. Mama had stayed behind in the house. Papa and Tandang Lino sat in front. Antonio suppressed a sigh on the back bench. Cupid plodded along, indifferent to Antonio's misery.

"You're not going to wake up Mang Fermin, are you?" Antonio asked Papa.

Papa looked at him over his shoulder. "We can't just trespass on his property. I don't want to get shot at."

Antonio's stomach churned.

As they approached the orchard entrance, Cupid suddenly stopped. "Go on, you brute," Papa told Cupid. "Move!" But Cupid just stood there.

"Antonio," he said. "Get out and see if something is stuck in the axle."

Antonio got out. He looked at the axle, which looked fine. He looked under the wheel for a rock that might have gotten lodged, but found nothing. He reached out to rub the water buffalo's neck but Cupid shied away from his shaggy arm.

And then, he heard, distinctly, a high-pitched voice saying,

"Foolish boy. You're back again."

"Did you hear that?" Antonio asked the others.

"What?" Papa said.

"A man's voice."

"Maybe Fermin's out."

"No." Antonio was certain it wasn't Mang Fermin. Cupid turned and snorted. In his eyes, Antonio saw his anxiety mirrored.

"Well, it wasn't me," Papa said. "Go on, get in."

The cart was already moving when Antonio pitched himself ungracefully back in.

"The *nuno* was out by the water," Antonio said.

"Alright," Papa said, but he kept on heading the direction Antonio had hoped he wouldn't: Mang Fermin's house. He would just as soon face a hundred *nunos* than a single Mang Fermin.

Antonio waited with Tandang Lino in the cart while Papa went to the door. A faint light glimmered through an open window. A tomb-like darkness shrouded the rest of the house.

The bats were strangely inert. Silent. Antonio realized that he hadn't heard them move or fly. He wasn't sure if he liked that better or not. With their silence, he half expected them to swoop down on him from nowhere.

Tandang Lino spoke, startling Antonio.

"This place used to be happy," Tandang Lino said. "Open to the sun. In the summer, the mabolo blossoms were so thick they looked like bouquets. And now, look at it." He paused. "Fermin's father could coax a fruit out of a rock. He had a gift for making things grow. But Fermin, no. That man makes things rot."

"*Tao po!*" Is someone there? Papa said at the door. "*Tao po!*"

Mad Juana slunk into view like a half-starved predator.

"And his sister," Tandang Lino said beside Antonio in the cart. "A shame. She was the most beautiful girl in her class. Soft-spoken and demure. Did you know she was engaged the year she started going crazy?"

Antonio shook his head. "To whom?"

"To a sailor. Some people say he broke her heart, and *then* she went crazy. But I think she was already losing her mind. As he boarded his ship, she told him she'd drown herself if he didn't stay."

"What did he do?"

"He hid and let the shore police take her away."

Antonio looked back at the doorway. Mad Juana had stepped aside, and Mang Fermin now stood there. His eyes flicked towards Antonio, who compressed himself even smaller into the cart.

Raised voices reached Antonio's ears. He could make out the words, "gate," "your worthless son," and "get out."

Papa came back in a foul mood, like the times when he had lost at the gambling tables. "He wants us off his property. The tide is high and we can only access the beach through the orchard. Antonio, you will have to remain hairy the rest of your life."

Tandang Lino raised his cane and whacked Papa on the head with it. "*Aray!*" Papa said. "What was that for?"

"You give up far too easily, Romy," the old man said. "We shall go through the beach."

"At this time of night?" Papa said.

"At this time of night."

High tide now covered the beach that had been, just hours ago, a stretch of sand. Beyond it, *nuno sa punso* dotted a hill. Antonio, his father, and Tandang Lino stood in waist-deep water, a thin moon putting forth little light. Antonio tried to pull Cupid forward, but he only dug in his hooves and snorted.

"Strange," Antonio said. "Normally, he'll cross water."

Antonio walked a little closer to the hill. Cupid was trained to come at a whistle and he tried that now. But Cupid only snorted and stomped, refusing to move.

"It must be the *nuno*," Papa said.

When he proposed that Antonio should carry Tandang Lino on his shoulders, Antonio balked like Cupid.

"We can float Tandang Lino on a raft," Antonio said.

"And *where* is this raft?" Papa said.

"Can you swim, Tandang Lino?" Antonio said.

"Antonio!" his father said.

"Can't we just undo the spell from across the water?" Antonio said.

Tandang Lino shook his head. "I need to see the actual mound."

"What if I can't remember which one it was?"

Tandang Lino drew himself up, adding a fraction of an inch to his contorted height. "You are just full of questions, aren't you? And none of them are the essential ones you should be asking your conscience. Let's go."

First, he had to get on Antonio's shoulders.

Antonio submerged himself to his neck, and waited. When nothing happened, he turned. Tandang Lino's hand trembled as it stretched and touched Antonio's shoulder.

Antonio groaned inwardly. And then consoled himself with the thought – *At this rate, maybe the tide will go out and then we can just cross the sand.*

"I used to climb coconut trees when I was young," Tandang Lino said.

My, but his knees were bony! They dug in Antonio's back as he climbed up like a feeble crab. Inch by inch, the old man eventually made it so his legs were on Antonio's shoulders.

The wave pulled back, then returned with such force that it nearly knocked Antonio off his feet.

"Careful now," Papa said.

With every step Antonio took, the waves got more unruly, causing Antonio to stagger around. On his shoulders, Tandang Lino swayed like a flimsy tower.

"What are you doing?" Tandang Lino said, clawing at Antonio's face. "Why aren't you walking straight?"

Antonio willed his legs to move, but all he managed to do was sway Tandang Lino around.

The old man whacked Antonio with his cane. "Would you stop that?" he said. "You're making me sick!"

"My legs!" Antonio said. "I can't move them. It's like someone is holding them in place!" Finally, Antonio could move again. He walked forward, only to have a wave crash into him.

"*Hay naku! Hay naku!*" Tandang Lino cried, before they both fell facedown into the water. The old man resurfaced, sputtering and refusing Antonio's offer for to carry him on his shoulders again.

They waded over to the landmine of *punso*. Antonio could see his footprints all over one mound. His hair-cursed skin tingled.

"*Makikisuyo po, nuno, makikisuyo po,*" Tandang Lino said, stopping a few feet away. "I've brought back this boy. He has been careless, and he has something to tell you."

Tandang Lino looked at Antonio expectantly. "What should I say?" Antonio asked.

"Tell him that you will be respectful of other people's property from now on," Tandang Lino suggested.

Antonio opened his mouth to say the words, only to be pulled to the ground by a foot-tall, *nuno.* He looked like an old man, shriveled like a prune. His hair reached to his waist, and his nose was long, like a *talong* or eggplant. Pulling on Antonio's cursed "beard," he said, in a high-pitched voice, "Get out, get out, you trespassing lout!" And then he scurried like a rat into the mound.

Antonio turned to Tandang Lino and Papa. "Did you see that?" he asked in a similar high-pitched voice, and they nodded, their eyes fearful.

The hair on Antonio's arms grew even thicker in the moonlight. He could feel the follicles pushing themselves out of his pores.

"What is happening?" Papa asked. "Tandang Lino, help him, please."

"You have angered the spirit greatly," Tandang Lino said in Antonio's ear. "You must ask for forgiveness!"

Antonio's words poured out of him like a repentant child. He begged for mercy, he begged for a chance to attend his high school graduation, even if it meant having to endure boring speeches, for wasn't that enough of a punishment in itself?

He heard laughter, but looking up, he saw Tandang Lino's grim expression and knew it wasn't him. To his astonishment, Papa was sobbing in the background.

The stranglehold on him loosened, and he bent over and expelled a huge breath. But the hair was still there, in all its glory.

"Very well," Tandang Lino said. "It's done."

Papa sniffled and cleared his throat. "But he still has hair on his arms," he said.

The old man closed his eyes as though searching for something in the wind. "Yes, but I no longer feel anger in the air. The spirit has been pacified."

10

"ANTONIO, WAKE UP."

Antonio opened one eye. He was being shaken at the shoulder, followed by a sharper admonition: "Antonio!"

He sat up and looked around, bewildered. Mama stood over him at his bedside, a frown on her face. Through the open window, daylight was beginning to filter through the thick *kasuy* boughs. He tried to lie back down on his woven *banig*.

"Oh no, you don't," Mama said, pulling him by the scruff of his shirt.

"It's still dark outside," he mumbled.

"Remember your promise to Papa," Mama said. "You would farm without complaining."

He sighed. "I'm up. I'm up." Mama left him.

Scratching his head, he froze. He remembered last night and slowly lowered his hand.

His hand still had hair, but was not as hairy as the night before. He whooped so loud that Mama ran into his bedroom again.

"What's the matter?" she asked.

"Mama, my hands...my arms...I'm free of the curse."

She stared at his face. "Well, I'm not too sure of that," she said, then left him.

He scrambled out of his bed and searched for the broken mirror that usually sat on the top of the dresser. He picked it up and held it in front of his face.

Antonio's heart sank. He still looked like a gorilla, with hair growing *everywhere*, it seemed. The prospect of having to shave like Papa depressed him.

He tried to shake out of a tired fog. The house was still closed up, quiet and dark. He unlocked the door to the back, the lock jiggling unsteadily, worn out over the years. As his bare feet made contact with the cold, damp earth of the *batalan*, or outside kitchen, he shivered.

Stumbling to the grain bin, he handed some corn to the cat, who sniffed at his offering and yowled loudly. He threw hay at the chickens and put a bucket of milk out for Cupid. He wanted to feed the dog, but remembered they didn't have a dog.

"What in heaven's name are you doing?" Papa's voice boomed at him from the direction of the house. His eyebrows were knitted, his fists planted at his waist. He grabbed the bucket and set it onto the steps of the shed where they often ate their meals. "You've just wasted a week's worth of milk."

"I'm sorry," Antonio said. "I guess I'm just so tired."

"Your face," Papa said, "it's still…"

"I know."

"Last night," Papa said, straightening out the grain bin, "you scared us."

"I'm sorry."

"Ah, Antonio, I wish you wouldn't break your mother's heart." Papa looked away. "Your mother and I may be old and useless, Antonio, but we're all you have. Do you understand?"

"Yes." Antonio wished Papa would go ahead and be done with his sermon. It was too early in the morning for one. When Mama called out, "Breakfast!" he ran off before Papa could say anything else.

Antonio went to school with a handkerchief tied around his face, pretending he had the mumps. His best friend Jose met him at the hallway, a curious expression on his face. Antonio did an about-face and walked away as quickly as he could.

"Wait a minute," Jose said, grabbing him by the shoulder. "What happened?"

"Nothing," Antonio said, shrugging his hand off.

"Right," Jose said, keeping pace. Without warning, he grabbed the handkerchief and pulled it down. His eyes widened. "Oh my…"

"Promise you won't tell anyone," Antonio said, covering his face again.

"What *really* happened?"

Antonio told him.

Jose nodded his head. "I had a cousin who angered a spirit and got warts."

"Did he take a bath regularly?"

"Come to think of it, no." He squinted at Antonio. "Are you going to attend graduation *that way*?"

"I have to. My parents are forcing me. They say it's my punishment for stealing a mabolo. One mabolo! Although," Antonio lowered his voice, "it was worth it for what I discovered."

"You've always wanted to look like an ape?"

"No, no." Antonio paused. "Mang Fermin has a record player!"

"Go on. I'm waiting for the good news."

Antonio punched Jose on the arm. "You know how much I've been wanting to see one of those!"

"Tell me about it."

"Someday, Jose, I'm going to have my own record player."

Jose raised an eyebrow. "And you laughed when I wanted my own basketball hoop."

The Dasalin schoolhouse stood two stories high and consisted of timber walls, a galvanized roof and hardwood floors. It had a spacious wraparound porch and classrooms whose doors led directly to this porch. Even on the last day, Arnell Fernandez, a classmate whose family operated a *sari-sari*, or variety, store just a few doors from Antonio's house, held an open tobacco case full of candy.

"Is that you, Antonio?" Arnell asked, as a handkerchief-wearing Antonio passed him.

"Yes," came Antonio's muffled reply.

"Want to buy candy?"

Antonio looked at the candies and fingered the coin in his pocket.

"Tell you what," Arnell said. "I'll sell you two candies for the price of one."

Antonio tossed the coin to Arnell and ate Necco wafers as he walked into class. When the school bell rang, the teachers put Antonio's graduating class of twenty-three to work, deep cleaning. Antonio didn't mind too badly. He preferred cleaning the school over math equations any day. Students wiped down desks, swept the floor, and polished it with coconut husks, and swept the floor. As he banged erasers together outside, creating a cloud of dust, Grace Mijares appeared in the hallway.

If any girl's name embodied her personality, Grace did. She walked like she was a princess and the school was her palace. Grace's father, Mr. Mijares, owned the tricycle fleet at the station. They lived in a riverfront *hacienda* whose driveway alone was about as long as Antonio's family farm.

Today she had her hair up in a bouffant, like the latest style, and her creamy Chinese *mestiza* skin glowed.

"That's a good idea," she said.

"What is?" Antonio said.

"The handkerchief around your nose." She eyed him curiously. "Is it true? Did you really knock over a *nuno sa punso* last night?"

"Who told you that?"

"I overheard your friend Jose Pineda talking to a boy in my class."

"That rat," he said, gripping the erasers tightly.

"I think that was brave of you," she said.

He blinked. "You do?"

"Jose said you had to fight off the *nuno*."

"Well, actually…"

"And that," she said, leaning close, "underneath that handkerchief are scratches from your encounter with the *nuno*."

Bless you, Jose. You're a good friend!

He shrugged. "I *almost* didn't survive, but it was nothing."

"Nothing?" She squeaked. "I think that was something."

"Thanks."

She handed him a notebook, and he stared at it stupidly.

"It's my autograph book," she said. "Would you please sign it? If you're not too busy, that is." She glanced at his powdery-white hands and the erasers.

He tried to grab the notebook without letting go of the erasers, but they were too much of a handful. The notebook and the erasers slipped. Grace giggled. "I'll get it from you later," she said.

He stood there a good minute with a silly smile on his face. Grace wanted him to sign her autograph book. She thought he was brave.

His teacher came out. "Are you about done there, Antonio? There's more to do inside."

"Yes ma'am," Antonio said, floating all the way back to the classroom.

THE TEACHERS DISMISSED students early with the admonition to "wash behind the ears." They were to return after supper for the graduation ceremony in the school yard.

As Antonio helped clear dishes from an early supper, a car engine emitted a low rumble outside. Antonio left plates stacked on the table, dodged Trining's disapproving eye, and ran outside to see who it was. On his way, he passed Lolo Sonny in the *salas*, listening to the radio with a peaceful smile.

Papa stood in front of the most beautiful car Antonio had ever seen. It was red as a rooster's comb and long and majestic like a boat. Tito Oscar, Papa's younger brother, was leaning against the side of the car. When Tito Oscar saw Antonio, he gestured for him to come over.

"Ah, you are becoming a man now, Antonio. Look at that mustache."

Papa and Antonio exchanged glances. Thankfully, Antonio didn't have to wear the handkerchief anymore, even though he still had some leftover.

"Give the front seat a try, Antonio," Tito Oscar urged. He was ten years younger than Antonio's father, but Tito

Oscar could have passed for his son. His eyes glittered with excitement. Antonio liked him; he always had a smile and knew how to enjoy life.

Antonio didn't wait for a second invitation. He ran down to the open door and slipped into the driver's seat. The engine was turned off, but there were keys in the ignition.

"Go ahead," Tito Oscar said. "Fire it up."

Papa watched from the opposite window, his face pinched like he was sucking on something sour. "Just don't break it," he said.

"It's not that fragile," Tito Oscar assured them. He showed Antonio how to start the engine. When Antonio turned the key, the car made a wrenching noise. Alarmed, he bumped the steering wheel and set off the horn.

Tito Oscar laughed. Papa's frown deepened. "What a waste of good money," Papa said.

"This deal came along and I just had to take advantage of the good price," Tito Oscar said.

"What does Alice think of it?" Mama asked as she walked over, wiping her hands on a linen cloth.

"She was skeptical at first," Tito Oscar said, "but then I told her I'd be able to bring her to the hospital quicker than the horse-pulled *karitela* and now she likes the idea."

Tita Alice, Tito Oscar's wife, was pregnant with their third child. Their two older children were girls. Antonio hoped for a boy cousin this time.

Tito Oscar went in to see Lolo Sonny. Antonio continued to sit in the car, pretending he was racing down the expressway. After a few minutes, Papa, sounding annoyed, said, "Antonio, it's time to come in and get ready for your graduation."

Tito Oscar came out of the house and leaned his elbows on the open window. "You want a ride over to the school later?" he asked. "We can take Lolo Sonny, too."

"Sure," Antonio said. "Is that alright, Papa?"

Papa shrugged. "I suppose."

"Kuya Romy," Tito Oscar said as he came out of the house. "I'll also need two bags of fertilizer."

Papa had already turned on his heel. "You know where they are."

Antonio stroked the steering wheel one more time and got

out of the car reluctantly. Someday, he wanted to be like Tito Oscar. He'd go for his dreams and make them happen.

Tito Oscar picked Antonio up an hour later. As Tita Alice wasn't feeling very well, she stayed home. Tito Oscar's daughters, fourteen-year-old Irene and seven-year-old Christine, came. Irene sat in the front passenger seat.

"Join your sister in the back, Irene," Tito Oscar said.

"But Papa," Irene said, "that wasn't a very far drive from the house."

"Yes, but it's Antonio's special day. And you can entertain Lolo Sonny."

Irene pouted but moved to the back.

Antonio helped Lolo Sonny get into the car, one arthritic leg at a time. Once Antonio got him situated, he got in the front passenger seat, sliding his hand over the smooth dashboard leather. He tapped his foot to the music that played on the radio.

The car was a marvelous machine.

They passed Antonio's classmates who were heading to graduation on foot. A few came in tricycles emblazoned with the colorful Mijares Enterprises logo on the back.

"Watch this," Tito Oscar said, grinning.

He pushed on the horn. It boomed like a barge, making the tricycles swerve and veer to the side. His classmates and their families turned to watch their progress.

"Wave, nephew," Tito Oscar said with a laugh. "Your classmates think you are someone famous."

Antonio waved and smiled.

They found a parking spot beside a battered-looking jeep, just as Jopet, Grace's 16-year-old brother, was pulling in, radio at full blast. His jeep dated back to World War Two, left behind in Dasalin by an American unit and no longer operable until Mr. Mijares bought it for his son to work on. Jopet had a metal roof welded on which had begun to rust over. But it was still a beauty.

"Nice set of wheels, Antonio," Jopet said as he got out of his jeep.

"Thanks," Antonio said. Then he asked, casually, "Where's your sister?" He tapped Grace's autograph book in his hand.

"Somewhere," Jopet said, shrugging, still riveted towards Tito Oscar's car. Antonio left Tito Oscar and Jopet talking about engines and took his grandfather and cousins over to chairs reserved for the audience. Antonio joined Jose at the student seats after he made Irene promise to save two spots for his parents.

A motorcycle roared into view. Grace sat sideways on the back of Timo Sandoval's motorcycle. Antonio's heart sank. So much for his high hopes about Grace being impressed with him.

A row over, he heard a girl say to another, "I hear they're going steady."

The other girl said, "I hear she'll break up with him because she's going to Manila."

Jose turned to them. "You're both wrong," he said. "She's Antonio's girlfriend." The girls looked at Antonio and giggled. Jose gave him a thumbs-up sign.

Antonio's parents arrived. He half-rose in his seat to show them where the girls and Lolo Sonny were sitting.

Tito Oscar, as Dasalin's *baranggay* captain, gave the first speech. He was funny and gave them advice about starting out in life, telling everyone that he was the prime example of why education was so important. Everyone laughed. They knew he didn't go to college, but look at him, he was rich anyway.

Antonio's eyes kept drifting shut through the other speakers. Yolly Nakpil, the valedictorian, spoke. She was an already quiet girl who became even quieter when her father died two years before. She talked about being responsible now that they were high school graduates and to honor parents by following their advice. Resisting the urge to roll his eyes, he shifted his attention to Grace, a few rows ahead. Timo whispered something in her ear, making her giggle.

Antonio glowered in his seat.

When he heard clapping, he joined in enthusiastically. Yolly was finally done! From the stage, Yolly looked at him sharply, before sitting down with the guests of honor.

Finally – finally! – the principal handed out the diplomas, declared them graduates, and then it was mercifully over.

"We made it!" Jose pumped Antonio's hand up and down in a hand shake. "No more making cheat sheets for you."

Mama embraced Antonio, then looked from him to Jose.

"He's just kidding, Mama," Antonio said.

Jose said, "What about that time when...?"

"Hush," Antonio said. "You won't ever let me live it down, will you?"

Tito Oscar shook Antonio's hand. "Now that you're done," he said, "you should work for me."

"He won't be able to," Papa interjected. "He'll be working for me."

Antonio bristled. How could Papa just *assume* he would just keep working at the farm? "I'd love to work for you, Tito Oscar."

Tito Oscar patted Antonio's shoulder. "Only if it's alright with your father."

Papa scowled. "Like I said, he's working for me."

Antonio clenched his jaw. He didn't need Papa to tell him what to do. "I need to talk to a classmate," he said, and marched off, just so he didn't say anything rude to his father. Wrapped up in his thoughts, he ran into Yolly Nakpil.

"Sorry," he muttered.

She had shoulder length hair pulled back loosely and a dusky complexion, one they would call *morena*. Pretty but unapproachable. Her dark eyes regarded him haughtily.

"Great speech, by the way," he added.

"Oh?" She arched her eyebrow. "You weren't even listening."

"Of course I was listening."

"You were staring at Grace and Timo the whole time."

Antonio's mouth fell open. "How did you...?"

She smirked. "You see a lot of interesting things from the stage."

Grace appeared in his line of vision. When he turned to excuse himself, Yolly had already walked back into the crowd.

"Grace," he called out.

GHOST MOON NIGHT

She glanced his way and smiled, meeting him halfway. "Here's your autograph book," he said.

Timo joined them and glared at Antonio. "What does he want?" Timo asked.

"He's giving me back my autograph book," Grace explained, taking it from Antonio.

"Antonio knows how to write?" Timo snickered.

"Oh Timo," Grace said. "Don't be rude." She thanked Antonio and the pair walked off holding hands.

Antonio stuffed his hands in his pockets and returned to his family. Papa was talking to his neighbor classmate Arnell. "Can you work for me? Just until the planting season's over?"

"Why?" Arnell said, glancing at Antonio. "Can't your son help you?"

"I'll hopefully be working at another job," Antonio said.

Arnell should know what it was like working for one's parents. Arnell always groused about how his mother used him for free labor at her tiny, *sari-sari* variety store.

"Alright," Arnell said, "I can help you for five more pesos a day than last summer's pay."

Antonio thought his father would spit out his dentures. "Five more pesos!" My, how he grumbled. But Arnell simply stood there, just like he did selling candy at school, haggling and biding his time.

Eventually, Papa nodded. "Well, Arnell, at least I can count on you, even if you aren't a blood relative." He cast a sour glance towards Antonio.

Tito Oscar offered Antonio a ride back, but Papa said, "It's alright. He's walking with me." Mama got the ride instead. Antonio waited and waited all the way home for a tongue-lashing, but Papa was quiet. Finally, just as they reached the house, Papa turned to Antonio and said, "You think you're too good for farming, now that you've gotten your high school diploma?"

Antonio just looked ahead.

"Well?" his father demanded.

"No," Antonio said, "it's not that!"

"Then what is it?"

Antonio shrugged. "I don't know. I just know that something better is in store for me."

"How do you plan to figure it out?"

"I haven't thought that far. I just graduated, Papa."

Papa shook his head mournfully and went inside.

12

A WEEK LATER, ON Sunday, Father Sebastian woke to the crowing of a rooster. He waited to hear the familiar clip clop of horse hooves interspersed with the blare of a car horn, just outside his window, the shout of the vendor selling the warm and fragrant *taho* soy drink, stall owners setting up their wares in the church courtyard. But no, he heard only the rustling of leaves and the distant barking of a dog. He turned his head to the open window. It framed only blue sky, not a rain-stained stone rampart.

And then he remembered.

He was no longer in the capital city of Manila. Instead, he had been living in Dasalin for about a week. Beautiful, remote, odd Dasalin.

A village cursed with evil spirits once a month.

An involuntary laugh escaped his lips. Technically, would they be part of his parish, too, once a month? When a cloud darkened the window, Father Sebastian bit his lip. A heavenly reproof that he was being irreverent? He made the sign of the cross and murmured his apologies.

The sun came out again, its rays dispelling the gloom from his arrival that first day. All this Ghost Moon Night business needn't rule his life. It was just one day of the month. After saying his prayers, he washed in a basin and patted his face dry with a towel. In the mirror, age stared back at him. He had lines it seemed, for every road he'd ever taken in his life in the past 65 years. This very well may be his last road.

His fingers fumbled nervously over the buttons on his cassock. Chuckling, he realized he was acting like he'd never officiated at Sunday Mass before. He would go down and get a cup of coffee before getting on with his day.

He heard a knock and opened the door to Henry, who held a steaming cup of coffee.

"Thank you," Father Sebastian said, grateful but a little unsettled. How did this little man know he craved coffee?

Henry didn't smile. His face perpetually held a rather sullen expression that Father Sebastian decided he wouldn't take personally. The man was pleasant enough, efficient at any rate, always anticipating the priest's every need. Maybe he had a facial deformity.

"Your breakfast is ready," Henry said.

Once again, the priest thanked him. "I've been meaning to ask you, Henry, what have other priests done about Ghost Moon Night?"

Henry shrugged. "Nothing."

"Nothing at all?"

"Well, maybe a few…things."

"Like what?"

"They've tried to use it to guilt villagers into sinning less. But it all goes against the grain of tradition."

"Tradition?" the priest frowned. "I don't understand."

"Well, everyone gambles here. And if a wife gets out of line, flirting, for instance, with the cobbler…a man's justified in getting jealous. Everyone sins at one time or another. No one is perfect."

"Of course. Only the Savior was perfect."

"Exactly," Henry said.

"But why shouldn't the church help *encourage* a more perfect behavior?"

Henry's scowl deepened. "Because being righteous all the

GHOST MOON NIGHT

time is simply *impossible.*"

The irony of Henry's statement struck the priest with such force. "The sinners would haunt the earth and the righteous ones would be in heaven," Father Sebastian said. "I still think it's best if we all strive to be good and not languish with the bad. The Savior showed us the way."

"I will of course take your lead, Father," Henry said. With a little bow, he left the priest.

Father Sebastian brought his cup of coffee to the window and slowly sipped from it. The thought that someone at the diocese failed to mention anything about the curse was disturbing. And yet...how could he blame them? This parish still needed a priest. They needed a counterpoint to this curse's darkness. He could be that counterpoint.

But then Henry's words returned and a tide of confusion washed over him.

Closing his eyes, he muttered a prayer. "Father in heaven, if it is Thy will, help me know what to do to help the people of Dasalin. Send me a message, or a messenger."

A clattering noise made him open his eyes. Below, a water buffalo pulled a cart into the church courtyard. Father Sebastian watched as the boy who picked him up that first day – Antonio, yes, that was his name – pulled on the reins. Antonio tied up his water buffalo to the posts where villagers could hitch their animals for blessings, then stood by the beast's ear, as though carrying on a conversation.

Maybe this teen could help him. Father Sebastian looked up to the heavens, with a little nod and smiled.

13

WITHIN A FEW minutes, the priest entered the chapel. Antonio greeted him with a hearty "Good morning!"

"And a good morning to you, too," Father Sebastian replied. "You seem to be in good spirits."

"That's what Cupid told me, too."

"And Cupid is…?" Father Sebastian asked.

"My water buffalo." Antonio looked sheepish. "Well, he didn't exactly talk. He just looked at me kind of funny. Anyway, why shouldn't I feel happy? I finally graduated from high school. Plus, I'm no longer hairy!"

At his questioning glance, Antonio smiled. "It's a long story."

While Antonio covered the altar with a cloth, Father Sebastian prepared his sermon. Then Antonio sat down on a chair beside him. From the priest's vantage point, he had a clear view of the parishioners who were filing in. Antonio provided a whispered commentary.

"There's Mrs. Silva," he said, as a stout lady whose hair was pulled back in a tight bun walked in. "She's your parish patroness. She can raise money for whatever you need."

"Really?"

"Yes. In fact, she's trying to buy you a new altar."

"What's wrong with the one we have now?"

"It's not very obvious, but there's a crack in the middle. The last priest had the habit of pounding the altar whenever he wanted to make a point. You're not an altar pounder, are you?"

"No, not usually."

Mrs. Silva genuflected at the altar steps and approached the priest. "Father Sebastian," she said, pushing up the spectacles on her broad nose then squeezing his hand. "I'm so sorry I haven't been by to introduce myself. I'm Leonora Silva, at your service. Would it be alright if we put out the altar collection jar today at the chapel entrance?"

"Of course, of course," Father Sebastian said.

"Good! I cannot wait to commission the marble from Romblon. And then afterwards, we can focus on the *kuding fiesta*."

And with that, she was gone, back to the front pew, looking very pleased with herself. She handed a large jar to a young girl, who proceeded to put the jar in the back, on a table.

"My advice to you," Antonio whispered, "is to just get out of Mrs. Silva's way."

"I'm beginning to think that. What is a *kuding*?"

"The *kuding* is a swallow. It nests on our cliffs. Many in our village consider the bird to be sacred."

"And you don't?"

Antonio looked away, then back. "I don't know, Father. I used to believe in everything. Your parents tell you one thing, and you just believe it without question. But now..." He shrugged. "I wonder sometimes if all our rituals make a difference." Antonio bit his lip. "You won't mention that to anyone, will you? Around here, it's a sin to question our traditions."

"Your observation is safe with me," Father Sebastian assured him. "In fact, I agree with you wholeheartedly. It's been several years since I lived in the provinces and I forget that pagan rituals are alive everywhere. The city isn't immune to this. Many in the capital worship worldly idols."

As a couple walked in, Antonio's expression dimmed. "The two people coming in right now are Mang Fermin and his sister

Mad Juana, I mean Juana. I'm surprised to see them here. They never come to church." The pair sat on the very back pew, their arms linked tightly. Around the woman's neck was a collar and a chain. A family sitting there slid further down the bench. The man's scowl deepened.

"What is that around her neck?" Father Sebastian asked.

Antonio made a circular gesture at his temple. "She's crazy. At the market, she steals butcher knives."

"Ah."

"There's my family," Antonio said. "My parents and my Lolo Sonny, my father's father. Behind my *lolo* is Tandang Lino. He's the village elder. He's about as old as my *lolo,* but not quite. I think Lolo beats him by a year. Tandang Lino had the idea of launching the *kuding fiesta* decades ago, when he was a *baranggay* captain. No one reveres the *kuding* more than he does. Every planting season, he leads a pilgrimage to the top of Mount Dasalin to deliver offerings."

"When is the *kuding fiesta?*"

"Next month."

A tall boy and a surly-looking man came in. "That's my friend Jose Pineda and his father," Antonio said. "He has a basketball scholarship in Manila. Can you tell, with his height? Jose's father used to play basketball in college, but he got injured. Jose says he's tried to drink his disappointment away since."

A handsome man entered the chapel with a pregnant wife and two young girls. Suddenly, Antonio's voice rose a notch, with a hint of pride and excitement. "That's my uncle, Oscar Pulido. He owns a successful fishing business and he's the *baranggay* captain. That's his wife, my Tita Alice, and their daughters Irene and Christine."

Another family entered, prompting Antonio to say, "Speaking of success, there's Mr. Mijares and his family. And his daughter...Grace."

The priest looked from Antonio to the young lady and smiled. Then he noticed Mrs. Silva looking pointedly at him and at her watch.

"Thank you for the introductions," the priest told Antonio. "Shall we start Mass?"

When it came time for him to deliver his sermon, Father

Sebastian stood up. He had it all planned out, writing some of the points he wanted to talk about on a piece of paper. He realized the paper had slipped out of his cassock pocket. Turning, he saw Antonio holding it up with a question in his eyes.

Father Sebastian surveyed the chapel. His gaze lingered on each person for a fraction of a second. He was aware that he was causing a bit of a stir. Turning to Antonio again, he declined the paper with a shake of the head.

"Today," the priest said, "I shall talk about Ghost Moon Night."

There was a momentary, stunned silence. Everyone raised their hands to make the sign of the cross.

Antonio stared at Father Sebastian, unable to believe his ears.

"More specifically," the priest continued, "I would like to address how we can prepare ourselves for Ghost Moon Night."

Another flurry of crosses.

"I'm not talking about physical preparedness," Father Sebastian said. "I'm talking about spiritual. I've been told that the wicked come back from the grave and haunt this beautiful village. If you were to die tomorrow, would you be among the legion of wicked? Or would you truly *rest in peace*? Do you cheat your fellow man? If so, it is time to set your life aright. Do you cheat on your wife? It's time to forsake your ways."

The priest mentioned a few more sins. And then he launched on something totally unexpected.

"Perhaps," the priest said, "if this village spent a bit more time on good deeds instead of worshipping birds, this village would be better off."

Antonio glanced at Tandang Lino. The old man's eyes burned with anger.

When Father Sebastian was done, the parishioners erupted into whispers. All except for Antonio's mother and Lolo Sonny. Mama nodded approvingly and Lolo Sonny had his usual unconcerned smile.

After church, the congregation poured out into the morning heat. Antonio walked over to the chapel entrance to collect the offerings when he heard Tandang Lino say, "That priest doesn't know what or who he's dealing with."

Someone asked, "Does this mean we will have to abolish the *kuding fiesta*?"

The old man scowled. "I will find myself a different church before that happens!"

Another asked, "And the *langbuan*?" Listeners made the sign of the cross.

Tandang Lino frowned. "There are stronger forces to reckon with that this priest knows nothing, absolutely *nothing*, about."

Few people stayed behind to shake the priest's hand after Mass. Even fewer people put money in the altar collection jar, which luckily was already half-full with bills and coins. Antonio put the vestments away as Father Sebastian hung up his robe.

"I didn't do that very diplomatically, did I?" the priest said.

As tactfully as he could, Antonio said, "I just don't think everyone was ready for that sermon."

"I don't know why I said what I did. But I've come to learn over the years that when I am inspired to say something, I must say it."

Mrs. Silva barricaded the door with her ample figure and practically shoved the collection jar under parishioners' noses. "If you don't donate, you'll join the legion of the wicked," she said. She left the jar on a table, instructing Antonio to put it away in the vestments cupboard. Then she went outside to talk to Father Sebastian.

Antonio went to the vestments room to hang the Mass linen. As he left the room, he ran into his father.

"Are you done?" Papa asked. "We're ready. Lolo's getting restless."

"I can go as soon as I put away…" Antonio's words trailed off. The chapel was empty. And so was the altar collection jar.

"The money was here," Antonio muttered to himself, searching around the little table, near the holy water receptacle, and out in the foyer, but he couldn't find it.

He wiped the perspiration forming on his brow. *Where could the money be?*

Mrs. Silva returned shortly. "On second thought, Antonio,

let me count the money first. *Then* you can store it. If we're close enough to the amount, maybe I can cajole the marble makers into scouting a slab for me sooner."

"It's gone," Antonio said.

"What do you mean it's gone?" Mrs. Silva said. "Antonio! Where is the money?"

Father Sebastian came in. "What's the matter?"

Mrs. Silva pointed an accusing finger at Antonio. "This young man stole the altar money!"

14

"I DIDN'T STEAL IT!" Antonio said.

Mrs. Silva tapped her foot impatiently on the floor. "Then where is it?"

Antonio scratched his head. "I don't know. It was here, and then it wasn't here!"

They searched again. When they came up empty-handed, everyone looked at Antonio.

"I didn't steal it," he told Father Sebastian.

"There's only one way to find out." Mrs. Silva pinned him with her gaze. "Empty your pockets."

Antonio did so. Mrs. Silva looked around, then told Antonio's father, "Could you please do the same?"

Papa had a few things – some coins (but not *the* coins), Chicklet gum, and his handkerchief – but no altar fund.

Finally, the priest called off the search.

"I suggest you call the constable," Mrs. Silva said.

Father Sebastian escorted Mrs. Silva to the foyer. "I will take care of it. Why don't you go home and get some rest?"

The priest stood there pensively for a long moment. "Odd, isn't it, that the money should disappear like that?"

"I can keep helping you find it," Antonio offered.

"No, that's alright. Your family is waiting. But thank you." Antonio sat on the bench of the water buffalo cart, outside in the church courtyard, feeling more aggravated by the minute. Lolo Sonny sat beside him, while his parents stared him down.

"I swear, I didn't take the money!" he said.

"You shouldn't swear," Mama said.

Antonio turned to Lolo Sonny. "You believe me, don't you, Lolo Sonny?"

Lolo Sonny nodded, wiping his mouth with a trembling finger. "My *apo* is...a good boy."

"We'd better go, Romy," Mama said. "Your father's had a long day."

Papa cast another sour glance at Antonio, then got in the cart. When they arrived at the house, Antonio helped Lolo Sonny into the living room to listen to the radio. Antonio was ready to escape to his room when Lolo Sonny said, "*Apo*." Grandson.

"Yes, Lolo Sonny?"

"Can...you...please....turn...it...up?"

Antonio's frown disappeared. "Of course, Lolo." He turned up the volume and took a seat by his grandfather.

Lolo Sonny smiled. "Thank...you."

"You're welcome," he said. Bowing his head, he whispered, "I'm glad you think I'm good for something. Sometimes I don't feel like I'm good enough. I'm always letting people down." He couldn't stop the words as they flowed out. "I try to be a good son, but Papa never seems to notice that I'm trying. When I do help, instead of thanking me for the job I did, he tells me that I could have worked a lot longer. I try to be a good friend, but I just pretend to be happy when Jose tells me his good news. And we know I've failed miserably at being a good altar boy."

Lolo Sonny reached out a trembling hand and patted Antonio's head. "You're a...good...boy."

It reminded Antonio of the times, when, as a little boy, he'd follow his *lolo* around on his carpentry jobs. Antonio would make something out of scrap wood and Lolo Sonny would praise his creation. But sometimes, his work of art fell apart. Lolo Sonny always made Antonio feel better with a pat on the head and a centavo coin for a sweet.

"Thanks, Lolo," Antonio said. Suddenly, it didn't matter

that no one else in the world believed in him, so long as Lolo Sonny did.

As he left Lolo Sonny in the *salas,* he heard his parents talking in Mama's sewing room.

"We'll eat dinner after the cockfight," Papa said.

"Romy. You've already gambled away our last bit of money."

"Oscar is entering his prize cock, Ilaryo. He's a sure win, and besides, I promised Oscar that as his brother, I would go support him."

Mama said, "Will he pay your gambling debts, too? What if you lose again?"

"Did you not hear me? Ilaryo *will* win."

"That's what you said the last time."

"Don't worry. Oscar said he'll loan me money."

"No more loans. Please."

"Ilaryo is sure to win," Papa insisted.

Antonio sighed. Another night of bickering. He started to go to his room, but Mama said his name. He poked his head in the doorway of the sewing room.

"Are you going with your father to the cockfight tonight?" Mama asked.

Mama seldom went anymore, but Antonio usually did with Papa. He nodded. "I was planning on it."

"Make sure he quits while he's ahead."

"*Ay naku,*" Papa said. "Margarita."

Antonio looked at his mother, sitting at her sewing machine on the Sabbath day of rest. Working. Always working. He couldn't remember when the last time was he heard her laugh – really enjoy herself – or when the last time was that he'd seen her do *nothing.* His glance took in her prominent collarbone and thin frame, the permanent squint from threading one too many needles, the veins bulging on the back of her hand.

"I'll do my best," he said.

Before the cockfight, Papa left for a quick errand. Antonio

listened to the radio with Lolo Sonny while waiting. When he returned, Papa carried a burlap bag into the house and took it to Mama's sewing room.

"Margarita," Papa said, "I brought you a sliver of pork and *malunggay* leaves for dinner."

Antonio couldn't make out Mama's response, but it was good to hear Papa say, "I'm sorry. I know you worry about money. Oscar bought some fertilizer from me and he gave me a little extra. I wanted you to know that."

Papa came out with the burlap bag in hand. "Let's go, son."

Cockfight night was an occasion for many families. Men brought their wives and children. Some brought women who were not their wives. The covered pavilion sat on the edge of town, flanked on all sides by vendor stalls that ruined the idyll of the forest backdrop.

When Antonio was younger, he liked coming to the cockfight with his father. Everyone ruffled his hair and patted him on the back. Father always bought him corn nuts or Kropek shrimp chips.

"Pick the winner," his father would say. If Antonio picked a winner, his father hugged and made a fuss over him. But if he picked a loser, his father sulked for days. Eventually, Papa stopped asking.

Tito Oscar had already arrived. He sat on a second-row bench watching Kulas, his trainer, blow rings of cigar smoke at Ilaryo. Tito Oscar beckoned Antonio over and patted the empty bench space beside him.

"Would you look at Ilaryo?" a beaming Tito Oscar said. "I bred him specially from a line of champions."

His uncle's enthusiasm started to rub off on him. Ilaryo's graceful white plumage made Antonio think of a woman's long hair. Papa would get the last word over Mama. Ilaryo would surely win.

Antonio's father waved to get the attention of the *kristo*, the man who kept track of wagers. The *kristo* held wads of peso bills folded in his hand and wore a pocketed apron bulging with coins. Papa held out the burlap bag and for a moment, Antonio wondered if he was bartering vegetables. But no, they were coins. Enough to wager with. Enough to get something of worth.

Like a marble altar.

"Papa," Antonio called out hoarsely.

Papa ignored Antonio. The *kristo* snatched the bag. Antonio wished he had the gumption to tell him to give it back. He stood up just as Kulas delivered Ilaryo into the ring and unsheathed the long thin sparring blade attached to the rooster's heel. Tito Oscar and Papa had their backs towards him, intent on the duel. Disgusted, Antonio made his way out of the building.

Outside, Antonio crouched to the ground, scratching at the dirt like the roosters did, tasting despair in the roof of his mouth. The *sultador'*s call for the match to begin blared from the pavilion. The audience shrieked. They howled for bloodletting and death, calling out Ilaryo as the *lyamado,* or the cock favored to win.

Antonio imagined the cocks strutting in a circle, generations of fighting blood pulsing in their veins. The roosters would kick at each other, their spurs slashing into a soft belly. There would be a scattering of feathers and a flapping of wings, spectators' contorted faces egging them on, the smell of blood and money mingling in the pit.

The crowd gasped, then fell silent. Antonio raised his head and waited for that rousing cheer for Ilaryo, but it never came. He ran inside, pushing his way through the crowd and was shoved back, but still he kept on pushing.

There Ilaryo lay on the bloody ground, lifeless.

Tito Oscar and Papa dropped Antonio off at the house on their way to some place they did not invite him to. He didn't ask where they were headed and he didn't really care. Tito Oscar said goodbye. Papa remained silent. Mama peered at Papa's face through the car windshield. Weariness crept into her features, then she turned on her heel and went back into the house. Antonio followed her into the sewing room, where a pile of fabric was strewn around the machine.

Mama took up her post at her machine once again. "How was the cockfight?"

Antonio stuffed his hands in his pockets. "Papa lost."

"I'm sorry I made you go."

"It was worth a try." Then he said, "Mama?" Antonio wanted to share his suspicions about Papa and the altar money.

"What?" she asked.

But then what would that accomplish? Papa would probably be sent to jail and the burden of paying back the money would fall on Mama.

"Nothing," he said,

"Do you mind delivering a dress to Lara Yap for me tomorrow, Antonio?" Mama asked.

"No. I can do that."

Antonio glanced at a nearly-finished white dress hanging on a rod attached to the wall. Over the years of being around Mama's projects, he could tell how much more would be needed to complete this one; it needed hemming and finishing of the seams along the neckline. In the light of the overhead bulb, the sequins glittered in rainbow prisms.

"Who's that dress for?" he asked.

"Grace Mijares," Mama said.

"She'll look beautiful in it."

Mama raised an eyebrow. "Do you like her?"

"Well, she's pretty and rich. What's not to like?"

"There's more to a girl than that, Antonio."

"Of course I wouldn't like anyone who had straw for her brain. I have more sense than that. What's the dress for? Her wedding to Timo?"

"It's for the *kuding fiesta*. Her last public appearance before she heads to Manila."

"I thought," Antonio mused, "after the priest's sermon, that wouldn't be happening this year."

"Of course not. What gave you that idea? Not holding the *kuding fiesta* would be like not celebrating Christmas."

"I can't see Tandang Lino canceling it," Antonio agreed.

Mama started sewing, her brows furrowed in concentration, clamping pins between her lips as she took them off the fabric. She gave him a vague wave, indicating she was done talking.

71

Leaning over the window ledge in his bedroom, Antonio breathed in lungfuls of air, trying to get rid of the evening's grimness. He put his hand in his pocket and took out an object: a white, downy feather with specks of red. After Tito Oscar gathered Ilaryo in his arms, Antonio had grabbed the feather from the bloodied ground.

He blew on the feather. It remained aloft for one long moment, then disappeared into the darkness.

15

OUD VOICES WOKE Antonio. He opened his eyes to a dark night sky. Creeping out of bed, he looked out. In the dull glow of lamplight that spilled from their *salas* onto the front stoop, Antonio recognized his neighbors. Some held burning torches, some held flashlights. He heard Mama say, "I'll wake him up."

When Mama appeared in his bedroom doorway, Antonio said, "Are you turning me in?"

"What?"

"For the altar money."

She gave him a sharp look. "Why? Did you steal it?"

"No, I swear."

"This isn't about you or the altar money."

"Oh." He unclenched his fist. "What, then?"

"Fermin Abad has been murdered by his sister."

Shock rippled through Antonio. He knew Mad Juana was crazy, but crazy enough to kill the hand that feeds her?

"Your father and uncle found Fermin stabbed and lying face down in the river," Mama said. "Juana was crouched over him, holding a bloody knife. She tried to attack them, then ran

73

off into the trees. Unfortunately, they couldn't find her. Your father said to send for you to join the search party."

Antonio wearily lifted the *kulambo* mosquito net and slipped his flip-flops on.

First, Antonio stopped at his friend Jose's house. He threw a pebble into an open bedroom window. Moments later, Jose appeared. "What's the big idea, waking up a working man?"

"Sorry to interrupt your dreams of urinals."

Jose yawned. "What do you want?"

"There's a search party going on for Mad Juana. She killed her brother."

Jose's eyes bulged. "I knew it was just a matter of time!"

"Are you coming then?"

"I doubt my father will let me. Wait here." Antonio peered around Jose's cluttered room, waiting and hoping it wouldn't take long. But it didn't. Jose returned right away.

"He's asleep so let's just go," Jose said. "And look what I got from the kitchen." He held out a garlic clove.

"You fool," Antonio said, "we're not fighting a vampire."

"Have you seen her lately?"

Antonio conceded, "You have a good point. But I'm not putting a stake through her heart."

"What will we do?"

"You can recite math equations to her until she falls asleep. Works for me in math class."

Eventually, everyone returned to the clearing. No one had seen Mad Juana. Papa joined them. He had scratch marks on his face and a huge gash wound on his ear.

"Here's a weapon," Papa said, handing Antonio a shotgun. "Only shoot to injure if she gives you trouble."

Antonio nodded.

"Do you have another gun?" Jose asked.

"No," Papa said. "You'll have to share." The men fanned out, leaving Antonio and Jose to pair up.

"Don't worry," Antonio assured Jose. "If she's running after you, I'll try to shoot her, not you."

"With my luck," Jose said, "you'll shoot me instead."

Carrying a flashlight, Jose walked alongside Antonio. Under Mang Fermin's hut, a gargantuan sow lifted her head, peering up at them with her little pink-rimmed eyes, snorting twice.

"She looks like she's been crying for her master," Jose said.

"I highly doubt that."

Jose snorted back.

Suddenly, Antonio held up a hand. "Shhh. Do you hear that?"

"What?"

Antonio gestured for him to be quiet. Music drifted out of the hut window. He exchanged glances with Jose.

"It's music," Jose whispered.

"Yes, from the record player I told you about."

Antonio took a deep breath and walked to the open door. He pushed it open further, and it creaked on its hinges. Then he stepped inside. The uneven bamboo floor groaned loudly. He nodded for Jose to flash the light into the living room while he clutched the shotgun tightly in his hands.

The arc of light showed furniture and piles. Lizards skittering. A tall stack of books. Plates of rancid food. A record player.

"Shine it back there again," Antonio said.

"Where?"

"Yes, right there. Against the wall."

The record player sat on a table. A record revolved on it. Antonio recognized the song, a Tagalog version of "By the Light of the Silvery Moon."

Jose reached across and turned the record player off with a click. "There. It's off."

The song kept playing. Just the voice, no accompaniment.

"Why won't that turn off?" Jose asked.

"You just turned it off, didn't you?" Antonio said. The hair on the back of his neck rose.

"So if that's not the record player, who's singing?" Jose asked.

The pair turned around at the same time. Jose trained the light on the wall next to the window. It skimmed the wall, a shelf, a table, and a woman's white blouse.

The ray of light returned to the cloth, and to Mad Juana's grinning visage.

16

MAD JUANA CACKLED. "Do you like my singing?"

"The gun, Antonio," Jose whispered.

In her hand, Mad Juana held a knife. "But she's not threatening us," Antonio said. "I say let's just tackle her."

"Are you crazy?" Jose said.

"Fine." Antonio raised the shotgun to his shoulder, putting Mad Juana in its sight. His finger shook against the trigger.

Mad Juana's eyes widened, like a trapped animal's. She took two steps back, crashing against the wall and dropping the knife. She crossed her arms in front of her face. "No, no. Juana is scared."

"She dropped the knife," Antonio told Jose. "Go pick it up."

Jose shook his head. "I'm not going anywhere near her. What if she bites me?"

"Just get that knife!"

"Alright. I'm going to do it." Jose took a couple of steps closer to Mad Juana, then practically dove for the knife. As he fell on the floor, the stack of books teetered and crashed over Jose.

A trembling Mad Juana still huddled against the wall.

Antonio set the shotgun on the floor and unburied his friend. Jose emerged with the knife. "I have it!" He paused, flashing the light on the floor behind Antonio. "The question is, who has the shotgun?" And then the wall near the window. "And where's Mad Juana?"

Outside, the yard blazed with lit torches and flashlights arcing in wild patterns. Men spoke in urgent tones.

"What possessed you in there?" Jose asked Antonio. "You should have shot her!"

"I don't know." Antonio shrugged. "That look in her eyes... she was scared, not bent on killing us."

Papa approached them. "We'll take care of this. Why don't you both go on home?"

Red rimmed Papa's eyes. For the first time, Antonio realized how close Papa must have been to Mang Fermin.

By the time Antonio came home, Mama had already gone to bed and all the lights had been turned off. Before going to bed, he decided he needed to use the outhouse. As his eyes adjusted in the darkness, he could make out the pile of pots and pans washed for the day on the table. The pans smelled of soap and dripped on the floor.

He unlocked the door to the backyard. The ground felt warm under his bare feet. Entering the first of two stalls made from lashed bamboo, he conducted his business, whistling nervously.

A low whistle joined in. Harmonized.

Pulling up his pants with a snap, he unlocked the outhouse door. *Click-clang!* The sound reverberated throughout his stall.

His fingers shook as he pushed slightly on the door and peered outside, then closed it again.

Just open the door and run towards the house!

He pushed, but this time the door wouldn't move. Something or *someone* was blocking it. Perspiration soaked his shirt.

He shoved the door open, sending Mad Juana sprawled on her back. Jumping over her, Antonio crossed the dirt yard. Behind him, she couldn't keep up, but he could hear her grunting with the exertion. Antonio reached the back door and locked it. Then he ran into his parents' bedroom, waking Mama up.

"Mad Juana's outside," Antonio said. He started to kneel under the bed. "I need one of Papa's guns."

Mama sat bolt upright. "Papa has all of them," she said.

They both froze at the sound of knocking on the back door. Antonio and Mama looked at each other. "Where's Lolo?" she asked. "Make sure he's safe."

"I will!" Antonio said, running to his grandfather's bedroom. It was empty.

Antonio ran to the kitchen, where Lolo Sonny held the door open. Beyond him, Mad Juana's wild hair stood in grotesque relief. She had her eye on a pile of knives on the counter.

Lolo Sonny turned to Antonio and smiled. "See who's come to visit."

Mad Juana smiled, too. For one brief moment, her face was transformed into a pretty face. And then she looked at Antonio and snarled.

"Mama," Antonio murmured. "Go get Lolo Sonny."

"But...she just...got here," Lolo Sonny said.

Antonio pulled his grandfather's arm and escorted him towards Mama, who led him down the hall. Mad Juana had picked up a knife and was admiring her reflection on the blade.

"I am a pretty girl," she sang out, before stabbing the counter.

Antonio ran across the kitchen floor. His foot struck the wet spot where the pans dripped water, and he had to catch himself. He skidded to a halt and turned. "Come on, pretty girl. Catch me if you can!"

She lumbered after him, graceful as a gorilla. She slid, and her arm knocked the pile of pans on the counter. Like cymbals, they echoed as they fell on the floor. One of them, the big pot they used for rice, hit her on the forehead. Antonio watched her for a long moment, to make sure she was out cold.

From behind Antonio came the sound of footsteps. Papa appeared at his side, hefting his shotgun. Papa raised the shotgun and pointed it at Mad Juana. A commotion ensued in the doorway.

Lolo Sonny shuffled forward and touched Papa's sleeve.

"Romy...no."

"She murdered Fermin," Papa said.

"She...isn't right...in her...head."

Papa kept her in the gun's sight for a long moment. He took a deep breath. Lowering the gun, he said to Antonio, "Help me tie her up, son. Then call the constable."

17

THE CONSTABLE ARRESTED Mad Juana and took her to the mental hospital in Nagat. It was strange to not see her at her brother's wake. They were always together.

Papa, Mama, Tito Oscar, Trining, Lolo Sonny, Father Sebastian and Antonio came to Mang Fermin's house to pay their last respects. So did several dozen, probably lured by the free food which Tito Oscar paid for. Jose had to work.

All of Mang Fermin's belongings had been moved out of the house, including the record player. Antonio wondered who had taken it and where it had gone, but he thought it would be bad form to ask so quickly after the owner's death.

Their servant Trining brought in a basket of mabolo fruit. Antonio couldn't will himself to eat any. He kept expecting Mang Fermin to wake from the dead and berate him. Antonio caught her glance and moved away before she could recruit him to serve more food on the table. As he made his escape, he bumped into the coffin, nearly falling against Mang Fermin's bloated, powdered face.

"Antonio!" Papa scolded. "Be careful!"

Antonio tried to pry his eyes off Mang Fermin, but he

couldn't look away. The dead man's orange makeup melted in the heat, staining the cotton stuffed in his nostrils. His thin lips formed a snarl and his white burial shirt couldn't conceal a sunken chest. On his stomach, his withered hands resembled claws locked together. A necklace of curious workmanship – a seashell attached to a heavy black thread, encircled his neck.

Amidst the heavy scent of *kalachuchi* flowers that masked a sour embalming smell, Antonio caught a whiff of mabolo, and a voice that said, "You still owe me."

He backed quickly from the coffin, then bumped into Tito Oscar.

"Steady," his uncle said. "Are you alright?"

"I'm fine," Antonio assured him. "Sorry. I just need fresh air." He hurried outside where Papa stood talking to Constable Martillo.

"There's our brave hero," the constable said.

"Yes," Papa said, chest puffing out like a rooster. "What can I say? He takes after me."

No, Papa. I'm no thief.

Antonio's tongue itched. Not trusting himself, Antonio went back into the house.

He saw Father Sebastian standing at the food table and joined him. "How are you getting on?" Antonio asked.

"Well enough," Father Sebastian said, but his tone said otherwise.

Antonio studied the priest's face, then picked up two slices of *hamon*, plateful of *pansit* noodles and five pieces of *lumpia* egg roll. "Are you really well?"

The priest nodded. "I've never been fed as well as I have, and everyone has been nice. However, there's been one thing weighing on my mind. Henry tells me that he'll be taking a trip to visit some relatives soon." He cleared his throat. "He'll be gone on Ghost Moon Night."

Antonio dipped a *lumpia* in sauce and took a crunchy, flaky bite. "As long as he's not on the road, he should be fine."

"Henry showed me how to close the windows, batten the hutches, so to speak. There are so many of them."

"I can help you," Antonio offered. "I can even stay the night, if you'd like." He took a handful of the still warm noodles, cabbage, carrot and shrimp and took a bite. *Delicious.*

"Oh, but that would be such an imposition."

"Let me help you Father," Antonio said. "It's really not a bother."

"Very well, Antonio. I would be most grateful."

Just then, a man entered the house. He stood in the doorway, a broad-brimmed hat shielding his face. When he took off the hat, Antonio took a step back, startled.

Trining clapped her hands over her mouth.

"What is it?" Mama asked.

"It's Mang Fermin, come to haunt us!" Trining whispered.

There indeed was Mang Fermin in the flesh. Except meaner-looking.

Tito Oscar broke the ice, chuckling. "Everyone, meet Fermin's cousin, Isidro Abad."

Isidro nodded, unsmiling. Then he walked over to the coffin. "In life, you wouldn't welcome me, cousin," Antonio heard him mutter. "Now, you don't have a choice."

Papa approached him, "So, you got my telegram."

Isidro eyed Papa with distaste. "Yes, I got your telegram. Some friend you are, Romy Pulido, for wanting to buy your friend's land, with him not even buried."

Papa's face turned red.

"Romy," Mama whispered, taking his arm. "And how is this going to happen? We haven't any money."

"Oscar," Papa said.

Mama pursed her lips.

Antonio went back to the food table for another helping of *pansit* noodles. Isidro came over and piled rice and at least three spoonfuls of *adobo* stew on his place while Trining looked on, open-mouthed. Papa and Tito Oscar joined him.

"Thank you for considering our offer," Tito Oscar said.

"We've had an offer on the land," Isidro replied. "One too big to refuse."

"We're prepared to match that."

"It's too late. I already accepted an offer."

"Is it finalized?" Tito Oscar asked.

"No, but..."

Papa frowned. "Fermin gave us his blessing."

Tito Oscar touched Papa's arm. "Romy," he said. "Why don't we wait to talk about this until after the funeral? We'll be in touch, Isidro."

"There's nothing to talk about," Isidro said. He moved away and stood by himself against the wall with his heaping plateful. Father Sebastian talked to him briefly, then Isidro left the house.

The adults spoke in hushed whispers. "Come help me clear," Trining told Antonio.

Antonio followed her to the table. He pinched some *pansit* and popped it in his mouth.

"*Hay naku*, Antonio," she said. "You're making a mess."

Picking up empty plates and glasses, he asked, "How did Mang Fermin and Papa become good friends in the first place?"

"When they were little boys, their fathers were friends," Trining said. "Your Lolo Sonny and Fermin's father spent hours together, just roaming the mountains and fishing. They were both friendly and included anyone in their circle of friends. That trait skipped the next generation, I can tell you that. But your papa and Mang Fermin still ended up friends."

"And Isidro Abad, did he grow up here, too?"

"He left here as soon as he could. Fermin felt his cousin was trying to worm his way into his father's good graces. Fermin wanted all the land himself. He got it in his lifetime. But now... he can't take it with him, can he?"

The next day, at Mang Fermin's funeral, Antonio stood with his family and Father Sebastian at the edge of the Abad family vault. The brown casket, paid for by Tito Oscar, gleamed in the sun. As the men lowered it into place, Papa tripped, dropping his corner. The cover fell open.

Papa rearranged Mang Fermin, including the seashell pendant dangling from his neck. Then Papa put the cover back in place.

Father Sebastian officiated a brief funeral service just as the clouds gathered and raindrops began to fall. Antonio watched his father brush raindrops from his face, but they just might have been tears.

RAIN POURED AS Antonio drove the family homeward in the cart from Mang Fermin's funeral. Occasionally, lightning slashed the sky and thunder boomed. The cart wheels slipped on the muddy ground. Twice, Antonio had to jump out and push so they could get unstuck.

At their house, he helped Lolo Sonny change into dry clothes and seated him next to the radio while Mama heated up some soup. Antonio turned the radio on, but no sound came. He thumped the side of the cabinet twice, but still, nothing.

A frown formed between Lolo Sonny's brows.

"It's not working," Antonio told his grandfather. "Watch, I'll get it going."

Lolo Sonny smiled and passed a trembling finger across his lips.

Antonio thumped on the side, but it still didn't work. He pulled the radio away from the wall and checked the wiring. The electric plug left a black residue on his hand, and smelled of burnt plastic. "Probably from the lightning," he murmured. For the next several minutes, he tried to plug it in and turn it on, without success.

84

He pushed the radio back against the wall and turned to Lolo Sonny. "I'll see if they have a part at the store. Do you want to come with me and listen to the jukebox at Aling Dona's?"

Lolo Sonny nodded.

"In this rain?" Mama called out from the other room.

Antonio looked out the window, at the drizzle. "It's easing up, Mama," Antonio said, popping into the sewing room. Lowering his voice, he said, "Do you have any ideas how Lolo can get his music?"

"No," Mama said. "You're right. Thank you for doing that."

By the time Antonio and Lolo Sonny reached Aling Dona's restaurant, the rain had stopped. He took Lolo Sonny into the restaurant where Aling Dona greeted them.

"Out to treat your *lolo* to lunch?" Aling Dona said.

"Our radio broke," Antonio said. "I thought Lolo could stay here and listen to music while I get a part for the radio." He reached into his pocket, pulling out five peso bills, precious money he'd saved from all the times he'd chopped wood for a neighbor. It didn't feel as bad as he thought it would as he handed it to Aling Dona. "Could you please give him a bowl of mami soup, and play some music for him with the leftover money?"

Aling Dona took Lolo Sonny's arm and waved Antonio away. "Don't you worry. I'll take care of him."

Antonio's first memory of *Sandoval*'s as a little boy was of him standing at the doorway, gazing at everything: at the bags of fragrant *champoy* that made his mouth water; Bulacan pastries –*pastillas de ube, de leche* and *yema* balls –wrapped in jewel-colored cellophane; *sampalok* or tamarind candy, *hopia*, egg cracklets, powdered sugar in straws, *kropek*. One shelf brimmed over with school supplies: paper, pencils, lick-on stickers, and rulers. Another shelf held pairs of flip-flops, stacks of little colored cups and a pile of handkerchiefs. Mama had given him ten centavos and he splurged it on a little duck toy that broke as soon as they got home.

Years later, as Antonio stood there in Sandoval's entryway,

he thought of how frayed the store had become. Sandoval's had no competition and didn't even have to try to be good. Many spots on the shelves gaped empty. Dirty windows blocked the light from outside. A thick layer of dust covered flimsy-looking trinkets.

Nobody sat behind the counter, which was usually the case when he stopped in at Sandoval's. He set the radio on the counter and moved his hand to ring the bell when he froze.

Behind the counter sat a Philco record player. He heard a loud ring and realized he'd slammed his hand hard on the bell.

"I'm coming," Timo said, as he came in from the back, a folded-up newspaper in hand.

Antonio wondered, not for the first time, why Grace liked him.

"Well," Timo said, "if it isn't manure-boy."

"Is that record player for sale?" Antonio asked.

Timo glanced behind the counter. "It's in the store, isn't it?"

"How did you get it?"

"I didn't steal it with altar money, that's for sure."

Antonio clenched his fists. "Can't you answer me straight? I just want to know, was it Mang Fermin's?"

"A cousin of his came in, yes. He just wanted to get rid of Mang Fermin's junk, like the record player."

"How much are you selling it for?"

"More than you can afford."

"How much?" Antonio repeated.

"That would be eight hundred pesos."

"Eight hundred," Antonio repeated, the numbers swirling in his head. "But it's not new!"

"Listen," Timo said, "are you here to buy anything? Or are you just full of questions?"

"I...I came to get a new part for our transistor radio."

"What happened to it?"

"It burnt out in the lightning storm."

"Well, you're out of luck. Once that's fried, you'll have to replace the whole thing. You might as well buy a new one."

Antonio's eyes narrowed.

"Don't believe me?" Timo said. "Ask my father. He used to fix radios." Timo called his father in.

Mr. Sandoval looked at the radio, fiddled with it for a few

minutes, then looked up. "Sorry, Antonio, but this radio is dead."

"It can't be fixed?" Antonio said.

"It's not like the *langbuan*," Mr. Sandoval said. "It won't come back to life, no matter what you do."

Antonio left *Sandoval's* in a daze. He put the radio in the back of the cart and went to collect Lolo Sonny from Aling Dona's. He thought of the record player. How nice it would be to just play Lolo's favorite music when he wanted.

"I'm glad you're here," Aling Dona greeted him. "I played two songs for your grandfather a while back and he's getting restless."

Antonio thanked her and helped Lolo Sonny to the cart. He noticed that Lolo Sonny walked slower and could hardly get into the cart without a lot of exertion. "Something wrong, Lolo Sonny?"

"Just...my bones...getting old. Knee...hurting."

Antonio patiently waited for Lolo Sonny to get in.

"What did you find out?" Mama asked when they got home.

"Mr. Sandoval looked at the radio and said it couldn't be fixed," Antonio said.

"Oh, no." She shook her head as she unspooled thread for her machine.

Antonio spent the afternoon fixing Cupid's pen. Afterwards, as he came in, Mama asked him to fetch Lolo Sonny. Antonio found his grandfather in the *salas*, turning the radio knob. He turned bewildered eyes towards Antonio.

"It's not working, remember, Lolo?" Antonio asked gently. "It's time to eat, *po*."

"I...will..."

Several minutes passed. Antonio went outside to wash up. At the dining table, Mama looked worried. "Where is your grandfather?"

Trining ran in. "*Ate*," she told Mama, "please come!"

They all ran out to the chicken coop where Lolo Sonny sat inside, on his haunches. A hen sat on his head. "Come out now, please," Papa coaxed Lolo Sonny.

"No," Lolo Sonny said.

Papa turned to Antonio and demanded to know, "What's wrong with your grandfather?"

"He has to have music," Antonio said, "or he goes crazy. The radio broke today."

"Then fix it!"

"They don't sell just the part at the store, Papa. We'd have to replace the entire radio."

"We can't afford that."

"Tito Oscar can. Let me work for him, Papa."

"No," Papa said. "Let's leave Oscar out of this. The last thing I want is for us to be indebted to him."

"Why don't you want him to help us?" Antonio asked.

"He's loaned me money several times and I have yet to repay him. Alright?"

"Fine," Antonio said. "We could buy Mang Fermin's old record player."

Papa's head swiveled. "What?"

"Mang Fermin's old record player is for sale at Sandoval's." Antonio turned to Mama. "It's our best alternative. We can play music any time of the day."

"And how much is this player?" Mama asked.

"Eight hundred pesos."

Papa muttered under his breath while Mama shook her head. "Impossible," she said. "You know we don't have that kind of money."

"We can't keep taking him to Aling Dona's," Antonio said. "Lolo Sonny has a hard time climbing in the cart," Antonio said. He took a deep breath. "Listen, Mama and Papa. I can do it. I'll get a job. I'll save every bit. I bet I can do it in six months."

"Six months is a lifetime! Besides, we don't need a record player, just a radio."

Antonio persisted. "Six months to raise the money. Maybe I can do it sooner, who knows? I want to get him the record player. Then he wouldn't have to listen to Elvis Presley."

Papa shook his head. "You're a fool! You have no idea how hard it is to earn money. It will take years, and I need you here."

Mama intervened. "Romy, let him try. He can work both places. Maybe he can arrange to make payments so we can get the record player sooner. You see what happens without music?" She gestured at Lolo Sonny, who was being pecked by a cross hen. Mama reached in to shoo the chicken away. Lolo Sonny took her hand and started to come out.

"What about the farm?" Papa asked.

"I'll help when I can," Antonio promised.

"*Hala!*" Papa said. "That is not enough! I can see right through you. It's just another excuse for you not to work here."

"Papa," Antonio said. "Look at Lolo Sonny. Is this how you want him to be every day?"'

Lolo Sonny blinked. Little tufts of feathers covered his bald head. "Music?" he said.

Papa didn't say anything for a long moment. To Antonio, he said, "You have six months. The sooner, the better."

As Papa walked away, Mama and Antonio smiled at each other.

"Thank you," Antonio told his mother later, when they went inside.

"Your father can be hard-headed sometimes." She glanced at her sewing room door. "Can you do me a favor?"

"Anything!"

"Can you please deliver Grace's dress to her house?"

"Gladly," Antonio said with a grin.

19

GRACE MIJARES' TWO-STORY adobe house stood on a sprawling *hacienda*. Majestic coconut trees towered overhead and colorful butterflies flit about the hibiscus bushes lining the driveway. Antonio drove Cupid to the house, tethered him to a hitching post, and walked up a path to the front door. After he knocked, a gray cat came up the driveway and rubbed its fur against his legs.

"Well, hello there," Antonio said, crouching to pet it. The cat purred. Or maybe he heard hunger pangs. The poor thing looked like it could use a meal or two. A female servant holding a broom opened the door.

"I have a delivery for Grace Mijares," Antonio said.

The cat tried to squeeze past the servant, but the servant blocked it with her broom. "Mrs. Mijares says no cats in the house." To Antonio, she said, "Wait here, please."

She closed the door but a moment later, it came unlatched and swung open. The spacious living room had three sets of furniture, one by a large window that overlooked a river, and two that formed their own larger seating area near the door. Antonio imagined parties here, guests gathered around the grand piano that stood center stage, waited upon by servants. But then he also imagined a fun childhood, running through the back fields, catching dragonflies along the reeds in the sparkling water. Did Grace only sit on the *sala* sets or did she explore the world beyond?

The cat meowed and bounded inside.

"Oh, no," Antonio whispered. "You're not supposed to be in there. Come here, cat!" The cat prowled even further into the house. It climbed into a cabinet and started walking along a row of delicate glass figurines.

"Come here, cat!" Antonio whispered.

The cat looked at him, meowed, and kept walking along. It flicked its tail just right, sending a little girl figurine tottering at the edge.

Antonio ran inside, just in time to catch the figurine. He put it back on the shelf, only to see the cat brush up against an expensive-looking porcelain vase. Stretching, Antonio rescued it as well from sure disaster. He sensed that someone stood behind him, and he turned. Grace and the servant were watching him, open-mouthed.

Sheepishly, he set the vase on the shelf.

"I know where I've seen him," the servant said. "He's that boy who stole the altar money. And he's stealing from us, too!"

"What?" Antonio said. "I'm not stealing the vase! I was just trying to get that cat out. And I *didn't* take the altar money."

The servant saw the cat and screamed, whacking the floor with the broom. The commotion sent the cat sprinting across the polished hardwood floor and out the open front door. The maid ran after it and slammed the door shut.

"I hate that cat," she said.

Grace was doubled over, covering her face with her hands. Was she worried about the figurines?

Then she raised her head, giggling. "That…was…funny," she said. She wiped the tears from her eyes and smiled. "Nita said you have a dress for me?"

Antonio had always thought she was beautiful, but now she looked positively radiant. "I left it outside," he said, going to the door. "I just need to…go out…"

And make a fool of myself, he muttered. He came in, this time gently pushing the cat away before closing the door. "Your dress," he said, handing Grace the box with a flourish.

Grace took the lid off, made a gushing sound and picked up the dress, lifting it to compare against the length of her body. "It's beautiful," she said.

"Grace?" a woman's voice floated down to them. "What's this?"

"My dress is here, Mama," she said. "Come look!"

Mrs. Mijares came down in a bathrobe and curlers. "That *is* beautiful." She turned to Antonio. "Tell your mother she's a genius."

"Thank you, I will," Antonio said. He cleared his throat. "May I take your payment now?"

"How much is it again?"

Antonio looked at his mother's note on the box. "Two hundred pesos."

"Two hundred!" Mrs. Mijares frowned. "Why, that's too much!"

"Isn't that what you agreed to pay?" Antonio asked.

"I don't know what we agreed on, but I just know that's too much."

Antonio felt his face grow warm. "My mother charges fairly, and does a great job. Everyone knows. That's why people come to her."

"Maybe it'll cost less if she takes off the sequins at the hem?" Mrs. Mijares suggested. "Or this extra lace?"

"Mama," Grace said.

"No, *m'ija*," Mrs. Mijares said, shaking her head. "We can't afford this."

The room fell silent. "Fine," Antonio said, his heart pounding like crazy, sure that he would offend Mrs. Mijares. "I'm sure my mother can sell it to someone else."

"Mama!" Grace said again.

Mrs. Mijares turned her haughty face towards him. He could see why Mr. Mijares married her. She must have been pretty at one time. But right now, she was ugly. "Take this dress back," she said, shoving it toward him. "I can simply buy the one that came in to *Sandoval's* this week. It will be a lot cheaper, too."

"But I want *this* dress, Mama!" Grace protested.

"Grace, I already told you..."

"Aurelia." Mr. Mijares came down the stairs, taking out

a wallet from his back pocket as he did so. "How much?" he asked Antonio.

Antonio told him. Mr. Mijares pulled out some bills.

"You will do no such thing," Mrs. Mijares said, grabbing her husband's arm.

"I'm sure this young man has better things to do than to watch us bicker," Mr. Mijares said. "It's a lovely dress and your daughter wants it. What exactly is the problem?"

"But it's highway robbery!"

"It's a good value," Mr. Mijares said. "And we can well afford it."

Mrs. Mijares scowled but didn't interfere when her husband handed Antonio the money.

"Thank you," Antonio said, then walked out of the house.

Outside, the cat skulked, until Antonio stretched out a hand and let it come and rub its fur against it. "Why do you come around here? You picked a stingy place."

The door opened. Grace said his name. He stood up, and the cat scampered away.

"That cat really likes you," Grace said, smiling.

"I guess."

"Please tell your mother she is very talented. I appreciate all her hard work on my dress."

"Thanks. I'll tell her."

"And as for my mother…" She looked over her shoulder, then back at him. "I'm sorry."

He shrugged. "It's not a big deal."

"I better go. Thanks again."

Antonio stood there for a long moment after she went inside, a smile plastered on his face.

20

May
Twelve hours before Ghost Moon Night

THREE WEEKS AFTER his arrival in Dasalin, Father Sebastian rose at dawn in the parish house he now considered home. Henry came to his bedroom door with his usual offering of coffee. "Thank you!" Father Sebastian inhaled that rich aroma. He noted the clean shirt, the pressed pants. "You're dressed nice, Henry."

"Thank you. I hope you are all set for Ghost Moon Night?"

"As ready as I will be."

Henry smiled, if one could call that a smile. "I left instructions at the market for your evening meal. All you need to do is to fetch the ingredients at your usual vendors. Make sure you go early." He paused. "And you said Antonio Pulido was coming, correct?"

"Yes, he is."

"Then he'll help you close the shutters over the stained glass windows." Henry glanced at his watch. "Unless you want me to help you right now?"

"No, that's alright. Thank you. And have a safe trip."

Henry nodded. "I will. Thank you for letting me borrow your car. It'll be nice to have a car traveling with my cousin

94

GHOST MOON NIGHT

from out of town, you know?"

"Of course."

After Henry left, Father Sebastian stood at the window for a long moment nursing his coffee. Smiling broadly, Henry turned with a farewell glance and jaunty wave before getting into the mint-green parish sedan. Why, he almost looked happy to get away.

The priest willed himself to get ready for his very first Ghost Moon Night.

His hand trembled at the thought. He accidentally dropped the coffee cup which shattered against the hardwood floor. This was not a good sign. By the time he cleaned up and went down to Mass, he was flustered.

He paused at the vestry door, surprised. People were crammed onto the seats, in the side aisles and doorways. The lines to the confessional snaked around the stations of the cross and to the back.

A beaming Mrs. Silva approached him. "Father Sebastian!" she said. "Have you seen how many people are here right now? We need to take advantage of it."

"Take advantage of it?" he echoed.

"What better way to solicit altar funds than to ask a captive audience?"

"Ah yes, of course," Father Sebastian agreed.

"Would you like me to take to the pulpit and make the announcement?"

"Go right ahead."

When she did, someone grumbled, "Didn't it get stolen before?"

Mrs. Silva tried to ignore the comment, but someone else said, "How do we know we won't lose this money again?"

Drawing herself up to her full height, Mrs. Silva leaned over the pulpit and said, "That will *never* happen again, so long as it's under my watch, I can assure you. Now, are we going to worry about what has been, or should we keep working on getting a beautiful altar to replace this one?"

For the next fifteen minutes, Father Sebastian heard confessions in the booth while Mrs. Silva announced that so-and-so was putting money in the jar – who was next? He smiled. How did Antonio put it? Get out of Mrs. Silva's way and thank her? It was good advice.

As he sat on his side of the window, the first confessor came in. A woman who envied her neighbor.

"I was fine until the day she had a fancier house built," she said. "It blocked my view of the sea. I cursed the day they put on the last shingle. To make myself feel better, I started throwing pig manure into her yard. Right over her prized guavas. They grew so huge people were paying her money!"

He listened next to a man who borrowed money from his aunt but never repaid her. A young woman had unkind thoughts towards her beautiful cousin. The litany was as varied as their voices. He made it a point to not try to identify voices, to preserve the anonymity of his confessors, but sometimes he was tempted.

Especially with his last confession.

The man sounded like he was taking pains to change his voice. Once in a while, in the deeper tones of his confession, Father Sebastian heard a high-pitched cadence of a young voice.

"Forgive me, Father, for I have sinned," said the man. "It's been a month since my last confession."

"Yes, my child. Go ahead."

"Can I confess a sin I haven't committed yet?"

That gave Father Sebastian pause. "If you haven't actually committed it, then it wouldn't exactly be a sin."

"*If* I do confess it, though, and then do it, can I be forgiven?"

"Plenary indulgence has been reserved for martyrs, my child. And as far as I can tell you aren't in line for sainthood, are you?"

"No," came the glum reply. Then: "I'll still confess, though."

"Go ahead."

Seconds ticked past. The young man confessed, "I'm going to help someone do some dynamite fishing tonight."

"But tonight is…"

"Yes, I know, Father. Ghost Moon Night. The job will pay a lot."

"Dynamite fishing is illegal any time of the month, my son," Father Sebastian said. "Have you thought this through carefully?"

"I know, but I need the money. Besides, I was promised it would be safe."

"With the *langbuan* out?"

There was a knock on the priest's confessional door, startling him. "Just one moment," he told the young man.

It was Mrs. Silva. "We should probably start Mass, Father," she said, pushing back her spectacles. "Everyone's getting restless. And great news, we got a lot of donations!"

"I just need to finish up with this confession," Father Sebastian said. But when he spoke into the mesh wall separating him from the other confessional, no one answered. He couldn't discern a silhouette.

"Young man?" he said. "Young man?"

The priest came out of his confessional. The other door stood ajar, the booth empty.

21

Six hours before Ghost Moon Night

THROUGHOUT MASS, THE congregation seemed preoccupied. Several kept looking out the windows, doorways, and at their watches. Father Sebastian looked at his watch, too. Ten minutes to the noon hour and all this restlessness.

Father Sebastian himself was preoccupied. Who was the young man who was going to engage in illegal dynamite fishing? He surreptitiously surveyed the congregation. Antonio Pulido was nowhere to be seen.

Could it have been Antonio?

When the priest talked to him the previous week, Antonio said he'd be by in the evening, before sunset. Before Ghost Moon Night. Antonio had offered to stay the night, and he'd better make sure it happened. To keep Antonio safe.

What could possibly go wrong? His unknown confessor had asked.

Plenty. Father Sebastian had seen many fishermen relegated to a life of panhandling when their arms were blown off. Often, it was because the dynamite wouldn't light up and tossed away as a dud, but it exploded anyway.

The morning heat intensified outside, but no one seemed

intent on napping through Mass like other Sundays. They sat upright, springing up like identical coils when Father Sebastian pronounced his final blessing.

An altar boy, not Antonio, put away the Blessed Sacrament.

"Father Sebastian," Mrs. Silva said, on her way out, "I thought I'd keep our jar collection this time." She clutched a huge jar of coins to her chest.

"Yes, thank you. Oh, and Mrs. Silva? Did you see who was the last person to leave the confessional before Mass?"

"I'm sorry, no," she said. "I wasn't paying attention."

In the kitchen, the priest ate a simple snack of Sunflower crackers and coffee, then made his way to the street to flag a tricycle. One roared up to the curb, slowed enough to so the priest glimpsed a full sidecar, then sped up the road once again. This happened three more times.

Normally, he'd flagged a tricycle by now. But not on Ghost Moon Night apparently.

Father Sebastian missed the sedan. It would have come in handy, but he wasn't one to complain. He started walking towards town proper, passing yards with shade trees screening simple lives in little huts. The quiet street led the eye seaward. Fishing boats crested waves which looked like magical scales on a brilliant turquoise sea. He thought of the families that sat together Sunday after Sunday in the chapel, clearly caring for each other. Except for a few, most homes had little in terms of material wealth. But they took pride in their name, and their family's legacy of hard work and honor. He used to wonder why anyone would stay here and endure Ghost Moon Night. Now he knew why.

A tricycle, full like the others, slowed. Father Sebastian waved it along, but it stopped. "Would you like me to come back for you, Father?" the gray-haired driver asked.

"I imagine you'd have to turn away passengers at the station."

The driver smiled. "It's my tricycle and I can choose to take in passengers as I please."

"Just make sure your supervisor doesn't find out," a girl in the sidecar said.

"If I don't beat you to the market," the priest told the driver, "I will take you up on the offer."

In short order, the driver returned, introducing himself as Nando Nakpil, and the girl in his sidecar as his granddaughter, Yolly. She looked to be about eighteen, her hair drawn away from her face in a ponytail, emphasizing her pretty, long-lashed eyes.

"Do you not drive?" Nando asked the priest.

"I do."

"Henry shouldn't have left you without a car," Yolly said. "Not today of all days."

"He took the car to take a trip along the coast with his cousin who is visiting," Father Sebastian explained. "So long as I stay inside with locked windows and doors, I'll be alright, won't I?"

"Yes," Nando said. "But a car is still handy. We'll take you to the market. Then you'll see what Yolly means."

When Nando stopped his tricycle in front of the rice vendor at the market, Father Sebastian could hardly believe his eyes. It was as though a swarm of insects came through and stripped it clean, leaving only a skeleton of its former self. Tables that used to brim over with fruit, rice, and vegetables had bare tops. Only one butchered pig hung on a hook.

"Everyone wants to buy everything on Ghost Moon Night," Nando said. "The earlier one buys things, the better."

"I don't need much," Father Sebastian assured him.

"That's good." Nando glanced at the sparse offerings.

"Henry said my dinner ingredients are waiting for me."

"Let's hope so," Nando said. "Nothing ever seems normal today. People are meaner. Greedier. Some make the most impulsive decisions, like marrying near-strangers because they think they might die in the course of the night. Or leaving their belongings to one of their children. Passengers pay me a lot more, I'll tell you that. They're just so grateful to get around they will pay *anything.*"

"My grandfather won't say this because he's too humble," Yolly said. "He *could* gouge his passengers, but he doesn't." Yolly got out of the sidecar. "I'd better go down to the pharmacy for Mama's medicine. I'll be right back."

Father Sebastian went to his favorite *suki* or vendor, Aling Lorna. "I'm here to pick up my ingredients," he told her.

"Oh, Father Sebastian," Aling Lorna said. "I tried to save them for you, but my daughter accidentally sold your share to someone else. I am so sorry! There's this, however." She held up a shriveled bitter *ampalaya* gourd.

"Is there nothing else?" he asked. "A sliver of pork, perhaps?"

"Sorry, no. You could sauté the *ampalaya*. It's really good with egg and garlic salt."

"Do you have eggs?"

She shook her head.

In the end, he took the *ampalaya*, plus two tomatoes and a slab of cured *tocino* meat she remembered was stashed behind the counter. Yolly didn't fare as well.

"They didn't have medicine," she said, her mouth forming a grim line. "Can we go to the hospital later, Lolo?"

"What's your mother's illness?" the priest asked.

"She has a weak heart."

The priest said, "I don't mind if we stop by the hospital first."

"But it's the other direction, between Dasalin and the next village. Wouldn't you like to head back first?"

"If it won't take all day, I'd be curious to see that part of town."

"Thank you," Yolly said.

Pedestrians formed a line on the side of the road like ants. Tricycles jammed the street leading to the hospital. "Many go ahead and check themselves in if they so much as have a sniffle," Nando said. "Just to be on the safe side."

"Does that irritate the doctors and nurses?" Father Sebastian asked.

"Oh, not at all. They just charge for the bed, and everyone is happy."

"Happy" did not describe Yolly's face as she stepped away from the hospital counter. "No medicine!" Her eyes filled with tears. "How will Mama get on through the night?"

"Tomorrow will come soon enough," Nando said. "I'll get the medicine from the next town over."

By the time Nando dropped off Father Sebastian, it was almost four. The sign said the sun would set at six o'clock. "Thank you for giving me a ride," Father Sebastian said. To Yolly, he said, "I'll pray for your mother's health."

Yolly thanked him, though worry still etched her forehead.

"Will you be alright alone?" Nando asked the priest.

"I won't be alone for long. Antonio Pulido is planning to come over to help me secure the windows." Yolly appeared to stiffen when he mentioned Antonio's name. He asked, "Do you know him?"

She shrugged. "Not very well at all. I just know him from school." And that was all she said.

The tricycle sped away and Father Sebastian brought the food into the kitchen. He closed the door to the back, then went upstairs to close all the windows of the dormitory. When he was done, he looked down at his watch.

Five o'clock.

It took a whole hour just to do half the building. He looked out one window before closing it. There was no sign of Antonio or Cupid. Nobody else was on the street. No tricycles, no pedestrians. Everyone had wisely gone indoors for Ghost Moon Night.

Don't panic, he told himself. *Not yet.*

22

Thirty-five minutes before Ghost Moon Night

FATHER SEBASTIAN DECIDED, Antonio or not, it was time to close up the chapel.

The sun dipped low enough on the horizon to shine through the stained glass windows. For one spectacular moment, prisms formed around Michael the Archangel as he appeared to Mary; as Mary visited with Elizabeth; as a circle of worshippers surrounded the baby Jesus in the manger.

Savior, Father Sebastian prayed, *these people need you tonight, more than ever. Protect us from the evil that is about to descend upon us.*

As he prayed, a thin cloud formed a hazy veil in front of the sun, as though a curtain was being pulled across it.

"Alright, Dionisio," Father Sebastian told himself. "Enough praying. You need to *act* now."

He found the ladder just outside the main door. It was an old, rickety thing, made up of pieces of wood lashed together. He leaned it against the outside wall, under a window, then placed a foot on the bottom rung which promptly broke.

"*Hay naku,*" he said. Oh dear.

He glanced over his shoulder at the sun, then at his watch.

103

Thirty-three minutes before Ghost Moon Night. Five large windows. Ten shutters. One old ladder.

He went to work.

The other ladder rungs did not break. One step, two...and so on until he counted ten. At the top, he paused to steady himself. His sweaty palm slid across the glass. He reached for the shutter and closed the left one. Just as he was about to do the same for the right one, a voice shouted from below, "Father Sebastian!"

Father Sebastian slammed the shutter in one startled move. That beautiful depiction of baby Jesus in the manger shattered where the knob hit it. A piece about the size of his fist broke off, skimmed the ladder and made a plinking noise on the stone floor below. Through the hole, he could see twilight coming on.

"Sorry I'm late," Antonio said.

"You're here now," Father Sebastian said. "Don't worry about it."

"We'll need to patch the window. I'll be right back."

Just as the ladder must have shrunk and weakened with age and exposure to the elements, the shutters had shrunk, too, leaving a gap in the middle. Through the hole, Father Sebastian watched Antonio run towards the living quarters, then run back with something in his hand.

"I've got some cloth and flour paste so it could harden like plaster," Antonio said. "I hope you don't mind, but I had to cut an altar cloth."

"Not at all."

Father Sebastian moved as swiftly as he could down the ladder and offered Antonio his former post. The young man grinned and scaled the ladder effortlessly.

"It's not pretty but hopefully it should hold," Antonio said, as he came down and surveyed his work, a yellow-tinted circle in the setting sun.

Twenty-seven minutes before Ghost Moon Night.

Antonio climbed the ladder to close the other shutters, while Father Sebastian helped steady the ladder.

The church, boarded up and gray, looked desolate. The priest and teen walked around, checking the doors and reached the main entry with five minutes to spare.

"I'm sorry I was late," Antonio repeated. "I couldn't bring

GHOST MOON NIGHT

Cupid and the cart over until Papa was done using him to plow some paddies."

"Really, don't worry about it."

The water buffalo and cart stood near the gate that opened up to the church courtyard. "Will your water buffalo be fine there all night?" the priest asked.

"He should be," Antonio said. "If you had a pen, I'd stick him in it. But he'll be fine. *Langbuan* don't bother animals."

Antonio stood facing the courtyard, between the massive front double doors, one hand on each knob. Outside, the horizon exploded into a fantastic tapestry of oranges and reds, as though the sky was on fire. Father Sebastian craned his neck to admire the sunset and, truth be told, to see if these notorious creatures were out.

But he saw nothing else as Antonio shut the doors, which creaked loudly on rusty hinges, leaving them in darkness.

23

THE LIGHT OF flickering candles danced against the parish kitchen's wall.

Father Sebastian was finally getting used to the idea of not having electricity at bedtime. In Dasalin, he discovered, the power shut off arbitrarily. Sometimes as early as nine. Sometimes at eleven.

The kitchen was a spare room, with just a washstand for dishes and a two-pot stove. Smells from earlier in the day filled it, including the rich aroma of coffee. Father Sebastian went to make himself a cup but discovered that the can was empty.

He sighed. Antonio, making wax sculptures from the melting candles, looked up. "What is it?"

"I'm out of coffee," he explained.

"I'm sorry," Antonio said, "If I had some I would give it to you." He was intent on his task, forming a ball of wax, his tongue tucked in his cheek.

"How old are you, Antonio?" Father Sebastian asked.

"Seventeen."

"So you've experienced seventeen years of Ghost Moon Nights."

"Yes."

"Have you ever seen a *langbuan*?"

Antonio's glance darted quickly towards the priest, then fell back to the candle. "Not to be rude, Father Sebastian, but I'd rather not talk about the *langbuan* tonight.»

"Fair enough."

The priest started to drum his fingers lightly on the table, trying to replace his thoughts. But all he could think of was coffee, and that wasn't any more desirable.

"Do you really want to know?" Antonio asked, startling the priest.

"What?"

"If I've ever seen one."

"Only if you want to tell me."

"It's not like I have anything to hide. It's just...sometimes I wonder if some evil spirit listens in. I've seen *langbuan* before. A few times, too close for comfort. But I'll never forget my first time."

The candle flame danced under Antonio's breath, casting a yellow glow on his hands, shaping what looked like a person. A little boy. "I was eight. A typhoon raged in our town for days. One evening, the storm finally stopped. I ran to the back door so I could play outside, only to be grabbed by the scruff by our servant Trining. 'Don't you remember?' she said. 'It's Ghost Moon Night.'"

"I knew what night it was, but I didn't care. Not going out on Ghost Moon Night was just a rule meant to be broken. I wriggled away like a wild animal! I even bit Trining's wrist, and she let me go. I opened the back door and ran out. The door shut behind me, so hard it knocked a bamboo pole down from where it leaned against the doorway frame, sending it to the dirt floor. I stood there for a moment, pleased with myself, when I noticed something strange."

Antonio turned the little figure right and left. "I couldn't hear a sound. Not a cricket, not a frog, not a rustle of leaves. Even Cupid was silent. He usually snorted whenever I came out. It was like everything was...*dead*."

Something skittered above. Antonio's head snapped up and Father Sebastian followed his gaze. A lizard flicked its tongue out at a moth, capturing it. Antonio smiled. "Just a lizard."

Antonio turned the little wax figure around. "I went to the door and twisted the doorknob. It was locked."

"'Trining,' I said. Then, louder: 'Trining. Trining!' She didn't open the door. I heard something behind me: the wrenching noise of the water pump handle being lifted, then the gush of water."

"A sheet on the clothesline blocked my view of the water pump, but the breeze came up and moved it to the side like a curtain. I saw a woman bent over at the waist, drinking from the pump. She had long, black hair over a shawl and a skirt like the ones my grandmother wore in the old days. And then I heard the most horrendous noise." Antonio's grip on the wax figure tightened. "She growled like a wild beast."

Swallowing, the priest said, "What happened next?"

"I turned back to the door and pounded as hard as I could. Suddenly, I felt a strong gust of wind behind me. I was almost afraid to look, but I did. The *langbuan* stood there, so close I could smell her. *Naku*, she smelled, like a dead animal that's been left out in the sun for days. Her arms, her face, everything was flaking off. What I thought was a shawl spread out into an enormous pair of wings. She opened her toothless mouth and grinned."

"I screamed and leaned against the door, which opened and sent me hurtling backwards onto the kitchen floor. Above me, Trining hit the *langbuan* with the bamboo pole. The creature fell over. Trining threw the pole at her, dragged me in, and slammed the door shut."

"Someone touched me and I flinched, but when I saw it was Mama, I relaxed. I thought Mama would be angry with me, but she reprimanded Trining instead. Trining cried, oh, how she cried, telling Mama how sorry she was."

Antonio glanced at the candle, melted down to a stub. "Do you have a lantern? We may need it in a little bit."

Father Sebastian stood up and took a lantern out of a cupboard. "That's quite a story," he said.

"Yes," Antonio said. "Isn't it? I have more."

Suddenly, Father Sebastian heard a noise, like piano keys being played. His gaze met Antonio's.

"The stained glass window," Antonio said.

24

THE CHAPEL SMELLED of candle wax and holy water. Of fear. Antonio held up the lantern, with Father Sebastian following close behind. The lantern flame danced and hissed, casting a glow over an alcove. Antonio raised it higher, revealing an open portion in the middle of the stained glass window where, earlier, Antonio had patched it. It had been knocked out.

"Normally, the *langbuan* leave the church windows alone," Antonio murmured, as he looked anxiously at the hole.

"You'd think these creatures wouldn't want to attack the house of God," Father Sebastian said.

"Oh, I imagine they don't like what priests do, Father Sebastian."

The priest chuckled. "You may be right."

Plink!

A crooked finger jerked through the window's jagged opening.

"Quick," Antonio said, "we need to block the window with something."

"The ladder's outside."

Antonio looked around. "We can lean a pew across the

window." They each grabbed the end of one and threw it up against the wall, being careful not to hit the glass. Antonio held his breath and slowly exhaled.

"We could tie chairs together," Antonio suggested, "to reinforce it." He ran into the vestry room and grabbed some chairs and rope. Lashing them together, he leaned it against the pew.

There was a whisper of wings and the insistent rattling of shutters.

Antonio glanced at the window. His face glistened with sweat. "I need to get the ladder," he said. "We need to shine a light right there to ward it off."

"The ladder's outside," the priest said.

"I know."

Antonio paused at the door. "Shine a light as close as possible onto the hole." He opened the main chapel door and slipped out. Fog had rolled into the courtyard, swallowing him up.

Father Sebastian pushed the door shut and began praying, "Our Father, hallowed be Thy name..."

More glass shattered overhead. Father Sebastian's heart hammered in his chest. When he heard a knock on the door, he gasped, then ran over. He opened the door a sliver, then wider, to Antonio.

"Mang Nando's with me." Antonio said. "He's hurt!"

The tricycle driver who had given Father Sebastian a ride to the market staggered in and collapsed on the floor. Just a few steps behind him, Antonio swung the ladder at these winged, reptile-like creatures. He screamed as three of these monsters clung to him, dragging him by the shirt.

Father Sebastian crouched behind the door and made the sign of the cross. A *langbuan* flew straight at him. Slamming the door shut, Father Sebastian leaned against it, trembling. Something thudded against the door.

Go away!

There was another wood-splintering crash, followed by Antonio shouting, "Father! Father!"

This time, Father Sebastian opened the door. The ladder came skidding in, followed by Antonio. "Close it!" Antonio screamed.

The door slammed shut on a wing, which snapped like a branch. It released a noxious fume, like rotting meat. The wingtip continued to dance until it lay still on the floor.

Father Sebastian doubled over. Chills racked his body.

"Yolly and her mother are out there still," Nando said, as he lay on the floor. "Please. Antonio. Can you help her into the chapel?"

A kneeling Antonio raised his head. The teen's shirt had gaping holes. Scratch marks slashed his arms. He looked over his shoulder at the closed door. If he refused, Father Sebastian wouldn't have blamed him.

Instead, he said, "Where are they?"

"In that grated drain hole at the edge of the graveyard," Nando said. "The one by the Garcia mausoleum." He tried to raise himself from the floor, but fell. "I know it's a lot to ask. I would go back if I could."

"I'll do it," Antonio said.

"*Maraming salamat*," Nando said. Thank you.

Antonio turned to the priest. "Do you have another lantern?"

Father Sebastian nodded. "In the kitchen. I'll go get it."

Glass shattered. Claws showed through hole in the glass window. "Hurry, Father!" Antonio said, setting up the ladder next to the pew and chairs.

Within a minute, Father Sebastian returned with a lantern. Antonio held a tall candle holder from the altar. "Do you mind if I use this?" Antonio asked. "As a weapon?"

"Go right ahead."

"Set up the ladder and keep the light close to the window," Antonio said. "Don't let the *langbuan* intimidate you."

"I'm not intimidated," Father Sebastian lied.

Antonio smiled as though he knew what the priest was feeling. "Me neither." For one moment, he stood at the door.

"Thank you," Nando said. "May God keep you safe."

Nodding, Antonio rushed out. Father Sebastian locked it after him.

Holding the lantern, Father Sebastian scaled the ladder. When it rattled, he looked at it in alarm, then realized he caused it, he was trembling so much. He continued climbing, each rung rattling more with each step. Near the top, sweat trickled into his eyes. He took a deep breath and climbed two more steps.

Raising the lantern to the hole in the window, he listened. He only heard the hiss of the kerosene.

Below him, Nando scooted to a pew below the ladder and leaned against it. "Sorry. I would help but I can't move my leg muscles very well."

"What happened out there?" Father Sebastian asked.

Nando took a deep breath. "We were trying to take my daughter-in-law, Yolly's mother, to the hospital in my tricycle. Susan's had a weak heart and she couldn't breathe. Just outside the graveyard, a swarm of *langbuan* attacked us. Some people have said the attacks are getting worse, and I believe them. We had to abandon the tricycle. Together, we tried to make our way here, but Susan couldn't go on. Yolly took her into a drain hole and I ran the rest of the way here to get help."

Father Sebastian adjusted his position on the ladder. He lowered the lantern for a minute. A skeletal hand broke through the window.

Nando asked, "And that was…?"

"A *langbuan*!" Father Sebastian cried hoarsely. The hand circled his neck like a vise, choking him. Ice seeped into his veins, slowing the flow of his blood, paralyzing his brain.

Do something! a voice in his head told him, but he couldn't think *what*. His eyes flicked towards the image of the Savior at His birth, the Virgin Mary and Joseph surrounding Him. The shape of Joseph's head made Father Sebastian think of someone, someone familiar. A boy with a shock of hair over his eyes. Antonio.

Antonio! Antonio was in danger, and so was he and Nando.

Father Sebastian shook his head, achieving enough clarity of mind to raise the lantern and pressed it against the *langbuan's* arm. It jerked back so quickly, Father Sebastian felt the movement propel him backwards on the ladder. He wobbled, picturing himself like a marionette, broken in pieces, over the pews below.

"I have you!" Nando said.

Father Sebastian glanced down. Nando sat at the base of the ladder, holding on to its feet. Father Sebastian held up the lantern and heard angry hisses, a flapping of wings, and no indication that the *langbuan* were giving up.

25

EANWHILE, ABOVE ANTONIO, *langbuan* swirled in the fog. He could only make out vague shapes, alerting him enough of their presence to dodge them. At first, he felt like he was just going in circles, as thick as the fog was, but eventually, he made out a clump of gray shapes - tombstones in the graveyard.

He found Yolly in the drain hole, holding her mother in her arms and crying. Crouching down, he whispered, "Yolly."

She looked up and blinked, her eyes bloodshot. "What are you doing out here?"

"Rescuing you and your mother."

Yolly cradled her mother once again.

His glance flickered towards her mother's lifeless body. "Is she...dead?"

Yolly nodded and her eyes welled-up with tears. "Her heart just couldn't take it anymore."

"I'm so sorry."

"How did you know I was here?" she asked.

"Your grandfather sent me to get you."

"He's alive?" Her sobs stopped. "Thank God! I thought... I'd lost him, too."

"He's in the chapel. Let's go and join him."

"Antonio!" Yolly screamed, pointing over his shoulder.

He turned and faced at least a dozen *langbuan* who hovered with their grotesque wings. Then he held up the candlestick.

She held up the grate. "I can fight with you."

Three creatures dove for them. Antonio and Yolly swung their "weapons," catching claws and ripping them off. The *langbuan* shrieked, circled away, then dove for them again.

"Behind you!" Yolly screamed.

Antonio clubbed the *langbuan,* sending the body flying. It slammed into the ground.

Yolly shoved her mother's body onto the dirt above. "Come in here, where it's safer!" Their eyes met. "She'll want you to live," she said.

Antonio dove into the drain hole. He had to squish himself behind Yolly so she was practically sitting on his lap. They kicked away any hands that reached for them in the places where the grate didn't cover them.

"Ready to go the church?" he asked.

"I don't know. It's a long way to that door."

"We have another option," Antonio said. He whistled high and long. Cocking his ear, and hearing nothing else but the *langbuan* circling like vultures above, he whistled again. Soon, Cupid came trotting over with the cart.

"Good boy!" he said.

"Your water buffalo comes like a dog?"

"He's smart."

Still tethered to the cart, the water buffalo took a few steps forward, then backed up.

"Hold still, Cupid!" Antonio said.

"Cupid?" Yolly said. "If only he had a bow and arrow."

"I wish he did, too." To the water buffalo, he coaxed, "Come Cupid, come park the cart here."

He didn't see the *langbuan* until it was next to him and pulling his arm from under the grate. He tried to wrench his arm away, but the creature clung tight. An icy numbness spread to his elbow. Yolly kicked at the creature's head, decapitating it. The head hung from its neck, which oozed a black fluid.

"Oh my…" she said.

The *langbuan* let Antonio's arm go and picked up its head

and set it on its neck once again. The head bobbled around. Antonio's arm throbbed with pain. "Cupid!" he shouted, warding off *langbuan* hands with the grate. "Come here!" Cupid took a few steps, then more, until the cart blocked the ditch. The *langbuan* hissed, circled, flew away and circled again.

"You're hurt," Yolly said, touching Antonio's arm. A broken claw protruded from a bleeding cut.

"It's nothing...*aray!*" Antonio flinched as Yolly pulled out the claw. "Let's go."

When she nodded, he handed her the candlestick. "I'll get your mother. Beat them back."

"Alright."

"On the count of three," he said. "One, two, three!"

They scrambled out of the drain and onto the cart bench. Antonio thrust Yolly's mother in the back. He whipped Cupid, setting him off on a fast trot into the fog.

Antonio felt something brush his neck. His hair. Slithering around him like a serpent. Antonio could sense Cupid slowing down, taking uncertain steps. He shouted again and got him moving, until they emerged from the fog, in sight of the chapel doors. Relieved, he looked over at Yolly.

A *langbuan* yanked her by the hair from the bench. "Antonio!" she yelled. He threw down the reins and jumped up, punching at the hand that held her, but it didn't let go. Yolly twisted and swung her arms. Kicked. Made contact. Growling, the creature released her. She landed on Antonio and knocked the wind out of him.

Howling and hissing, a mass of *langbuan* converged. One grabbed Antonio's arm. Another covered his face, dug the heel of its palm on his nose until he couldn't breathe. He swung the grate against them, but they kept coming. His legs were pulled, yanked hard. Pain made him cry out as the monsters' grip dug into his skin, scratching, tearing at his flesh. He kicked and twisted, but they wouldn't let go.

And then he saw Yolly, yanked back up into the air by a *langbuan*. With a grunt, he kicked even harder, bashed at his attackers, struggled and fought out of their grasp. He leapt up and swung the grate at Yolly's attacker. Another *langbuan* pulled at Yolly, the first one hissing and pouncing on the other. They scrabbled and fought over her. She dangled for one heart-stopping moment, then fell, screaming.

Antonio broke Yolly's fall once again. She tumbled and slammed against the side of the cart and scrambled upright, her eyes widening as the *langbuan* returned, grabbing at them. Antonio's head spun as he rose to the air upside down. *Langbuan* covered him with their slime, death-stench, and those cold, cold claws, rising higher and higher. He saw Yolly, dangling from another's grasp and pulled away enough to reach for her. They clung to each other, kicking away at the monsters.

And then they were falling, to their deaths, Antonio was sure. His body sliced the air. The *langbuan* above him looked further and further away as he continued to fall.

With a loud crash, he hit the dense canopy of a tree. Scraping and skimming branches and leaves. His face, his arms, his legs, catching and snagging. Stinging his skin.

He watched Yolly fall alongside and land in a pile of broken branches and mangoes. For one moment, he lay there stunned. But the *langbuan* were coming, so he jumped to his feet, his body protesting the sudden movement. He grabbed a large branch and saw Yolly do the same.

"To the door," he said.

They ran towards the chapel, swinging branches at the flying mob. Yolly pounded on the door, while Antonio twirled around and swung at them, scattering body parts. Beyond them, he saw Cupid, being dragged by *langbuan*. Some hovered over the cart.

"My mother!" Yolly said.

"I'll get her," he said.

The chapel door opened. Antonio pushed Yolly in. "Don't open it unless you hear me say so." It shut behind him with a disconcerting thud.

Antonio whistled for Cupid. Cupid trotted over, dragging a half-dozen *langbuan*. Antonio swung up into the cart and grabbed Yolly's mother. As he jumped off, the *langbuan* seized him again.

"Let me in!" he shouted as he jerked away, tearing his shirt and flesh from the monster's grip. When the door opened, he launched himself and Yolly's mother into the chapel.

116

26

ANTONIO STAGGERED FORWARD. With each step, his breath caught at the pain that throbbed through his body. He sat on the floor, trying without success to find a position that didn't hurt.

Yolly and her grandfather wept as they held each other, illuminated by the lantern which Father Sebastian held at the top of the ladder.

Several minutes later, Mang Nando walked over.

"You're feeling better," Antonio said.

Mang Nando knelt beside Antonio. "And you're...oh, my dear boy. Thank you. Thank you so much."

"It was nothing." Antonio looked at Yolly. She lay on her side. Her cheek sported a dark bruise. "Are you alright?"

She nodded, brushing away tears.

"You were great out there," he said.

A ghost of a smile lifted the side of her mouth.

"No," Father Sebastian corrected, his voice echoing in the chapel. "You *both* did great."

The next morning, sunlight streamed through a hole on the stained glass window, the size of a large serving tray. Throughout the night, Antonio, Father Sebastian and Mang Nando took turns holding the lantern.

Antonio snuffed out the lantern flame, and surveyed the scene below. Mang Nando, Yolly and Father Sebastian slept on separate pews. Shards of stained glass covered the floor. A sheet covered Yolly's mother's body. He made the sign of the cross.

May her soul rest in peace.

He climbed down the ladder slowly, as each joint in his body seemed to turn on rusty hinges. As he approached the others, Yolly bolted upright, her face still swollen from crying.

"It's morning," he said gently.

She got up and shook Mang Nando awake. They spoke to each other in subdued tones. Nearby, Father Sebastian stirred and sat up. He glanced at the window, at Antonio, at the mourning pair. Getting up and walking around, he touched Antonio on the shoulder, then knelt beside Mang Nando and Yolly.

"Father Sebastian, can you please offer a prayer?" Mang Nando requested.

"Gladly," he said. He bowed his head and prayed for peace and comfort, expressing gratitude that He spared them. He gave thanks for another day, for their village, for the people who lived there, and asked Him to comfort those who mourned.

Antonio went outside to check on Cupid. His water buffalo snorted as he approached.

The cart was missing a wheel. Cupid's nose ring had been wrenched off. The cart yoke had split in half. And still, Cupid acted like it was just another happy day. Antonio hugged Cupid and buried his face in his neck, inhaling the familiar smell of mud and hay.

"He's an amazing beast, isn't he?" Father Sebastian said from the doorway. The priest joined him, glancing at the sunrise. "I'm not a young man. I just turned 65. But I have never, in my

GHOST MOON NIGHT

life, experienced anything like Ghost Moon Night."

"Welcome to Dasalin," Antonio said.

"You know, we should really do something about the curse."

"I always feel that way the day after," Antonio said. "But then your day goes on, one week turns to two, then to four. And you forget until it starts all over again."

"You should all just leave Dasalin."

"Try telling that to our villagers." Antonio smiled. "I once asked my father why we didn't just move. He said no one would buy our land so if we were to move, we would have nothing. But it's more than the land. Our ancestors fought for this land, and now we carry on their tradition. We are a village of fighters, and we won't be beaten by evil."

Father Sebastian gave him an admiring glance.

When they went back into the chapel, Mang Nando came up to Antonio. "I was just about to get you. *Makikisuyo lang.* Can you please go with us to the hospital? We need to take Yolly's mother there, and I thought your cart would be more... appropriate."

Antonio glanced at Yolly. She sat on the pew, eyes staring grimly straight ahead.

Father Sebastian offered breakfast, but the others declined. Antonio hurried and opened the shutters, after which the priest thanked him and sent them on the road. Antonio drove the cart and Mang Nando followed in his tricycle. Yolly sat in the back of the cart with her mother.

At the hospital, two nurses came out to help. Yolly touched Antonio's shoulder. In her eyes, he saw pain and sorrow and something more. "Thank you," she said, turning away.

"You're welcome." He watched her take Mang Nando's arm and walk slowly up the hospital steps. Then he drove the cart home, passing yards that seemed untouched by Ghost Moon Night. Everything seemed normal, just another dawn, until he saw a family of little children and a mother, crouched over a body, shrouded with a sheet near their doorstep. Suddenly, his words about their brave little village flashed in his mind. Courage and sorrow. They went hand in hand. Antonio's jaw clenched as he forced himself to drive on.

119

Mama was opening her sewing room window as Antonio drove the cart into their yard. She disappeared, then burst out of the front door. He stopped Cupid and let her catch up. Her glance traveled over his face, his shirt, his arms. Tears filled her eyes.

"*Anak*," she said. Son. She touched his skin lightly, and he flinched.

"Sorry, I'm kind of...sore."

"What happened?" she asked.

He told her about the window, Yolly's mother and their narrow escape.

"My brave son," Mama said. "But poor Yolly!"

"You know," Antonio mused, "Father Sebastian says we should all just move away."

"I've thought about that, many times," she said. "I've thought about it as I've lain at night in bed on Ghost Moon Night, when the windows are shut and the heat stifles. Pretending to sleep but in reality listening for *langbuan*. Sometimes I dream about leaving and moving to the city. I've heard that a good seamstress can make a good living sewing for rich folks." She looked at the rice paddies. "But then I think of the things we'd be leaving behind. No, I'm not ready for that yet."

Antonio let his mother pull him down into an awkward embrace. "Thank God you stayed safe," she said.

She went in to sew while he gave Cupid an extra pile of hay. Then he went in search of Lolo Sonny. The *salas* was empty. "Where's Lolo?" he asked Mama.

Mama pushed back strands of hair from her eyes. "Last night, we had to tie him up to a chair, or he would have ran outside. I finally untied him at dawn. He's asleep in his bedroom. Just let him rest."

Antonio groaned. *Lolo Sonny, tied up like an animal!* "I won't wake him up," he said.

"I'm just going to see him." He went into Lolo Sonny's bedroom. Closed up, with the windows shut, the room smelled sour. Lolo Sonny lay curled up on the bed under his *kulambo*, his breathing shallow and noisy. Sometime during his sleep, Lolo Sonny had kicked off his sheet. With his eyes, Antonio traced the rope marks on his grandfather's wrists. Antonio reached under the mosquito net and arranged it so it covered him.

As he came out, he met Papa in the hallway. Papa took in Antonio's appearance and blanched, then motioned for Antonio to follow him to the kitchen where they could talk. "What happened?"

Antonio repeated what he told Mama. Papa sat down heavily on a chair. "It seems that every month, the attacks are getting more and more vicious," he said. "Sounds like the new priest was lucky to have you there."

"I'm going to go change." Antonio turned but Papa called his name.

"I don't imagine you're able to help me with the farm in your condition?"

From the other room, Mama said, "Romy. Let the boy catch his breath for a minute."

"Don't worry about it," Papa said gruffly. "I'll go get Arnell. I just need to finish plowing the field today."

"I can still help," Antonio said.

"If you're sure." Papa paused. "Thank you."

In the kitchen, Antonio helped himself to some garlic fried rice and dried fish. He sprinkled some vinegar on the fish, mixed it with the rice and washed it all down with coffee. Suddenly, he heard shouts coming from the direction of their neighbor Arnell's house. He left his plate on the counter and ran out.

Two doors down, a crowd gathered. Arnell's mother, Aling Mila, knelt on the ground beside Arnell, who was crying, his hand wrapped in a bloody rag. There was blood everywhere, on his shirt, Aling Mila's blouse, his pants, the ground.

The constable drove up in a horse-drawn *karitela*. He and two men loaded a moaning Arnell in the back. Aling Mila made a big fuss about not being allowed to go with them. Finally, Constable Martillo waved her in, and the driver drove the horse into a fast-clipped trot.

"Did the *langbuan* get him?" a bystander asked.

"No, he was dynamite fishing," answered another.

"Ay, *por Dios!*"

"Poor Aling Mila! He's always giving her grief…"

Antonio glimpsed Papa's face. He looked stunned. Most likely thinking how the perfect Arnell had sunk so low.

27

THE FOLLOWING WEEK, the village held the *kuding* procession up the mountain, as they had every year before. Only after this could anyone plant their crops in Dasalin for the season.

When Antonio was a child, his father explained how Mount Dasalin got its name. "The mountain looks like a woman kneeling and clasping her hands in supplication, *dasal* or prayer," Papa said. "It's the side that faces the rocky sea shore. Her hair is the waterfall on the other side."

This year's procession went slowly behind Tandang Lino, who stopped every few feet to catch his breath. Everyone followed his frail figure: sandaled feet with too-long toe nails slipping in the dirt, a red handkerchief tied around his head, the hump on his back prominent under his faded *kamiso de chino*.

Beside Antonio, his best friend Jose didn't seem bothered by the slow pace. In fact, he whistled and looked around at the trees, insects and birds. Antonio was glad, too. He was still a little sore from Ghost Moon Night.

Tito Oscar was out of town, and of course Tita Alice – due to have a baby any time – couldn't bring her girls. Papa groused about Tito Oscar's family not being there. "Baranggay captain

123

and he neglects his duty!"

"He paid for the *kakanin* refreshments afterwards, didn't he?" Antonio asked, reminding Papa about the food waiting for them at the pavilion.

Papa shrugged. "Anyone can pay for things."

Not you, Antonio thought, but just bit his tongue.

Mang Nando drove his tricycle up, with Yolly in the sidecar. Antonio lingered at the start of the trail.

"Come on," Jose said.

Yolly looked up and smiled at Antonio. He smiled back, before turning to walk alongside Jose.

"Wait," Jose said. "You and her...?"

"I was just being friendly, is all," Antonio said. "This past Ghost Moon Night, we had a little... adventure together."

Jose wasn't even listening. He was too busy watching a snake slither into the grass. "What?" he said. Antonio shrugged and walked on.

Up ahead, Grace Mijares stumbled and fell to her knees.

Grace's mother, Mrs. Mijares cried, "*Anak!*" Child! "What's wrong?"

"I think I sprained my ankle," Grace said.

Mrs. Mijares called out to Tandang Lino. "Can you please help my daughter?"

Tandang Lino leaned the weight of his body against his walking stick. "You know I don't heal bones anymore." He held up his contorted hands. "*Rayuma.*" Arthritis.

"Go." Jose pushed Antonio forward. "You can play the hero."

"Are you kidding?" Antonio said. "I don't know what to do with a sprained ankle."

"Fine," Jose said. "Just come with me, then, and be my assistant."

"What are you talking about? You only do urinals."

"I've had to bandage my ankle a lot," Jose pointed out. "Here," he said out loud, "I can help."

Mrs. Mijares looked at him skeptically. "And you are...?"

"Jose Pineda, ma'am. I'm Grace's classmate. We were in math together."

"Well, this isn't a math problem," Mrs. Mijares retorted. She noticed Antonio standing to the side and glared at him, probably remembering the dress.

"I play basketball, ma'am," Jose said, "so I deal with sprains all the time."

"I'm alright," Grace said, standing up. "It hurts just a little."

"Jose helped Grace on her left side, and Antonio helped on the right. She took two steps and winced, but bravely kept going again.

"I'll help my daughter, thank you," Mrs. Mijares said. The two reluctantly handed Grace over.

"We shall go again," Tandang Lino announced. "If you can't keep up, then I would ask that you stay behind."

"That looks like a good spot to rest," Mrs. Mijares said.

"I can keep going, Mama," Grace insisted.

Jose nudged Antonio and whispered, "You should stay back there. If she stumbles again, you can catch her."

Yolly passed them then. Antonio smiled but she only nodded coolly. Had she heard what Jose said?

As the trail got steeper, the forest got darker. Denser.

Trees pressed in on Antonio, giant trunks of tangile with canopies that soared hundreds of feet up, lean ipil trees that looked like dwarves under its giant neighbors. Here, the air was cool and humid. Leaves and branches slapped at his face, his arms. Dew drenched his shirt and pants.

A snake reared its head, then slithered into the brush. Colorful birds swooped, landed and issued out calls of "*Tu-ko! Tu-ko!*" A lizard puffed out its throat, its eyes looking filmy under its first eyelids. Antonio ran into spider webs, disturbing spiders the size of a child's fist. Fat mosquitoes buzzed around his ears and bit his arms.

A half hour passed. Then an hour. Two. Tandang Lino may not have been fast, but he was steady. He stopped every so often, but for the most part, he kept going, shaming the rest of the group from resting too long.

Towards the top, the trail turned indistinct. Tandang Lino forged ahead, getting down on all fours over the rougher terrain. He stood up, only to stumble. Two men moved to his side to help him along, but he refused their help. After he made it over a rise, everyone took turns scrambling up to the top.

A few minutes later, Antonio stood on the bald, rocky summit of Mount Dasalin. Here, the wind blew steadily, cool despite the noon sun. Except for a sloping trail leading to a ridge that sheltered a large cave, the rest of the mountain face was a steep cliff. It dropped sharply down to a mangrove-lined beach, where little huts on stilts stood at water's edge. In the clear shallows, white sand sloped gently into a mass of coral, where the water deepened to turquoise. Small islands formed stepping stones in the horizon.

Everyone formed a half-circle behind Tandang Lino, who faced the cliff's edge, and sat on rocky ground. Antonio noticed that Yolly sat on the opposite side of the crowd. He thought about getting up and talking to her to find out how she's doing, but Tandang Lino began the prayer.

Arms outstretched, the old man recited the prayer Antonio had heard since he was able to sit on his father's shoulders and join in the pilgrimage: "Our most revered *kuding*, we are here to pay homage to you..."

Next, he replicated the call of the kuding.

"*Ku-diiing! Ku-diiing!*"

If a kuding responded, or showed itself, it meant that their town had the right conditions for planting. If not, the pilgrimage would have to be repeated in another week. Antonio hoped they would get it this first time. He could remember only one time when Tandang Lino had to take them back to the mountain. That year, Dasalin suffered a drought and worms attacked their crops.

Beside Antonio, his parents' lips moved in prayer.

Tandang Lino repeated his *kuding* call.

"*Ku-diiing! Ku-diiing!*"

In his mind's eye, Antonio imagined what lay over the edge of the plateau: sheer cliff that plunged to the sea. Swallow nests pockmarked the upper cliff wall, the limestone bleached white by the sun.

Suddenly, unearthly shrieks pierced the air. At first, Antonio thought girls were making the sound.

"What is that?" Mama whispered to Papa.

"*Kuding* sounding an alarm to their brood," Papa replied.

A brown cloud of birds rose up from the cave on the cliff and flew over Tandang Lino, whose arms were stretched out. His shirt, his bandana, the little wisps of hair on his bald head moved to the wind's onslaught. The *kuding* swooped down next

126

upon the villagers, who ducked, and then the birds disappeared over the cliff edge.

"Look!" someone cried.

From the cave, a battered brown hat emerged, followed by a black cassock. "Good morning!" Father Sebastian called out.

"Father Sebastian!" Tandang Lino exclaimed, spittle forming at his mouth. "What are you doing here? These," he made a sweeping gesture with his hand, "are sacred grounds!"

"I'm sorry, but I hadn't heard about the pilgrimage until an hour ago. So I drove my car up until it couldn't go further and took this route. Don't let me interrupt you."

Tandang Lino's veins bulged out on the sides of his face. He looked like he wanted to push the priest over the cliff. "You already have! Not only that, you've ruined something important, a town ritual on which many livelihoods depend!"

The priest continued to smile agreeably. "Oh ye of little faith."

"Pardon me?" Tandang Lino said.

Father Sebastian seemed to look straight at Antonio. "You work hard for something and you will get it. Not through bird calls. And not just the sweat of your brow. You need to rely upon God. He is the Almighty grantor of wishes. The source of all life here on this earth." To Tandang Lino he said, "Maybe it's time that this village depends on something more than just birds."

Tandang Lino opened his mouth as though to speak, but the priest plowed on. "And what about Ghost Moon Night and the *langbuan*? Why does this town cower instead of choosing to fight evil? But birds are so harmless. And monthly monsters are so harmless. A lie! Every time you revere these creatures, every time you worship them, you might as well worship the devil!" Father Sebastian wiped his brow with the sleeve of his cassock. "There! I'm done."

No one spoke for a good long minute.

"As I am," Tandang Lino finally said. "As I am." He walked away, back down the mountain path they had hiked.

"Tandang Lino," someone asked. "Does this mean we can start planting?"

The old man paused and raised a hand. The wind blew strong. Antonio couldn't smell the sea; the wind was blowing the wrong way for that. Instead, he smelled the lush secrets of the forest, and a little of the fear in the group as they hung onto the elder's words.

Tandang Lino held up a hand and closed his eyes. "Yes."

No one cheered as in past years after a successful kuding sighting. This one didn't feel earned.

Antonio could sense everyone's disappointment as they whispered among themselves. He liked Father Sebastian a lot. But he disagreed with him. Given time, maybe the priest would understand and learn to accept their traditions and rituals.

Tandang Lino turned and led them in the hike down the mountain. Antonio stayed back to talk to Father Sebastian, a lone figure facing the cliff.

"Father Sebastian," Antonio said, approaching him. "I should have mentioned about the pilgrimage. Then you wouldn't have driven off the birds."

"Do you believe that these birds affect your harvest?" the priest asked. "Truly, in your heart of hearts?"

"My parents have always said so, so I believe."

Father Sebastian nodded. "That's understandable. But someday, you'll need to decide for yourself who controls your destiny. These creatures or God."

28

O N THE FIRST day of planting, Antonio met Papa at the rice paddies at the crack of dawn. Already, the humid morning air made Antonio's shirt cling to his sweaty back.

"Thank you for coming to help me," Papa said.

Antonio glanced sharply at Papa, surprised at his humble tone. But it didn't last long.

"Come on," Papa said in his usual gruff way. "The sun moves fast."

Papa led Mama and Antonio past an open-walled shed. At Papa's hip, he carried a scabbard with a huge bolo knife. He stopped at the chicken coop, taking out a hen, which he inspected at length. He seemed to take forever, but Antonio knew better than to hurry Papa at this part of the planting ritual. Satisfied, Papa handed him the hen and reached in for another, repeating the inspection process. Antonio tucked both chickens under his arms and followed Papa to a corner of the nearest field.

"Are we ready?" Papa asked, to which Mama and Antonio responded appropriately, "As the spirits of the earth see fit."

Papa knelt down and recited words Antonio had heard

from the time he was old enough to remember: "Our beloved ancestors, our revered spirits of the earth, please accept from us this humble offering, the best of our flock representing the best of our efforts."

Antonio's mind wandered. The coolness of dawn had fled, replaced by heat that made it difficult to think. He lost himself in a daydream, imagining Yolly and him scaling one of the lower rock cliffs and daring each other to dive.

With a start, Antonio realized Papa had stopped talking and was staring at him, looking annoyed. Antonio handed him one hen. Papa took the bolo knife. As he held it at lap-level over the hen's throat, the blade glinted in the sun. He quickly chopped off the hen's neck, darkening the earth with its blood. He did the same to the second one, and left them on a slab for Trining to clean and cook.

Antonio thought of Ilaryo, his uncle's white rooster. For a moment, his throat tightened.

Next, Mama untied a burlap bag from around her waist and pulled out golden rice grains. She wore a faded, knee-length dress that trailed in the mud as she walked down to the seedbed. Then she stopped and released the rice grains onto the paddy.

The first planting, by the mother of the household. It symbolized Mother Earth bestowing her graces upon them. After that symbolic first planting, Trining fetched the chickens to roast them. Antonio and his parents fanned out, sowing rice grains from hand-held *bilao* baskets.

Mama went back to her sewing machine after their meal of *inihaw* or roast chicken. Papa and Antonio stayed outside and sat under a mango tree eating soft pillows of doughy *palitao* sprinkled with shredded coconut.

Antonio was enjoying his third *palitao* when Papa spoke. "In a few weeks, we'll be ready to transplant," he said. "Without Arnell, it will be doubly hard. I'm planning on you to help me."

It was not a question. Antonio stiffened. They'd talked about this before. Antonio had already told him he was finding a different job. Was Papa being deliberately obtuse?

"If I find a job, I won't be available, Papa," Antonio said.

Papa's expression darkened. "But you have a job, right here!"

"Papa, I need a job that would earn me enough money for

Lolo's record player."

"How am I to take you seriously?" Papa cried. "I don't think you don't even know your own mind."

"Did you, at my age?" Antonio countered.

"Yes. Farming is what my father did, and his father before him. I knew that these fields would someday be mine, just like they will be yours someday."

"Papa, there are other jobs than farming."

"*Hala!*" Papa said. "You mustn't speak like that to your father. You'd better get your head out of the mud, son, or you will be sorely disappointed. What can a farmer's son do?"

"Mr. Mijares runs a good business." Antonio paused. "Tito Oscar, too."

Not surprisingly, Papa said, "Oscar is simply a lucky man with a lot of charm."

"And a nice house by the sea. He's wealthy."

"Wealth!" Papa's lip curled. "I'll show you wealth. Get up!"

"Why...what...?" Antonio stammered.

Papa just kept walking along the dirt dams that would keep the water in the paddies. Antonio followed until Papa stopped at an intersection of paddies.

"Son," he said, "do you know how many generations of Pulidos have farmed these fields?"

Antonio shook his head.

"Five," Papa said. "Our ancestors carved a life out of this valley. Death, sickness, pestilence – nothing deterred them. Outsiders – the Spaniard, the Japanese, the American – tried stealing this land. This land is the product of *sacrifice*. For you and me."

"I never asked for anyone to make any sacrifices for me," Antonio said.

"You're right," Papa agreed, "but you can't change the past. The offering is there for the grateful to take."

"But I *am* grateful!"

"Then show it!" Papa got red in the face. "Antonio, I want you to look! To really look. What do you see?"

After a minute, Antonio said, "I see a brown field that's been re-seeded, muddy and bare."

"Is that all? It's not just a brown field," Papa insisted. "It's mud and water slapping against the water buffalo's hoof, the sowing of seeds into the prepared dirt. Seedlings ready for transplant. Rice stalks swaying in the breeze, the hulls bursting and ready to harvest. It's the sun drying piles of grain and its rhythmic sifting onto the woven *bilao*."

Papa stopped speaking, slightly out of breath, and glanced at Antonio. "Well?"

"Papa," Antonio said. "Farming isn't always poetic."

Throwing his hands in the air, Papa said, "If my words do not move you, then you are hopeless!"

Something within Antonio busted loose. "Hope!" he lashed back. "You speak of hope, and how can I have hope as you slave over this land? You see more than a brown field? Well, I do, too."

"It's the monotony of chores and slimy mud, prying off a dozen leeches, fingers cut and bleeding from plucking and transplanting wet seedlings, flies getting in my eyes and nose, enough sweat to fill a bucket. It's a back so sore I can't even lie down properly at night. It's having just enough money for you to gamble away, almost not enough money to buy seeds for the next planting season and to keep some crop for our table. The honest truth is, if it weren't for Mama's earnings, we would most likely starve!"

Papa was right; like an untethered water buffalo, Antonio was unable to stop himself from charging stupidly headlong. Papa looked like an empty hull of rice, slack around the mouth and the eyes. Defeated. Antonio had pushed it beyond the limit, and he knew it.

Antonio shoved his hands in his pockets. "I'll think about what you said, Papa, alright? But I would like to try something else. For Lolo Sonny and a new record player."

"And then after the record player, what then?"

"Then I'll think about it some more."

Papa didn't say anything but just shook his head. He looked up at the sun and said, "Let's keep working."

FTER HIS DECLARATION, Antonio had to make good on his word and find a job. The next morning, he came to breakfast wearing his Sunday best. Papa refused to look up from the newspaper. He must have told Mama the gist of the conversation. She looked at Antonio and said, "How about an apology?"

Antonio waited for Papa's.

When Mama sighed, Antonio decided to just get it done and over with. "I'm sorry, Papa," he said.

Papa grunted but refused to lower the newspaper. Antonio looked at Mama as though to say, "See? What's the point?" but she looked mollified.

Lolo Sonny was oblivious to all this. He looked worn out and pale. His eyes lacked the usual spark. Antonio helped him put some food in his spoon, but after about five bites, Lolo Sonny refused more.

Despite Papa's objections, Antonio felt better about his decision. If he raised enough money, he could buy the record player for Lolo Sonny and hopefully make him feel better.

Trining brought in a steaming basket of *pan de sal*. Antonio welcomed the diversion. He grabbed a roll and got smacked on the hand with a fly swatter.

"We haven't blessed yet," Trining said.

Trining's insolence irked Antonio. But Mama acted like nothing was amiss, and waited pointedly for Antonio to fold his arms. After Mama offered the blessing, Antonio dunked his bread into his coffee and took a big bite.

"Careful," Mama said, "or you'll dribble on your shirt. What's the hurry?"

"I have a lot of doors to knock on today," Antonio said.

"If you show manners like that, no one will want to hire you." Papa said. "I don't want you to bother your Tito Oscar for a job."

"I know, I know."

Papa belched loudly and hid behind the paper again.

Antonio excused himself and went out, shaking his head. *I won't be like him*, he vowed.

Antonio flagged down a tricycle and asked to be taken to the bus station, where the businesses were clustered between small villages like Dasalin. As he got out of the tricycle, he saw Yolly seated in her grandfather's sidecar waiting for customers at the queue. She had been watching him – he caught her glance – but quickly lowered her eyes to her lap. He willed her to look up. Last Ghost Moon Night, hadn't they shared a remarkable experience? They might not be the best of friends, but surely she could trust him now? He wondered how she was faring, with her mother's passing. When she wouldn't look up, he went on to Aling Dona's restaurant, confounded by girls.

"Well," Aling Dona greeted him, "you look decent for a change. Have you come to play music or eat?"

"Neither," Antonio said, although he itched to play the latest song on the jukebox. "I've come to apply for a job."

She shook her head. "Sorry, I have nothing."

"I can man your jukebox," Antonio offered.

"No, thanks." Aling Dona smiled encouragingly. "But good luck with your search. If you end up empty-handed at the end of the day, at least come in for a bowl of soup. I can donate that much."

He thanked her and walked on down the sidewalk, into an alley which emerged into the harbor road. Here, a cluster of tricycles waited for patrons who were shopping at the wet market.

Under the open-sided stalls with tin roofs, a hive of customers buzzed over vendor stalls. Piles of oranges, guavas, and mangoes filled bins; newly hulled white rice smelled fragrant; *pechay* and other vegetables tried valiantly but failed to stand up to the heat, looking limp in parts; cow stomach, pig heads and various cuts of meats left a slimy trail of blood along the side of the stall to the wet ground. Flies swarmed over a gigantic tuna head, and what looked like the fin of a shark, as well as mussels, squid and other fish. The whole place smelled like fish.

Antonio went over to the biggest fish stall of them all, Tito Oscar's. Here, the fish seemed twice as big as the others, and a young girl stood over the stall with a stick and streamers meant to keep the flies off. Pedro, Tito Oscar's vendor, came out from the back and hailed Antonio. Antonio wished Papa wasn't so pig-headed about him working for Tito Oscar.

Antonio sidestepped puddles of standing water and let a harried housewife pass him, then kept walking. Two aisles over, a sign caught his eye.

Wanted: butcher apprentice

Antonio hesitated. There had been whispers. The new butcher never went outside in the mornings and only slaughtered animals in the evening. People said he was an *aswang*.

A vampire who sucked blood.

Antonio wanted to pass on, but he needed a job. As he deliberated whether to apply, a butcher knife impaled itself on the meat counter. The butcher walked towards him, with red-rimmed eyes and fangs. Antonio blinked and the image was gone, replaced by a greasy complexion, beady eyes, rodent teeth and a huge double chin.

"You look like you just saw a ghost," the butcher said, snort-laughing like a pig.

"I was just looking at your job opening."

The butcher eyed him. "You look too delicate for such

bloody work."

"I'm not," Antonio assured him.

"Hmmph," the butcher grunted. "Let's put it to the test, shall we?"

Already, Antonio was having second thoughts about showing his interest. He eyed the market's exit and considered bolting for his freedom, but the butcher grabbed his arm. "To the back," he said.

30

NTONIO DIDN'T THINK he was squeamish, but the smell of blood and the sight of cow carcasses lined in a row, hung from the rafters with chains, made his stomach turn. One rod held gigantic beef sides. Another held blood-stained whole pigs. Yet another had smaller, headless animals that looked like goat.

The butcher asked him questions: how old was he, was he still going to school, who was his father? All the while, his pudgy hand kept hold of Antonio's arm. He brought Antonio up close to a pig, hung upside down, which looked like it was still alive, its flesh was so pink.

In one swift movement, the butcher unsheathed a knife and held it up to Antonio's face. Antonio flinched and took a step back.

"I still need to drain this pig," the butcher said. "Will you do the honor?"

He handed the knife to Antonio. Mercifully, he let his arm go, too. "You cut right here," he said, indicating a spot in the pig's throat.

Tentatively, Antonio swallowed and held the knife at an

JEWEL ALLEN

angle next to the pig's skin. He took one breath. Two.

"Not queasy, are you?" the butcher said, his beady eyes dancing and his double chin quivering.

Pressing the knife blade against the pig's throat, he took a deep breath and pushed down. The blade was so sharp it passed through its skin quickly. Blood, dull red, began to cascade down to a bucket underneath.

The butcher squealed, making Antonio jump. "Oh, glorious, glorious fluid of life. Would you look at that?" Bending down, the butcher put his mouth directly in the flow of the blood. Blood gurgled out and down the side of his face, to his ear.

Antonio blinked. His imagination had once again ran away with him. The butcher was looking at Antonio. There was no trace of blood on his face or mouth.

"Well," the butcher asked. "What do you think?"

Thrusting the handle of the knife into the butcher's hand, Antonio didn't answer, and instead ran past the other stalls on down to the market exit. Outside, he breathed lungfuls of air until his heartbeat slowed down.

In the dirt lot next to the market, he saw Timo carrying the record player out of his family's store to his motorcycle. "Wait!" Antonio shouted. He sprinted across the road and dodged a tricycle to get to Timo. "It's not sold, is it?" he asked.

"It's not, Farmboy," Timo said, "but it very well could be by the end of the month."

Antonio frowned. "Why are you taking it away then?"

"It's broken. Someone dropped a bag of flour on it and broke the stylus."

"I'll...I'll buy it then," Antonio said. "For a fraction of a price."

"Nice try, but no thanks. My cousin will fix it and it'll be good as new. It's still going for the price I told you."

Timo straddled his motorcycle, balancing the record player in front of him. Antonio cringed at Timo's carelessness. At least Timo strapped the record player to the seat.

"Don't drop it," Antonio said.

Past the rows of tricycles waiting for riders, a door opened to a small building that was marked "Mijares Enterprises". Grace came out in a lovely pink dress and approached Timo.

"Ready?" Timo asked.

GHOST MOON NIGHT

Grace made a face. "I can't fit on your motorcycle with that thing on your lap."

"I can give you a ride," Antonio offered.

Timo chortled. "In his cart? What a tough choice, huh, Grace?"

She looked like she was considering it.

"You're not seriously thinking of riding in Antonio's mudcart, are you?" Timo asked.

Grace folded her arms across her chest. "Then put that thing back in the store."

Timo glowered but carried it back to the store while Grace waited by the motorcycle.

"You look nice," Grace told Antonio.

"Thanks," he said. "I'm looking for a job."

"You should apply here," she pointed at the Mijares building.

"That's where I'm going, in fact." Antonio headed on over.

"*Hoy!*" Timo called out. "The mental hospital's the other way!"

Someday I'm going to own that record player, Antonio vowed, as he ignored the taunt. *Just to shut Timo up.*

Antonio walked into the Mijares building, then entered the first door, marked "Owner".

It was a small room with spare furnishings: a rattan desk, a cabinet, and two chairs. A woman with bright red lipstick sat behind the desk filing her nails. She moved with a practiced air of putting the file away. But when she saw it was only Antonio, she continued. An electric fan clicked and whirred in the corner.

"Can I help you?" she said. She blew on her bangs and studied a fingernail closely.

"Can I please see Mr. Mijares?"

"Mr. Mijares isn't here," she said. "He's out to lunch."

"Can I make an appointment?"

She shrugged. "Depends. What do you need?"

"It's about a job."

"I don't know. Mr. Mijares is a very busy man."

"Yes, he is," a man chimed in.

"Oh," the secretary said, looking past Antonio to the open door. "It's just *you*."

Antonio recognized the man from high school, Bubuy

139

Alvarez, three years his senior. He had what looked like scars from fighting, but Antonio knew he just had a bad case of acne. His greatest claim to fame was that he once masterminded the theft of the watering can from Mr. Basilio's practical arts classroom, in broad daylight. It may not sound like a big deal, but if anyone knew Mr. Basilio, they'd consider it was the heist of the century.

Bubuy sauntered in, an unlit cigarette hanging from his lips.

"You know Mr. Mijares doesn't like you smoking in the building," the secretary said, smiling.

"You won't snitch on me, will you?" He winked at her, then glanced at Antonio. "Are you Romy Pulido's son?"

"Yes."

"I know your old man."

"Oh?" Antonio said.

"Not a very smart gambler."

Antonio stiffened.

Bubuy eyed Antonio's clothes and shoes. "Are you selling something?"

"I want to apply for a job. As a tricycle driver."

"Do you, now?" He took the cigarette out of his mouth and gestured towards Antonio. "I have a test. If you pass it, I will recommend that Mr. Mijares hires you. What do you say?"

Antonio glanced at him warily. "What do you want me to do?"

"A driver didn't show up for work today but he owes Mr. Mijares money. I need you to go to his house and repossess the tricycle."

"That's it?"

"Yes." Bubuy smiled, flashing tobacco-stained teeth.

"Alright."

31

A TRICYCLE DRIVER DROPPED Antonio off in front of a fenced yard on Palanca Street. From where he stood, he could only see the house, no tricycle. He let himself in through the gate, then skirted around to one side.

The tricycle was parked in some overgrown weeds. Antonio stuck his hand in his pocket and felt the key that Bubuy gave him. "He won't be nice about it," Bubuy had warned him.

A mangy dog half-ran, half-dragged itself from the backyard to where Antonio stood. The dog's tongue lolled out slightly, and one of his eyes twitched.

"Is your owner home?" Antonio asked.

The dog watched him with his odd eye. There wasn't anything menacing about his posture, so Antonio took one step, and another step until he could get past it to the side yard.

"Just turn the key and drive it off," Bubuy had said.

It sounded pretty simple. However, Antonio hadn't counted on the heavy chain wrapped around the tire spokes, bolted to the ground, a large padlock keeping it all in place. Antonio knelt and tried to pry up the bolt. No such luck. He looked around for a tool to use, anything, when the window just directly to his right opened up. To his surprise, Yolly Nakpil stood framed by it. Her eyes flashed with shock, then anger.

"What are you doing here?" she said.

"I thought this place looked familiar," Antonio said, groaning inwardly.

"This is my grandfather's house but yes, I live here. Why?"

He hesitated, then said, "I'm here to take back this tricycle for Bubuy Alvarez."

"You're not the first one to try. Leave before I call my dog on you!"

He looked at the mongrel. "What happened to him anyway? He looks like a truck squashed him."

"Some stupid kids took him and strung him up by the leg."

"Do you save every poor dog you encounter?"

"Do you follow the bidding of every bully you meet?"

He focused once again on the tricycle. "If you'll just give me the key to this padlock, I'll be on my way."

"Do you even know why Bubuy wants the tricycle back?" she asked.

"He said the driver didn't show up at work, and he owes Mr. Mijares money. If I had known it was Mang Nando, I'd have come to your front door first."

"Then you are the biggest fool for believing him!" With that, she retreated and slammed the window shut.

"Great," he muttered. Aloud, he shouted, "I told Bubuy I would take it. I'll let him sort it out with your grandfather."

The window opened again. "Don't you dare," she warned.

"Watch me," he said.

He looked around the yard for a tool. There was a pile of junk out in the back, and he marched over to it. The pile had scraps of wood and tree branches, and a long silver bar. He grabbed the bar but it wouldn't budge. Yanking hard, he fell on his back as the whole thing collapsed. As it was, the metal thing wasn't even useful; it was an old rusty bicycle frame, cannibalized for parts.

He had no time for this nonsense. Marching back to the tricycle, he began yanking at the chain. It didn't budge. Whoever buried the bolt it was connected to had done a good job.

"Stop it!" Yolly shouted from the window.

"Unlock it," Antonio shot back.

GHOST MOON NIGHT

"No."

So he continued working on the chain.

Suddenly, she yelled, "Caloy, attack!"

32

THE NERVE OF the girl! The dog would have ripped Antonio's ear off had he not put up an elbow and knocked it backwards. He scrambled up, ran around the tricycle, and stood on the driver's seat. The dog snapped at him again, but he wasn't tall enough to reach Antonio's ankles.

"Call him off!" Antonio told Yolly.

"Only if you promise to get off our property," she said.

"Not until I get what I came here for."

"Fine, you can get rabies for all I care!"

The window closed again. Caloy bared his fangs and Antonio could have sworn he was foaming at the mouth. Fortunately, he was a little dim. If he'd been smart at all, he could have walked around to the sidecar, gotten up on the seat, and attacked Antonio easily.

"Yolly!" Antonio shouted. "Yolly Nakpil!"

The window remained shut.

He remembered the key in his pocket. He fished it out, his eyes searching for the motorcycle ignition. Still perched on his spot with the crazy dog trying to eat him, he crouched down and put the key in the ignition. Nothing happened. He tried it a few more times with the same result.

"What are you trying to do now?" The window had opened and Yolly was watching him with a smirk.

"What's wrong with this tricycle?" Antonio asked. "Did Mang Nando destroy it?"

"Even my dog can figure that out better than you. Have you ever heard of kick-starting?"

"Of course," he lied. He studied the side of the motorcycle. He *had* seen tricycle drivers kick something before the engine turned over and rumbled. The only problem was, a shark of a little dog wanted to take a bite of his ankle if he dared kick the lever.

"Even if you did drive it off," Yolly said, "the tire would stay here with the chain. Do you have money to get it fixed?"

"Well, Bubuy didn't say I had to bring back the tricycle in one piece," he pointed out.

"Knowing Bubuy, he'd charge you triple for the tire."

"So just be nice and toss me the key to the padlock."

"How much will Bubuy pay you if you get this back to him?"

"Nothing. He just promised to hire me."

Yolly made a face. "All that trouble for nothing?"

"Yolly," a voice called from the hut. "Yolly." Louder now. "Can you hear me?"

Yolly looked over her shoulder. "Yes, *Lolo*."

"Who's out there with you?"

She gave Antonio a sidelong glance. "It's Antonio Pulido. He's here to steal your tricycle for Bubuy."

Antonio glared at her.

"Tell him to come in," Mang Nando said.

Yolly frowned. "Are you sure, *Lolo*?"

"I'm sure."

She looked at Antonio for a long moment. Then she said to the dog, "Leave him." The window shut once again.

Antonio stood at the front stoop and waited. Yolly opened the door, unsmiling, but at least she was civil. She led him through a dark house. Antonio expected it to be oppressive like Mad Juana's hut, but a sweet scent of *pandan* leaves filled the air, from the sheaf dangling near the front door.

Yolly led him to a bedroom, where a candle flickered in the corner, casting shadows on Mang Nando, who was lying on a frayed woven mat. She stood against a wall, watching Antonio like a cat.

"Antonio," Mang Nando said, his voice barely above a whisper. "Is that you?"

Antonio knelt beside him. "Yes, it's me."

"I've been sick since…since the *langbuan* touched me." Mang Nando was racked by coughing, and for a minute, he couldn't speak. "So," he whispered, "You work for Bubuy now?"

"Not yet," Antonio said. "I would like to though."

"I probably shouldn't do this, for I hate to gossip, but I would recommend against it."

"You work for him," Antonio pointed out.

"No. I work for Mr. Mijares. Bubuy is an unpleasant side effect."

"What do you mean?"

"Power does some strange things to men, is all I will say." Mang Nando shifted slightly on the mat. "You think I don't want to return the tricycle? I tried to, yesterday, and I tried to pay the boundary fee, but he wouldn't let me."

"Why wouldn't he?"

"Why, indeed?"

The old man closed his eyes and appeared to fall asleep, but all of a sudden, his eyes opened and he spoke. "If I let you take the tricycle, and you start working for Mr. Mijares, will you look out for an old co-worker like me?"

Antonio didn't hesitate. "Yes, of course."

"Yolly takes care of me well, doesn't she?" Mang Nando said. "Some said, when her father died, I was doing her and her mother a favor, taking them in, but it's been the other way around. I don't know what I'd do without her. She could drive my tricycle while I'm sick, but Bubuy wouldn't hear of it. He doesn't want girls to take over, I suppose, even though I think Yolly is as smart as they come."

"I already have a job, *Lolo*," Yolly said.

"Ah, yes, she works at the bank," he told Antonio. "Like I

said, she's very smart." To Yolly, he said, "Unlock the chain, *apo*, and let Antonio take the tricycle."

"Are you sure, *Lolo*? After what Bubuy did to you?"

"Yes, I'm sure. We'll leave it up to God. A letter might not hurt, too." He looked at Antonio. "Perhaps you would be so kind as to give Mr. Mijares a letter for me?"

"Do you know how to *stop* this thing?" Yolly asked Antonio as he straddled the motorcycle.

Antonio was tempted to say, *of course*, but instead he bit his tongue. "How?"

She showed him how to squeeze the lever at the handle. "At least you don't have to worry about balancing the motorcycle. Just go slow, and if you forget how to stop, find a vendor stall to crash into."

"That'd be an expensive way to stop," he said.

"Better than hitting people," she said.

He thought he saw a glimmer of a smile, and then it was gone. "Right. Well," he said gruffly, "thanks."

"I would say *you are welcome*, if I mean it, but since I don't, I won't."

"You know," Antonio shouted as the tricycle took off wildly, giving him a slight whiplash, "you'd be attractive if you weren't such a smart mouth!"

33

ANTONIO COULD FEEL everyone's eyes watching him enter the station parking lot on the tricycle. He circled once, twice, three times slowly because he wasn't sure where exactly to park. Finally, he settled for a spot between a pink tricycle and a vendor stall full of fruit.

"Do you mind?" the woman vendor said. "I don't want fumes on my fruit!"

"I won't be long," he said, taking the key out of the ignition. Down the sidewalk, Bubuy stood, smoking a cigarette. Two men stood behind him, ugly like their boss.

Bubuy held his hand out for the key. "Well, look who's driving a tricycle. I don't remember you being on our payroll."

"You told me to fetch it from Mang Nando," Antonio said, "so I did."

"And so I see. Did his granddaughter put up a fight? Or throw that dog at you?"

"Yes to both."

"Did you bring a hack saw to break the chain?"

"No. I tried to ask nicely, but when that didn't work with his granddaughter, the old man called me in and decided to let

148

me take it."

"Just like that?" Bubuy snapped his fingers.

"Well, we talked. But yes, eventually, he let me."

"That doesn't sound like the troublemaker that I know. Ah, but oh well." He gave the tricycle a cursory glance. "It looks like it's in one piece. Fellows, put this tricycle away." Bubuy went back to smoking.

"You said if I brought this back, you'd give me a job," Antonio reminded him.

"Try me next year," Bubuy said. "Maybe then I'd have some turtles available." His men laughed.

"You promised!" Antonio said.

"I'm tired of this conversation," Bubuy walked away. "Fellows, keep him away from me, okay? You know where pests go."

The two men advanced towards Antonio, flexing their biceps. Antonio looked into their ugly faces. Anger flared inside, but he tamped it down. They weren't worth it.

"So Yolly was right," Antonio said, stalking off and shaking his head. "*All that trouble, for nothing.*" He shoved his hands in his pockets, running smack into someone else.

"Sorry," Antonio muttered.

"Where's the fire?" Mr. Mijares said.

Mr. Mijares sat in a large chair, regarding Antonio across a gleaming desk that smelled of furniture polish. Antonio found it hard to believe that someone as delicately lovely as Grace Mijares could descend from such a man. He was large, not fat, but built of solid muscle. He had a broad forehead and a pencil-thin mustache.

Someone knocked on his office door. "Come in," he said. The secretary came in, set down two steaming hot cups of coffee, and left them alone once again.

"Go ahead," Mr. Mijares said, gesturing with a little nod towards the cup nearest Antonio.

Antonio blew at the hot drink first and took a sip. It was well past lunch. The drink felt good on his empty stomach.

"This is a very curious letter," Mr. Mijares said, picking up Mang Nando's letter and letting it fall on the desk. "Don't you think?"

"I wouldn't know," Antonio said, setting the cup down. "I've never read it."

"You could have. It wasn't sealed or anything."

"It's not my business what Nando Nakpil wants to tell you, sir."

Mr. Mijares leaned back. "So. You brought back that tricycle for Bubuy."

"You know about that?"

"I saw you pull in. Did you tell Bubuy about this letter?"

"No."

"Why not?"

Choosing his words with care, Antonio said, "I figured whatever it said about Bubuy wasn't going to be nice."

"It actually doesn't say anything bad about Bubuy."

"Oh."

Antonio watched the electric fan whirr in the corner, wondering what Mr. Mijares' point was, but he didn't press. His cup still had a lot of coffee. No need to hurry their conversation along.

Mr. Mijares leaned back. "You seem like the type of young man who could be relied on to carry out an errand."

"I hope so," Antonio said.

"You want something and you go for it, am I right?"

Antonio nodded. "Yes."

"I knew that before today. You delivered that dress to my wife and she refused it. But you didn't give in."

Of course now it would come back to haunt him. Antonio's spirits sank. "I'm sorry," he said.

"Don't be. It's refreshing, finding someone who would stand up to my wife. And to Bubuy. Thank you for giving me the letter. I will make sure to reinstate Nando. He's a good man."

Antonio hesitated. "Mr. Mijares?"

Mr. Mijares had already pushed out his chair; the conversation was done. "Yes?"

"I was actually hoping to get a driving job with you."

"Very well, talk to Bubuy."

GHOST MOON NIGHT

"I already did, and he said no."

"Why?"

"I honestly don't know."

"He can be a pig sometimes. I really have to watch him. Tetchie!"

"Yes, sir?" the secretary asked from the doorway.

"Get Bubuy, will you?" Mr. Mijares said.

When Bubuy came in, Antonio stood up to leave, but Mr. Mijares motioned for him to keep sitting.

"I'm hiring Antonio," Mr. Mijares said.

Bubuy hedged. "We don't have any available tricycles, Boss."

"There's one almost done with repairs at the shop. Tell Efren to finish it *pronto*, and have it available for Antonio. I want this young man making money for me immediately."

"I'll see what I can do," Bubuy said sullenly.

"If you don't get that ready," Mr. Mijares said, "he can use your tricycle until then."

Outside, away from Mr. Mijares' presence, Bubuy grabbed Antonio's shirtfront. "I don't like being made a fool."

You do that well enough on your own, Antonio thought.

"We'll get you a tricycle," Bubuy said. "But you'll have to work doubly hard as a new recruit. Or find another job."

Antonio nodded. "I'll work hard."

"Efren!" Bubuy shouted into a shed. "I need that tricycle!"

A man wheeled out a tricycle with a white sidecar. It was plain, but it was Antonio's to use. When he'd saved up a little bit of money, he would add decorations. He'd seen a few around that he liked: a small statue of the infant Jesus, a rosary. Maybe he could even have pretty pictures painted on. He kick-started it and it roared to life. Driving it in a couple of circles, he sped on out of the tiny circular station and down to Yolly's house.

If Yolly was surprised to see him, she didn't show it. She simply led him back to the bedroom where Antonio gave the old man the hundred-peso bill.

"What's this?" Mang Nando asked.

"It's from Mr. Mijares. He says to come back to work soon."

"Praise be to God," Mang Nando said. "Thank you. You must have represented me well. What did Bubuy say?"

"Nothing," Antonio said. "I didn't show him the letter."

151

Mang Nando smiled. "Thank you."

At the door, as Antonio was leaving, Yolly called out, "*Hoy!* Hey!

Antonio turned. She was leaning against the frame. "Thank you," she said. And before he could reply, she disappeared inside.

34

THE NEXT MORNING dawned stormy, the perfect weather for sleeping in, but a smiling Antonio bounded down the stairs, two steps at a time. Papa eyed him curiously over breakfast. "What's got you in such a good mood?" he asked.

"I got a job driving a tricycle for Mr. Mijares," Antonio announced.

Mama raised her cup of coffee. "Congratulations."

Antonio braced himself for his father's reaction.

"A plum job for a high school graduate," Papa said.

Antonio left the breakfast table before his father could ruin his good mood, then he checked in with Lolo Sonny. To his relief, his grandfather was in better spirits. Trining had been taking him to Aling Dona's to listen to the jukebox and that seemed to help.

"Things are looking up, Lolo," Antonio said, sitting beside the old man for a minute. "Soon, I'll get you a record player, and you can play *kundiman* music over and over."

At the street corner, Antonio hailed a tricycle. By the time he reached the station, the rain poured in thick sheets. Bubuy's henchmen took their time getting out Antonio's tricycle, making Antonio stand in the rain. But he didn't really mind. When he got the tricycle, he took a deep breath, kick-started it, then drove it to the queue of tricycles waiting for passengers. Hopefully looking as if he'd done it a million times.

Mang Nando came over. "Well, that's a mighty fine tricycle, Antonio," he said.

"Thank you."

He handed Antonio what looked like a folded up plastic sheet. "I have a spare poncho. Would you like to use it?"

Antonio gratefully took it.

"I heard that a bus is supposed to roll in," Mang Nando said. "Here it is now, in fact." A small bus of about ten rows of benches with the sign "Manila to Tuguegarao" pulled in, belching two puffs of black smoke.

"You want to watch how it's done?" Mang Nando said. "Follow me."

Mang Nando and several of the other drivers pounded on the side of the bus as it pulled in and parked. The conductor got out, traded a couple of jokes with some of the men, and undid ropes holding the luggage to a roof rack.

As passengers came around to claim their bag, tricycle drivers helped unload it, pointing at their tricycle. Mang Nando carried two suitcases as though he were a young man, and followed an old lady. Antonio was next in line. As a man came round the corner of the bus, Antonio's smile died on his face.

It was Mang Fermin's cousin.

"Well, what are you waiting for?" Isidro Abad said to Antonio. "I haven't all day."

"Where to, Mang Isidro?" Antonio asked.

The man stared. "How do you know my name?"

"I saw you at Mang Fermin's wake."

"Ah, yes, that cheapskate affair."

Antonio tightened his grip on the tricycle handlebars. Mama said Tito Oscar paid for all the food at the wake and the coffin. He decided to keep the conversation to a minimum so he'd not be tempted to slug Mang Isidro. "Where to?" he repeated.

"Fermin's orchard."

The rain turned into a drizzle as Antonio drove the tricycle down to Mang Fermin's orchard. Since the funeral, a gate had been built at the entrance, a padlock keeping it shut. Mang

GHOST MOON NIGHT

Fermin's cousin took out a key and opened it. "I'm meeting a buyer today," the cousin said. "Wait for me."

The man disappeared into the dark orchard. At his approach, bats scattered, but he just kept going.

Antonio waited.

Another tricycle pulled up and two men got out. They were dressed nicely, in light-colored chinos and ties, like they had come from the city. "Is Isidro Abad here?" one asked Antonio.

Antonio nodded. "He went into the orchard."

Antonio watched as the pair walked into the orchard, scattering the bats. Unlike Mang Fermin's cousin, the two put their arms out to ward them off, retreated, then ran back into the orchard, their arms covering their heads. Then men didn't make arrangements for their tricycle driver to wait. Within minutes, he took off.

An hour passed. The sun now seared Antonio overhead. He stripped off the poncho and moved to the shade. Finally, the two men emerged. One said, angrily, "What a bully! We're already doing him a favor, and he ups the price!"

The other commiserated. "I almost wanted to call the entire thing off."

"Too bad we can't. We'll lose our deposit."

Reaching the tricycle, the pair got in. "Back to the bus station."

"What about Mang Isidro?" Antonio said.

"What about him?" one of the men said. "Let him walk." They laughed.

Antonio glanced at the orchard. "Sorry, he hired me. I have to wait for him."

One man cursed. Antonio studied him more closely. He wore a pair of dark sunglasses with his chinos. His fingers were immaculately manicured.

The other man wasn't as well-groomed. He sported a shaggy black beard and no manicure. Sweat stains marked his shirt's armpit area and a middle button had come undone. His jeans were frayed at the hem.

"Why are you buying this property?" Antonio asked.

"We're buying it for our boss," Manicured Guy said.

"For what?"

"You ask a lot of questions," Black Beard said.

155

"Just curious," Antonio said.

"We own a lumber company."

"Oh."

"You sound disappointed," Manicured Guy said.

"I thought maybe you were putting up a hotel." *Or something fun,* he amended in his head.

"Did you hear him?" Manicured Guy ribbed Black Beard. "There's an idea."

"Are you kidding? No one will put up a hotel in your village, not with your curse."

Antonio shrugged and shielded his eyes from the noonday sun. All those trees, cut down. He imagined the sun coming through and kissing the earth. Little shoots of trees coming up, able to survive for the first time.

"What will you do with all the bats?" Antonio wondered aloud.

"Hope they fly away," Black Beard said. "And if they don't, we'll smoke them out until they do."

Mang Fermin's cousin joined them then. He had a stack of books and a suitcase. Thick dust had been lifted off where he had touched the items. He struggled carrying them all to the tricycle, but neither man offered to help, even when one of the books tumbled to the ground and opened to a page covered with handwriting. It looked like a journal of some kind dated with the year 1900. He dumped the other things into the sidecar, at the feet of the property's buyers, and picked up the journal.

"Do you mind?" Mang Fermin's cousin looked pointedly at Black Beard. "I have to be in the sidecar with all of this."

The Manicured Guy shoved out Black Beard. "He'll ride behind the driver."

By the time Antonio took them to the station, the Manicured Guy's hair looked like a stiff broom. The pair left first, then Mang Fermin's cousin collected all his belongings and began to leave.

"Excuse me," Antonio said. "You need to pay."

"Charge the other men," Mang Isidro said. "They have plenty of money."

"But they're gone."

"It's your problem, not mine." The man turned towards the bus.

Antonio took three strides and got in the man's face. "You kept me waiting for hours. You need to pay."

"I have a bus to catch. Let me pass."

"When you pay."

Mang Isidro set down the books and suitcase, then shoved a couple of bills at Antonio. "Fine. Here!"

"Thank you," Antonio said, counting out the fare. "Let me get you some change."

"Listen, just keep it!" Mang Isidro marched on with the suitcase and books in hand. He disappeared into the bus, which let out two loud honks on the horn. Antonio noticed he'd left the journal on the ground. He held it up and tried to catch the man's attention. Mang Isidro opened his window and leaned out, snatching the little notebook from Antonio's hands.

Antonio turned to his tricycle and found his path blocked by Bubuy and his men.

"What was that all about?" Bubuy asked, his eyes following the bus as it left the station.

"He left a journal," Antonio said.

"I saw you collar that man and demand that he pay you. It's not something all drivers are willing to do."

"I wouldn't have demanded payment had his ride not taken my whole morning," Antonio said.

"I like it," Bubuy said, surprising Antonio. Then he walked off, followed by his henchmen.

Mang Nando went up to Antonio. "What did Bubuy tell you?"

"He said he liked how I negotiated payment from one of my passengers."

Following Bubuy with his gaze, Mang Nando said, "Did he, now? You should be flattered. It's not every day that Bubuy gives a compliment."

"I suppose." Antonio noticed that Mang Nando's eyes were troubled. "Something wrong?"

"Oh, nothing." Mang Nando smiled. "Just getting fanciful in my old age. I think Bubuy's plotting something."

Antonio looked past Mang Nando at the old man's tricycle. It was empty. Just like he felt right at that moment.

35

B Y THE TIME Antonio came home, Aling Mila's *sari-sari* store was closed and the roads empty. It was almost eleven o'clock and he'd come home on foot, tired to the bone. Mr. Mijares had a rule where a new driver had to leave the tricycle at the station while he was under "probation."

His back ached, his hands felt like they were still gripping and shaking over the motorcycle handle bars, and he smelled like a wet dog from all that rainy-sunny-rainy-sunny weather. He tried to get a ride home from another driver, but none of them were going his way. Mang Nando had already left or he'd have asked him.

But his pockets bulged with some bills and loose change. A good start towards Lolo's record player.

Light drew him to his house like the moths dancing around its feeble porch light.

Something moved by the doorway. Antonio's eyes narrowed.

"Well, if it isn't Mr. Moneybags!" Jose greeted him, stepping out into the light.

"And if isn't *Arinola* Man," Antonio said, referring to Jose's job as a urinal cleaner.

"I've been promoted to trash cans, I'll have you know," Jose crowed.

"Congratulations."

"Your mother says you've joined the ranks of tricycle drivers."

Antonio sat on a bench, not even expending the energy of swatting mosquitoes away. "Yes. And my body can feel it, too."

"You're getting old, my friend."

"And wiser, I hope."

"Sorry to break the news, but you're just getting older."

"And you?" Antonio smiled. "Are you enjoying your last little window of freedom before you get buried in homework?"

"I'm trying," he said, sighing. "But my boss keeps calling me in. Speaking of work, are you too busy for an odd job at the hospital?"

"Doing what? Open heart surgery?"

"Even better. Cleaning out the holding room."

"Holding room...?"

"The room that holds the dead for burial."

Antonio thought about the butcher's job opening. He really didn't want to do *this* job.

Jose lowered his voice. "Some of them died, you know, at the hands of the *langbuan*. So if they were evil in their past life, they're most likely just *langbuan* at rest."

"What do you take me for?" Antonio said. "*Tangangot?*" A gullible fool?

"So, what do you say?" Jose said. "We can take breaks together. I leave for Manila in a week, you know."

"And I can't wait to throw a party *after* you leave."

"Liar." Jose punched him on the arm. "So?"

"When is the job?"

"Sometime before dawn. Just once. Somebody else usually cleans it."

"Sorry, I can't. I'm too tired."

"It will pay thirty pesos."

Thirty pesos. The number resounded in Antonio's head. It was just a little drop in the bucket of what he needed, but he'd be closer to his goal. But working at the morgue! Already, Antonio's imagination ran wild. What more when he's tired?

Thirty pesos.

He glanced at Lolo Sonny's darkened window. Most likely he was asleep already. More pesos meant Lolo Sonny could enjoy his music sooner.

"Let me at least eat," Antonio said. "I'm starving."

Papa and Mama were still up. In the lantern light, Mama was hard at work on her sewing machine while Papa read the newspaper. Papa looked up, then hid behind the main section of *Manila Bulletin* with a harumph.

"How did your day go?" Mama asked.

"Great," Antonio said. "I think I'm getting the hang of driving a tricycle."

"Did you have a lot of passengers?"

"Enough to keep me busy."

"Any interesting passengers?" she asked.

"One of them was Mang Fermin's cousin."

Papa lowered the paper. "Isidro Abad?"

Antonio nodded.

"What did he want?" Papa asked.

Antonio's stomach grumbled. "Can I have something to eat first?"

"*What* did he want?"

Antonio gritted his teeth. "He sold Mang Fermin's property to two men who work for a lumber company."

"He told me he wouldn't do anything without consulting me or Oscar," Papa grumbled.

"Why would he consult with you?" Antonio asked.

Papa flicked the newspaper shut, his eyes flashing with anger. "We've only been Fermin's friends since childhood!"

"Jose's been my best friend for a long time but I don't see his family asking me what to do with his coconut basketball hoop when he leaves."

"You don't know anything about our friendship," Papa said.

"You're right," Antonio said. "I don't."

"Then maybe you shouldn't make any judgments based on

160

things you don't know about."

Antonio stalked out and seethed as he rooted in the kitchen for something to eat. Banging pots and pans. *And who was the high school graduate? Not Papa.*

There was some stale rice and the dregs of *kare-kare* oxtail soup in an earthen pot. He grabbed a spoon, added rice to the pot and started eating.

Mama joined him. "Be patient with your father. He's been under a lot of stress lately."

"Yes, he's under a lot of strain planting rice."

"His best friend has just been *murdered.*"

Antonio paused as he chewed. "Sorry." He sighed. "You're right. But I don't see why Papa can't be nice to me."

"Let Papa worry about himself. You can only control your reaction."

Antonio threw the spoon into the pot, wheeled around and stalked out of the kitchen. Mama said, "Where are you going? Antonio, talk to me."

"I'm working at the hospital tonight."

Papa entered the kitchen. "What about farming in the morning?"

"What about it?" Antonio shot back. "I'll be there."

"Antonio, don't you talk to me like that."

"Good night, Papa," Antonio said, joining Jose without looking back. "Come on."

"What was that all about?" Jose asked.

Antonio refused to talk until he was sure he was out of his father's earshot. He walked silently for a few minutes, then crouched on the ground. Crossing his arms over his head, he groaned.

"This looks serious," Jose said.

"Just let me...just wait...alright?"

"No problem," Jose said. "As long as your tantrum only lasts a minute, we have time for this."

Antonio unburied his face. "Who says I'm throwing a tantrum?"

"Not me."

Shaking his head, Antonio let out a little laugh. "You're crazy."

"So, what's the problem?" Jose asked.

"You heard my father. He's the problem."

"Maybe we should trade fathers for a day and you won't think your lot's too bad."

"Maybe. On second thought, never mind." Antonio picked up a pebble and threw it across the road. "You're right. And it's not just him. It's me, too. Just kind of fed up, you know?"

"So are you going to talk about it?"

"What, and be late for my hospital job?" Antonio stood up and shoved Jose at the shoulder. "Let's go."

36

ANTONIO HUNG BACK while Jose fiddled with side door to the hospital. The building had two stories above ground. Light shone through some windows. Many were dark. The holding room was in the basement.

Six feet under. How appropriate.

"Your mother looked pretty worried when you left," Jose said.

"I don't want to talk about it," Antonio said.

"Alright. It's just, you know, if something were to happen to you tonight, and that's the last exchange you had with her..."

"What could happen to me tonight?"

"You're right. Holding rooms are usually...lifeless. Boring."

"Hush, will you, and let me get to cleaning it," Antonio said.

"I'm trying."

After a minute, Jose said, "Did I tell you I'm going to be billeted across the street from Grace? I told you, you should go to college. Think of what you'll be missing."

"Well, too late now."

"Next year, promise me you'll look into it."

"We'll see."

The lock clicked and the door opened, releasing a fusty smell of rubbing alcohol, disinfectant, and soiled linen. Jose led Antonio down an empty hall and a flight of stairs. Antonio noticed gouges on the wall.

"What are these marks?" he asked.

"Oh that?" Jose shrugged. "They say Japanese made them with bayonets during World War II. They used the hospital as a sick bay. Come to think of it, they could also be fingernail marks left by *langbuan*."

Antonio pried his glance from the wall and forced himself to keep walking. "Very funny."

"It's a pretty straightforward job," Jose said, pulling on light chains, until the basement hallway lit up. "My boss said to clean the surfaces that don't have anything on them, sweep the floor and wash out the sinks."

"I don't do anything with the bodies, correct?"

"Not unless they rise up and put you in a choke hold." Jose chuckled.

He showed Antonio where a bucket and soap were and led him to a set of double-doors. "Here you are," Jose said. "Lights go off in an hour. When you're done, come up and find me."

"Aren't you coming in with me?" Antonio asked.

Jose was already backing away. "What, and ruin all your fun?" And then he was gone.

Antonio turned the knob and opened the door, the stench of death hit him.

Where was the chain pull?

He let his eyes get used to the darkness, but couldn't make out any shapes near the door. Splaying his fingers against the inside of the door, he kept moving his hand until it reached the wall.

Something soft touched the back of his hand. He withdrew his hand so fast, he nearly hit the other door with his elbow.

"Is someone here?" he said, his voice hoarse to his ears.

He heard the sound of someone giggling. His stomach flipped.

This isn't worth thirty pesos, he told himself. And then: *just turn on the light! But what if someone or something is here with you? Then you can at least know who or what your companion is.*

With the help of a sliver of light from the hallway, Antonio

164

could make out the shape of tables and cabinets on the wall.

Let's try this again.

Sweat trickled from his neck to the back of his shirt. He moved his hand haltingly across the door until it reached the wall. Feeling for a chain pull. His fingers connected with something long and he yanked at it.

Light. Glorious light.

And the soft thing by his hand? A pair of rubber gloves hanging on the wall.

He smiled. Until he heard the dripping behind him.

Drip. Drip. Like the pig at the market, blood dripping into the bucket. The image came unbidden to his mind.

Slowly, he turned his head.

The faucet was dripping, leaving a discolored trail on the sink tub in its wake. Two empty cots stood in the corner. Nothing was out, except for some buckets.

Grabbing his soapy bucket, Antonio went to work. First, he cleaned the sinks, two of them spattered with flecks of what looked like blood. As he scrubbed with a wet rag, the sink turned bright red.

Antonio blinked. The sink reverted to a white, worn-out tub.

He needed sleep badly. His imagination was running wild.

Rinsing the rag and wringing it out, he next worked on the counters, the gurneys. The smell in the room gave him a headache. Maybe he could at least open a window. He walked over to a window and opened the latch. It was the kind which slid up. He tried to raise it, but it wouldn't move. Glancing over his shoulder, he thought, *At least the door is open.*

Well, it *had* been open. Now it was closed. He hoped from the breeze.

Better finish this cleaning job and get out of here.

Lastly, he took up the broom and started sweeping. He started in one corner and moved in front of a cabinet. At his feet, a pile of dirt had accumulated. He knelt to sweep it into the dust pan and a drawer above him began to open.

Slowly.

Antonio swallowed and tried to not panic. *It's probably empty. I'll just shut it.*

He lifted his arm but it wasn't long enough to reach it.

Holding the dust pan in his right hand, he started to stand up. He saw a balding head, shrunken skin. The corpse's eyes were open, staring at something in the distance. The man's mouth was frozen in an expression of terror.

Antonio jumped back and hit the counter, spilling a trail of dust in his wake. His heart felt like it was going to burst right out of his chest. Walking back to the drawer, he pushed it until it clicked firmly shut.

There.

Another drawer, this time to his left, started to slide open. This corpse had masses of hair. He lost more dust this time, as the pan clattered to the floor from his clammy grip.

With trembling hands, Antonio swept up the dust on the floor. Threw it in the trash can. Grabbing the soap bucket, he moved to the door and pulled on the knob. It was locked.

He pushed and pulled on the knob. It wouldn't budge.

Then he heard it again. The sound of giggling. A shiver ran up his neck. His clammy hands slipped on the knob.

The knob came off.

Antonio stared at it, then at the opening where the knob had been. He slipped his fingers through the hole and jiggled the door. Shook it hard.

Still, it wouldn't open.

"Pull on it." The voice was that of a young girl's and it came from over his left shoulder.

Antonio rattled the door again.

"I told you to pull."

He turned his head. A girl in pigtails and a school uniform stood in the corner. She giggled. When she did so, the points of her teeth showed. Like fangs.

Antonio screamed and yanked at the door. When it opened, he threw himself out into the hallway, ending up in a kneeling position. The knob was no longer in his hand. It sat in the hole which, earlier, didn't have a knob.

Now it did. *Another product of his overactive imagination.*

He took in a deep breath. Another. And then he heard footsteps coming down the hallway. They got louder and louder. Closer and closer. Antonio leapt to his feet, ready to run the other way.

But it was only Jose. "What are you doing?" he asked

Antonio, who ran past him and up the stairs.

Jose caught up with him down the hall. "What happened?"

"Has anyone ever seen ghosts in the holding room?" Antonio said.

Jose nodded. "Some people have said a little girl appeared to them. She may have been a victim of the Japanese. She likes to play tricks on people."

"You could have warned me before I got stuck in that awful room. Have you ever seen her?"

"No, but I'd like to." Jose grinned. "Everyone who's seen her says she's harmless."

Antonio shook his head.

"Come on, you survived. And you've seen worse, right? Like the *langbuan*?" Jose nudged Antonio. "You're tough. You want to do this again if my boss needs you?"

"So," Jose said, "would you be willing to do this again if my boss needs you?"

"I don't know. If I haven't found another job yet, maybe."

"I hope you come back," a little girl's voice said.

Antonio looked over his shoulder but saw only an empty hall.

"GOOD MORNING!" JOSE greeted Antonio as he emerged from his house a few days later.

Antonio grunted. It was too early to be cheery.

"I waited for you at my house," Jose said. "I thought you'd left for the parade already."

Antonio blinked. "Today is the *kuding fiesta*, isn't it?"

"How could you forget?" Jose asked.

"I'm working today. It doesn't really matter."

"But we've always watched the parade together! And I leave tomorrow. Can't you skip work?"

Antonio started walking to town. "Not today. I'll see you at the church maybe, between passengers."

"Haven't you heard?" Jose caught up with him. "Tandang Lino moved the parade to the town plaza. He doesn't want the priest to profit from the procession."

"Profit?"

"You know, have the table at the church entrance for his altar fund. Mrs. Silva is very distraught over not being able to get donations for the altar fund."

"Father Sebastian doesn't seem too concerned about that."

"Not if you ask Mrs. Silva. She tells everyone that Father Sebastian is considering a move to another parish. At least the *barrio fiesta* tonight hasn't been scrapped. Hooray for the kissing booth!"

For once, Jose was right. Except for a few people who wanted to shop, go to church or run some other errand, everyone went to the *kuding* parade. Antonio dozed on and off while he sat at his tricycle watching the trickle of passengers flag down the next in queue.

Bubuy and his men, whom he aptly nicknamed Asim (Sourpuss) and Ngungot (Grump), came out of the office building and walked straight towards Antonio. They looked like they wanted to rough someone up.

What did they want now?

Antonio forced himself to remain sitting on his tricycle even though he had an aversion to apes.

"Pulido," Bubuy said.

Antonio nodded.

"A little bird told me that a novice tricycle driver set a record in yesterday's haul. Isn't that right, Asim?"

"Yes, bossing!"

Bubuy's eyes zeroed in on Antonio. "And that would be you."

"And if it is?" This was news to Antonio.

"It means that I need for you to slow down, take things easy."

"That's stupid," he blurted out.

Bubuy cocked his head and cleaned out his ear with his little finger. "Excuse me?"

"I mean, why would you want me to slow down? If I earn more, it means more money for Mr. Mijares."

"Well, yes," Bubuy said. "But it makes *me* look bad. Did you ever think of that?"

He already looked bad, as far as Antonio could tell, but he didn't say so out loud.

"I'm supposed to be the smart one," Bubuy continued. "At

this rate, you're showing me up. Making me dispensable. Mr. Mijares will think he won't need someone to train the trainees."

"That's your problem, not mine."

Bubuy moved to grab Antonio's shirtfront. But this time, Antonio was ready. He grabbed Bubuy's fist and twisted it behind his back.

Asim and Ngungot rushed forward. Antonio shoved Bubuy to the ground.

Bubuy scrambled to his feet. "Why, you louse…"

"Speak for yourself."

"And I was just about to make you an offer."

"Anything you have to offer probably won't interest me."

"Oh?" Bubuy smiled. "How about a record player?"

"What?" Antonio stared.

"I was talking to Timo Sandoval yesterday. He showed me this beautiful record player and said you'd set your heart on it. He cut me a great deal. So I bought it."

Antonio felt like his breath had been knocked out of him. "That rat!"

"Come now, relax," Bubuy said. "Getting all heated up for a box with wires and knobs." Bubuy studied his finger nails. "Would you like to have it? Because I have a trade."

Antonio's eyes narrowed. "What exactly is this trade?"

"Remember how I told you that I knew your father from the gambling tables?"

"Yes."

"Two years ago, he owed me money and gave me a sword instead. He said it belonged to his father. Sonny Pulido, decorated hero from the Spanish-American War. The old man had gone senile, and no longer needed it."

Antonio remembered that sword. As a boy, he used to ask Lolo Sonny if he could play with it. Papa always told him the sword was valuable and not a toy. Come to think of it, Antonio hadn't seen it in the last two years. Papa said he'd kept it in the *baul* with other family treasures.

"So I looked into getting the sword checked out," Bubuy said. "I wanted to make sure your father was telling the truth about its value. Imagine my surprise, when I found out it isn't as he claims."

Antonio's grip tightened on the chair arm rest. "What do

you mean?"

"Fourteen years ago, in 1942, your grandfather testified in a secret tribunal. Because of what he said, a man got executed by the Japanese. He had three daughters. Without a man in their home to protect them, they disappeared, too."

"Are you saying Lolo Sonny was a Japanese informant? That's impossible! He would never..."

"Wouldn't he? Your grandmother was still alive then. The Japanese took her because they knew he had information they needed. They would exchange his wife, in one piece, for the information, or they'd chop her up slowly in front of him, and not kill her, but then kill him – if he didn't."

"That never happened!" Antonio staggered to his feet. "You're lying! I won't have you smearing my honorable Lolo Sonny!"

"Oh, really? You know the Javier family?"

Antonio recognized the name. Once, at dinner, Papa told him about how the man's brother and daughters just disappeared during the war. Lolo suddenly got up from the table and walked out. No one knew why.

Could it possibly be that Lolo Sonny...?

Antonio felt sick. He glanced at Bubuy's smug, knowing expression.

"I won't smear him," Bubuy promised. "If you work for me."

"You mean drive tricycle?"

"And a little more. You collect the default boundary for twelve weeks."

"I'd just as soon get another radio," Antonio said.

"Fine. Why don't you?" Bubuy pushed his chair away from the desk. "It's much easier to replace a broken radio than, say...a broken reputation."

Slack-jawed, Antonio stared at him.

Bubuy's eyes turned to flint. "You seem like a smart person. But I'll be clear so there's no misunderstanding. Work for me and your grandfather will get a record player *and* keep his war record spotless. If you don't, everyone will know all about his collaboration with the Japs. If he's lucky, he'll only be shunned."

"That's blackmail!"

"Yes, isn't it?" Bubuy took a cigarette out of his pack and

tapped it impatiently on the desk. "So? Will you do it?"

Antonio thought of his grandfather's war medals on their *salas* wall. Lolo Sonny would never know what people said about him. He hardly cared or knew what was going on nowadays. But every generation from here on would. If his grandfather were sent to trial…the thought was hard to bear.

"Yes," he heard himself say, as though the voice came from a stranger. "I'll do it."

"Great," Bubuy said, grinning like a shark. "Great! Well. It's slow here. To celebrate our deal, why don't you take a few hours off and go to the parade? We'll go over the details later."

Antonio stood behind a crowd about ten-deep to watch the *kuding* parade. But his mind was a million miles away, thinking of what he had agreed to do. And then the present called him back when he saw the water buffalo pulling a cartload of war heroes, including his Lolo Sonny. Lolo Sonny beamed as he sat there with his friends, about a half-dozen of them in their smart-looking uniforms from the Spanish War.

When people began to whisper, Antonio craned his neck to see what was going on. The whisper turned into a loud rumble as Father Sebastian arrived in his rusty old car. He parked at the curb and got out, waving at the crowd. No one but Antonio and Mrs. Silva waved back. Mrs. Silva shouted into the crowd, "Don't forget to donate to the altar fund!"

The village elder, Tandang Lino, sat on a chair surrounded by other old people. His glance flickered towards the priest, and then he turned his attention back to the parade.

A water buffalo, scrubbed clean for the occasion and decorated with flowers, lumbered forward with a cart. In that cart, Grace Mijares held on to a rail, a little crown on her head glinting in the sun, her white dress glowing like a magnolia. Timo, standing behind Grace, looked like a water buffalo in a stiff shirt.

Grace smiled and waved, throwing flowers to the crowd. Antonio caught a magnolia-blossom and cradled it, soft and velvet smooth, in his palm.

"Thank you, Grace!" Antonio shouted. Grace waved and smiled. Timo scowled.

Tito Oscar and his family drove past in his car, followed by the constable and the doctor. Four pretty girls, wearing sashes that represented the planting seasons, waved at the crowd. After the girls, a float arrived carrying someone dressed as a giant kuding, with a fabric body and feathers. He strutted around, cocking his head, circling back to a giant nest.

The crowd began to jostle each other, raising their arms up high and crying, "Here! Me!"

The kuding grabbed something from the nest, threw back his arm and launched the object. A boy raised his hand and the egg hit him squarely on the palm, egg trickling down his arm down to his armpit. The crowd laughed.

"Me! Me!" Many raised their hands. The *kuding* lobbed eggs left and right.

Now the kuding threw back his arm and launched another egg into the crowd. Everyone gasped as the egg hit the parish priest squarely on the face. Father Sebastian wiped the mess off with a hand and opened one eye.

Everyone looked at the bird, then the priest and back.

Father Sebastian laughed and the tension in the crowd went away. Seconds later, the fire brigade tiptoed behind the priest, dumping water over his head. Someone else joined in, and soon, a water fight raged.

Amidst the festivities, Antonio noticed that a dripping wet Father Sebastian quietly approached Tandang Lino. The priest tried to shake his hand but the elder refused.

"I would hope we can put our disagreements behind us." Father Sebastian smiled. "I apologize if I started off on the wrong foot. I can…"

"Father Sebastian!" Tandang Lino barked. All heads swiveled their direction, listening. "I wish it were that simple. You tell me you're sorry. Village life goes on as before." He paused. "Farmers have come to me with a disturbing report. Their seedlings are not growing as before."

This was the first Antonio had heard of this. He searched for Papa in the crowd and when their eyes met, Antonio went to stand beside him. "I haven't noticed any problems in this year's harvest, have you?" he asked Papa.

Papa averted his eyes. "I think they are smaller."

"No, they're not."

Papa said, "If Tandang Lino says they're smaller, they must be. Other farmers might be having problems. Anyway, keep your doubts to yourself. I can already see the cogs turning in your brain."

Suddenly, Antonio saw the years stretched out ahead of the village, worshipping the *kuding*.

At Tandang Lino's death, someone else would lead the village up the mountain for the annual procession. Crops would grow or fail, and the sacred *kuding* will always take credit or blame. Nothing would change. Everything would be as it always had been. Unless someone were to step in and make the change. Father Sebastian was trying, not successfully.

Who would make that change among the villagers? Probably no one in Antonio's lifetime.

38

THAT EVENING, ANTONIO waited for Jose at the entrance to the *kuding fiesta*. His back ached from driving tricycle all afternoon, but it had settled into a dull pain. After his shift, he came home wanting to quit his job. However, when he saw Lolo Sonny, confused and feeble, he pushed those thoughts aside. Dinner was a disagreeable affair, with Papa glaring and Mama looking like she wanted to cry. Most likely about gambling debts. Antonio left the table as soon as he finished his pork steak.

The *fiesta* was a welcome diversion. A breeze from the sea cooled the air. The grounds had enough torch lights for ambience but not too much as to detract from the breathtaking night sky.

"You look like you're ready to have fun," Jose said.

"You better believe it," Antonio agreed.

They passed a little lean-to, where Aling Cora was telling fortunes.

"Let's get our fortune told," Jose suggested.

"Why waste money on a quack?" Antonio said.

"Aling Cora knows what she's talking about. She once told

my mother that I would be tall. And look at me now."

Antonio rolled his eyes. "Knowing your father, that's hard to predict."

"I'll pay, so now you have to do it."

"Fine."

But the lines were long, so they wandered off to other games first. They stopped at the *hampas palayok*, a game where one hits a suspended clay pot filled with candy. The younger children took their turns first. When only a little chunk came off, Mrs. Sandoval from the village store allowed the teenagers to have a try at it.

Mrs. Sandoval's son Timo took the first turn. His mother tied a handkerchief around his eyes and turned him around a few times. Timo hefted the bamboo pole, pulled back his arms and hit the pot squarely, breaking the pot and scattering the candy all over for the children to gather. Timo smiled and turned, looking smug with one eye uncovered.

"Don't worry," Mrs. Sandoval said. "I have another *palayok*."

Jose helped blindfold Antonio. "Now the key is to hit the pot, not Timo. Wait. Actually, it's the other way around."

"What was that, young man?" Mrs. Sandoval asked.

"Oh, I was just coaching Antonio on the finer points of this sport. How he should try to be like your son. Very athletic."

Mrs. Sandoval smiled.

Jose turned a blindfolded Antonio once, twice, thrice, then he let him go. Antonio pulled back the bamboo pole and swung as hard as he could. He hit the ground, rattling his arms and making his ears ring.

"Come on, even a one year old could do better than you!" Timo said.

"Antonio gets two more turns," Mrs. Sandoval said.

"I only took one," Timo whined.

His mother replied, "Yes, but he's not as gifted as you."

Antonio tried again, and missed. Timo laughed. Jose turned Antonio just a half circle, then had him face the same way as before.

"Do you think he'll hit it this time, Timo?" Jose asked.

"I don't think so," Timo said.

"Go for it," Jose said in Antonio's ear.

Antonio took a step forward, then three steps to the right.

About where he heard Timo's voice last. He raised the bamboo and hit his target. *Thwack!*

"*Aray!*" Timo said.

Antonio took off his blindfold, threw it at an advancing Timo who was rubbing his head, and ran off to the other side of the *fiesta*. By the time Jose and he blended in the crowd, his side hurt from laughing.

"You should have seen his face, when you hit him," Jose said, howling.

"I shouldn't have done that," Antonio said. "On second thought, it felt really good." He grinned.

Next, the two friends lined up to do the grease pole contest. The object of the game was to be the first to ring a bell at the top of an oil-greased pole. Whoever won would get ten pesos.

"You have to do it," Jose said.

Antonio nodded. "For ten pesos, I will."

Timo stood at a pole, flexing his muscles and scowling at Antonio. "You owe me."

Antonio smiled, then turned to Jose. "He keeps reappearing, like a bad dream."

"I can't see how he'll win," Jose said. "He's too fat."

"What did you say?" Timo sauntered over.

Jose said, "I worry that the pole won't hold up your weight."

"Are you saying I'm fat?"

"Yes."

The operator got in between them before Timo could swing a fist. "Settle this on the race, children. Alright, get ready and stand by a pole."

Antonio stood at a pole and looked up.

"On your mark, get set..."

Timo already started, the cheat!

"...go!"

ANTONIO HAD TO start three times. Each try, he slid down to the bottom like a heavy piece of lead.

"Someone forgot to tell me this is kind of impossible," Jose said, grunting. "And here I am, in good shape!"

Antonio heard his friend try again, and slide back down. Meanwhile, he hadn't gotten up too far, but at least his grip was holding. On the next pole over, Timo grunted like a pig. At the thought, Antonio shook with laughter.

"Come on," Jose told him. "You need to take this seriously!"

Antonio looked down and Jose was grinning. Somehow, Antonio found a toe hold on one of the bamboo rings. With that, he eased himself up a foot, and another, until he was just another arm-length to the bell.

Every muscle in his body ached, especially in his legs. He didn't think he could keep going. He used his nails to grip the pole.

To his right, Timo was just a foot away from being ahead of Antonio. Antonio couldn't let him win, especially with his next words: "You think you can beat me? Then you're crazy like your *lolo*."

GHOST MOON NIGHT

Antonio clenched his jaw. With one aggressive lunge, he reached up until his fingertips touched the bell. Then he slapped it as hard as he could, sliding down the pole and digging his feet in to slow his descent. At the bottom, his hands and feet burned, but the ten peso bill and Timo's defeat made it all worth it.

Yolly Nakpil walked past, by herself. It seemed like she was smiling, he wasn't sure.

"Go say hi to her," Jose said.

"Quit being such a pest. I'm going to say hi to Father Sebastian instead." Antonio began walking and realized Jose wasn't beside him. "Are you coming?"

"I will in a minute." Jose veered the other direction. "I need to talk to someone."

Father Sebastian and Mrs. Silva sat at a table loaded with *bibingka* cakes covered with a brown sugar topping, *puto* muffins, and red *kuchinta* sticky rice cakes. "How's the altar fund coming along?" Antonio asked.

"Great," Mrs. Silva said. "Would you like to buy something?"

Antonio smiled sheepishly. "I'm sorry. I'm saving up for something important."

"What could possibly be more important than a new altar for Father?" Mrs. Silva said.

"A record player for my *lolo*."

"You don't understand, Mrs. Silva," Father Sebastian said. "If you had a jukebox, perhaps you will entice this young man."

"Even my jukebox habit has to wait now," Antonio said, sighing.

Antonio wished them good luck and wandered the *fiesta* grounds. Two groups were playing tug-of-war. In another area, two men tried to outbalance each other on the bench dance, *sayaw sa banko.*

Where was Jose?

Idly, Antonio picked up a fruit from a stall.

"Are you going to buy that or not?" An old woman vendor asked him. She was his mother's favorite *suki* vendor at the wet market.

"No."

"Unless you're buying it, hands off! How am I supposed to sell it to someone when it's so *lamog*...bruised."

"Alright, alright." Antonio backed off and walked the

179

opposite direction. The direction of the dance and music. He loved music, but not so much dancing. He set off to find a place where he could listen to the music. *Where was Jose?*

"Antonio Pulido?"

He felt a tap on his shoulder and turned to see Constable Martillo, with a somber expression on his face. Instinctively, Antonio looked back at the fruit vendor. If she wanted him to leave, he could have just asked!

"Will you come this way, please?" the constable asked.

"What?" Antonio said. "Why?"

The vendor watched them, her mouth gaping open.

"No questions, please," the constable said. "Just come this way." Not that he gave Antonio a choice. Grabbing Antonio's arm, he led him away.

Antonio's heart raced. He tried to rack his brain for anything he may have done to break the law. Earlier that afternoon, a disgruntled passenger complained about the fare. Could that have been it? Or maybe Mrs. Silva had a change of heart and filed a theft report for the altar fund? On the constable's hip, a pair of handcuffs dangled.

Eventually, they reached a tiny fenced corral with benches which opened to the stars. Antonio frowned.

Inside the fenced area, Yolly, in pedal pusher jeans and a white blouse, sat on a bench. As Antonio and the constable approached, she shook her head, smiling. Looking embarrassed.

Antonio knew how she felt. The words outside the corral said, in bold letters: "The Love Jail."

40

ANTONIO HELD UP his wrist for the constable to handcuff it. Yolly did the same. "I'm sure this is illegal," she said. But she was smiling.

"Relax, young people," Constable Martillo said. "Antonio, you could either pay five pesos and insult the lady, or you might as well enjoy it. Either way, by paying for you to be jailed, your friend has already donated towards the village safety fund."

"I'd better stay handcuffed," Antonio said. "I don't want to insult *this* lady. I've seen her when she's mad."

Yolly's expression looked half-happy, half-sad. Probably thinking of her mother.

Constable Martillo hummed as he left them.

"So, here we are," Antonio said.

Yolly smoothed her jeans with her free hand. "Yes, here we are."

"What would you like to do?" Antonio gestured towards the crowd. "There's plenty to do here."

"We should do the pole-race together," Yolly said.

They laughed.

"We can walk and just look around," Antonio suggested.

At the plaza, which also served as a basketball court, Jose was playing a game and winning. He waved and Antonio shook a fist. They joined the crowd watching them at the sidelines.

"You've been friends with him a long time?" she asked.

"Forever."

"That's nice. My best friend moved away when we started high school. Rowena Bautista. Remember her?"

"Sure." Antonio nodded. "She was always drawing pictures. Why did she move?"

Her face darkened. "Ghost Moon Night. At that time, I thought she was crazy to move away. But now..."

They moved on to watch dancers flap their arms like ducks in an *itik-itik* performance.

"I'm really sorry about the tricycle," he said.

She gave him a sidelong glance. "I hope so. I really hated you there, for a while."

"Hated!" he echoed.

"I thought I knew you after Ghost Moon Night. But then you showed up and took the tricycle. Like a thug."

"And it wasn't even worth getting you mad at me. You were right. Bubuy didn't want to give me a job. Mr. Mijares hired me."

"So, you're working for him now? How is it?"

Antonio thought back to the deal he made with Bubuy in that small, cramped office smelling of cigarette smoke. "I haven't been there long."

"If you need help, I'm sure Lolo Nando will be glad to help you."

What if I'm beyond help?

A feeling of dread pressed down on Antonio's chest, but he just shook it off. "Thanks."

A live band played "Mambo Magsaysay" in the dance "hall," which was a small patchwork of plywood sheets on the ground. Someone strung flags of colored paper over the dance floor. Antonio tapped his foot and smiled. He liked this song. And apparently, so did Yolly, as he caught her tapping along, too.

"We might as well dance, if we're going to be handcuffed to one another," he said.

"Might as well."

GHOST MOON NIGHT

They joined the ten couples who danced the mambo. Suddenly, Yolly's steps faltered and Antonio caught her free hand.

"I was just thinking of my mother," she said. "She loved to dance."

The mambo segued into "Tennessee Waltz" by Patti Page. Antonio took Yolly in his arms and waltz-counted in his head so he wouldn't step on her. *One-two-three-four.* It didn't matter after all. They didn't really follow the music, but the steps felt right.

"I'm sorry about your mother," he said.

"It's alright," she said. "She's in a better place. She's probably dancing with my father right now."

"To 'Tennessee Waltz'?"

She smiled. "To 'Tennessee Waltz'."

They were both silent, and then she said, "You'll think this is strange, but many people underestimated my mother. Like people underestimate Caloy. They thought, because of her heart condition, that she was the frailest thing. But she wasn't. She said what she thought and never apologized for it."

"I find that hard to believe, since you're such a quiet, mousy thing," he teased.

"Yes, that's me, mousy." She smiled, then looked up at the night sky. "After my father died, Mother did what she could to support our family. I learned early on that if I needed something I had to work for it."

He twirled her at the end of the song. Then they just waited for the next one.

Back in Antonio's arms, Yolly said, "Father Sebastian said my mother might have died on Ghost Moon Night, but we won over the *langbuan*. Did you know that he wants to get rid of the *langbuan* forever?"

"If he discovers how to do that, more power to him."

"He told me he's been talking to some people." She touched his arm. "Creating enemies. Apparently, Tandang Lino doesn't agree with his *kampanya* to make our village less superstitious."

"Father Sebastian grew up in the city. Can you blame him for not believing?"

"He must think we are all strange."

"Strange. Yes, that's how you are."

Yolly pretended to pinch his ear.

Constable Martillo walked over to them, keys jangling in his hand. "Alright, sweethearts. Sorry for the interruption, but you're free to go."

After the handcuffs came off, Yolly rubbed her wrist and smiled. "Thanks for putting up with me."

He smiled, too. "It could have been worse." His eyes followed her as she turned and disappeared into the crowd.

"It could have been worse?" mimicked Jose, appearing at Antonio's elbow. "Ah, Antonio, you need to get out more."

Jose grabbed Antonio's arm and pulled him towards the outer edge of the *fiesta*. Right in front of Aling Cora's *manghuhula* stand. No one was in line. A curtain partially concealed a woman sitting behind a small circular table with only a candle for light.

"Come on in," Aling Cora said.

Jose walked to the curtain, then looked back. "Aren't you coming?" he asked Antonio, who hung back.

"I don't really want my fortune told," Antonio said.

"Why wouldn't you want to? Don't you want to see who you'll marry? How much money you'll make someday? If you will ever get as handsome as me?"

"No, thanks."

"Why not?"

Antonio didn't know why, but the little bamboo stand, the curtain, the dark interior, and the flickering candle made him want to run off.

"Well, just come in with me," Jose said.

Antonio followed Jose in. There was only one chair. While Jose got his fortune told, Antonio remained standing. Aling Cora had flowing white hair and a squat nose. She turned Jose's palm upwards, then started to give his fortune.

Jose would play basketball for a national team someday. He would marry a beautiful girl and have six daughters. No sons. (Jose groaned at this prediction.) Someday he would pen a novel.

"Really?" Jose asked. "Wait till I tell my English teacher who almost tried to flunk me. Will it be funny?"

"No," Aling Cora said. "Everybody will die in the end."

Jose grimaced and stood up. "Thank you." To Antonio, he whispered, "You're right, she doesn't know what she's doing.

184

Just play along with it."

Antonio sat on the chair and extended his arm. Aling Cora peered at this palm and made a puzzled sound. She raised the candle and the flame danced wildly.

"I see success. Happiness with a beautiful girl." She paused. "But I also see a lot of dark things. Death. Misery. Destruction."

Antonio swallowed and told himself, *she's just a fraud.*

"Are you sure you're not talking about my future novel?" Jose interjected.

"Shhh." Suddenly, Aling Cora's eyes grew wide. She practically shoved Antonio's hand away as she said, "I can't see anymore. I'm done for the night."

Curiosity nagged at Antonio, but he didn't dare press her.

Jose protested, "But..."

"Go away!" She chased them out of her tent with a broom.

"What a rude woman!" Jose said. "That bit about a dark novel was unbelievable. You were right. It wasn't worth that money, was it, Antonio? Antonio?"

Antonio was already walking away, into the dark night.

THE NEXT DAY, Antonio picked Jose up to give him a ride to the bus stop. "*Uy,*" Jose said when Antonio showed up at his house, "it looks like someone's in love."

"Stop it," Antonio said.

"You looked so miserable dancing with Yolly. If I had more money, I'd have shackled you two for the rest of the night."

"You have a crazy imagination."

Antonio parked at the curb and got out. Jose took his suitcase and shoulder bag and stood there blinking like an owl. "Well, I guess this is goodbye," Jose said.

"Don't be so dramatic," Antonio said gruffly. "You'll come home again soon."

"During breaks, I suppose."

Jose patted Antonio on the shoulder, loaded his luggage in the bus hutch, and boarded the bus. Antonio started up his tricycle and parked it at the curb, his teeth worrying his lower lip.

Lucky Jose.

Antonio looked around the station, at several familiar faces of people who had grown up in Dasalin all their lives, or had married into families here. The rest, he didn't recognize. They came from other outlying villages and used Dasalin's station as a hub, which made it possible for a tricycle driver to make a living. Did he see himself driving tricycles the rest of his life here, or was there really something better in store for him?

He shook off his thoughts and buckled down to work. Last night, Bubuy had given him a new list. He unfolded it now.

Sixteen names. Sixteen people to strong-arm today.

Antonio sighed. He wondered what excuses he would hear. *A wife in the hospital. A son's wedding. A daughter finishing nursing school.*

He found one driver, Efren Giron.

"I'm sorry, but my wallet got stolen yesterday," Efren said, not meeting Antonio's eyes.

"At the *sabungan?*"

Efren stared. "How did you know?"

"Papa told me you lost a lot of money last night."

"Have pity on me, Antonio," Efren pleaded. "If you take my money, my family won't have anything to eat tonight."

If Efren was squirming, it was his own fault. He had gambled the money. It wasn't Antonio's problem. Antonio didn't say anything and just stood there. Finally, Efren pulled out some bills and gave all but one to Antonio. Antonio ignored the tears in Efren's eyes and moved on.

Antonio came to the seventh name and sighed. Nando Nakpil. He hoped Yolly wasn't there to give him a tongue-lashing like some of the other times he had collected late fees on her grandfather.

Mang Nando was alone, waiting in the passenger queue. When he saw Antonio, he already started pulling out some money from a cigarette carton. Antonio almost stopped him. *Don't worry about it,* he wanted to tell the old man, noting his stooped back and leathery lined face. But he didn't.

Within an hour, he had collected all the fines. He went into Bubuy's office to deliver the money. At the doorway, he paused. On the shelf behind Bubuy sat the record player.

"Very nice," Bubuy said, looking pleased as he spread the bills and coins on his desk. "I had a hunch you'd be good for this job, and I was right. Not only are you earning far more than what you could as a regular driver, that record player will soon be yours."

Antonio felt like a noose just tightened around his neck.

On his way home, he took a different route, this time along Mang Fermin's old place. He slowed down and admired it. It looked so different. Light and airy. A copse of trees had been cleared in front of the property, revealing little bright green seedlings, piles of scrap wood, and a little pond that sparkled in the sun.

Jose leaving for college. A priest wanting to change their traditions. And now this. There had been too many changes in Dasalin lately.

42

A WEEK PASSED. FATHER Sebastian had driven to the market early and was parking his car when Antonio dropped off Aling Rosal and Aling Kamia for morning Mass.

"We expect you at our house punctually at seven tomorrow," Aling Rosal told Antonio, her dentures quivering as she jabbed the ground with her umbrella tip. Her sister, Aling Kamia, nodded in agreement, pinning Antonio with her rheumy eyes.

"Don't worry," he said, "I'll be there."

The two spinsters counted out their money to the centavo, gave it to Antonio, and shuffled off to Mass. Despite their abrasive attitude, Father Sebastian liked them. They came faithfully to Mass every day and they always brought treats to him because, in their opinion, he "needed fattening up".

Father Sebastian had been thinking about talking to Antonio, but there was so much danger in what he had to say. Back and forth he went, vacillating. Finally, he called out, "Antonio!"

"Yes, Father Sebastian?"

"I need to talk to you about...about something important. But I have Mass right now. Can you meet me for lunch?"

"I can, of course. At Aling Dona's?"

Father Sebastian hesitated. He needed to meet him somewhere more private. Where other people couldn't hear. "How about the parish kitchen?"

He could tell Antonio was curious. But the priest couldn't say more. Besides, it was time for Mass.

Father Sebastian pulled the last of the curtains shut in the kitchen.

"You must not say a word of this to anyone else," he said as he joined Antonio at the table. "Can I count on you to keep our conversation confidential?"

Antonio nodded over his bowl of soup. "Of course. You have a friend in me."

"And I am grateful." The priest smiled weakly. "I can use all the friends I can get. Let me put it this way. Some have suggested, in subtle and not so subtle ways that I should leave the parish."

"That's ridiculous. We need you here."

"Well, they have and will probably continue to do so. So long as I 'rock the boat'."

"Over the *kuding fiesta?*"

"That and Ghost Moon Night." Father Sebastian sighed. "*Especially* Ghost Moon Night."

"That's odd. Our village should have no quarrel with anyone who tries to rid it of the curse."

"That's what I thought, too. But then I started looking into the curse, its history and any news clippings. I went through our village records, and found nothing. Granted, you have a small village."

"Nothing?"

"Not a scrap of news, no reports, no records, no journals from former *baranggay* captains." Father Sebastian paused. "Don't you find that odd? It's as if Ghost Moon Night doesn't exist!"

"Well, everyone *knows* about Ghost Moon Night," Antonio said.

"How do you learn from the past if you don't record it?"

GHOST MOON NIGHT

Father Sebastian said. "For the past seventy-five years, no one has come forward with any solutions to Ghost Moon Night?"

"I think they have. My uncle always talks about how it's come up in council meetings before."

"And your uncle, what is his position in the town?"

"He's the *baranggay* captain."

Father Sebastian said, "Ah," and leaned back. "Perhaps that connection will come in useful. Had I known he was your uncle, I would have tried harder to see him. He's gone a lot."

Antonio nodded. "He'll actually be gone this Ghost Moon Night and asked me if I'd be around to help with my Tita Alice that day. She's not due for two weeks. You won't need me that day, will you?"

"Not that day, but I do need you to help me with something else." Father Sebastian paused. "I need you to help me figure out a way to destroy the *langbuan*."

Antonio stared. "I'm sorry, but I have no idea how to do that. I already told you all the things we've tried."

"Yes, yes, I know all about that. But you're a smart boy. You know people here. They will probably talk to you. No one wants to talk to me about the curse. Someone even told me that if my plan doesn't work, the *langbuan* will come after them the next Ghost Moon Night. So they refused." Father Sebastian clasped his hands together. "All I ask is that you share any information you can with me. I know you're a busy young man. So maybe you can write it down and give it to me Sunday?"

"I'll be honest," Antonio said. "I don't know when I'd do it."

"I understand." The priest sighed. "Just if you can."

"I will."

Father Sebastian walked Antonio to the door. Maybe Antonio wouldn't be able to help much. But it felt good to unburden himself to someone else.

The priest said a little prayer of comfort, and even before he said "Amen," peace washed over him. As long as he was doing the right thing, he knew he'd be alright, no matter what happened.

June
Six hours before Ghost Moon Night

A NTONIO WENT TO the Mijares building during his lunch
break. "Is Bubuy here?" Antonio asked Mr. Mijares'
secretary, Tetchie.

"I think so," she said, not looking up from her typewriter.

Antonio went to Bubuy's door and knocked. When no one
answered, he opened the door. Bubuy, Asim and Ngungot were
playing cards on the desk.

"Did I tell you to come in?" Bubuy asked, flicking ash from
his cigarette in a tray.

"No," Antonio said, "but when you didn't answer at my
knock, I figured I should just let myself in."

"Did you hear that, boys? He's making himself at home.
Even though I didn't say so."

"I just had a quick question," Antonio said.

"Well then why don't you say so?" Bubuy slapped his hand
of cards down. "You're distracting me."

"Can I take home my tricycle today? I should be past my
probation, shouldn't I?"

Bubuy puffed on his cigarette. "Let's see, is the year-mark
over?"

"I was talking to Mang Nando and he said probation is two weeks."

Bubuy crushed his cigarette butt in the tray. "As of today, it's three months."

"We'll see what Mr. Mijares has to say about it." Antonio walked to the door. Before he could reach it, Asim and Ngungot got there, barring his way.

"Why do you bother Mr. Mijares with trivial stuff?" Bubuy asked. "Two weeks, three months, it's all the same to me. You're pulling in your weight, so why not? Boys, make a note he has his tricycle overnight."

"Thank you," Antonio said through gritted teeth.

Mang Nando passed Antonio just as he was queuing up for passengers. After they waved at each other, Antonio craned his neck, to see if Yolly was in the sidecar. She wasn't.

With his usual flurry of last-minute shoppers, Antonio left work at three. On his way to Tita Alice's house, he drove his tricycle on the road to the coast, passing Mang Fermin's orchard.

It seemed like more trees had been hacked down. Past the remaining trees, he could see glimmers of the coast. The other night, Papa was grousing that the land would soon be denuded, and how would they make up for the lack of trees, but Mama said his was a needless worry. The lumber company planted seedlings as soon as they chopped trees down, and they had other lumber sources elsewhere.

A woman flagged him down just past the orchard. Antonio didn't want to stop. If the errand took longer, he'd be too pressed for time to go to Tita Alice, and already he was later than he'd planned. He passed the woman, then groaned. He turned his handlebars and circled back.

"*Manang*, where to?" he asked, recognizing her as a ticket seller from the bus station. She gave the address, clear at the other side of town. He'd have to drive at a fast, steady clip if he was to make it to Tita Alice's before sunset.

"Thank you!" the passenger said as she got in. "I was getting worried that no one would stop for me and I'd have to walk home." Antonio politely nodded, a worried sensation settling in his gut. *Hopefully, Tita Alice is alright.*

They passed pedestrians hefting bags of vegetables from the market. Other tricycles zipped recklessly around Antonio and other tricycles. Villagers pounded nails into boards across windows. Many fed their animals early.

Antonio eagerly parked the tricycle in front of his passenger's house and revved up his engine, anxious to go, but the passenger still needed to pay. By the time Antonio left her house, it was nearly five o'clock. He circled the end of the street and thought about stopping at his house first.

No. Just get to Tita Alice's as soon as possible. You promised Tito Oscar you'll be there for her.

The sun dipped lower in the horizon, a glowing orb in its last push for life. Bats began to come out to feed on evening insects. Antonio leaned forward and drove his tricycle as fast as he could to Tito Oscar's house.

Usually a servant or two came out but no one greeted him at his uncle's gate tonight. He reached over the waist-high gate to open it from the inside. He heard a pitter patter of feet, then a dog lunged and snapped at his hand. Thankfully, it missed.

The black dog had a huge head, broad chest and a tapered hip, one of those fighting dogs. His uncle's family must have just gotten it recently because he'd never seen it before. Through the window, he saw his uncle's daughters watching him. The older of the two, Irene, disappeared. Moments later, she ran outside.

"Antonio!" she said. "Where have you been? Mama's not doing well at all."

"Put away the dog, Irene," he said. "Then I can come in."

As she put the dog away somewhere in the back, Antonio looked towards the sea, at the setting sun. In just a few moments, Ghost Moon Night would descend upon them in earnest.

And so would the *langbuan*.

TITA ALICE LAY on her bed, soaked in sweat. When Antonio sat at her bedside, she said, "My husband. Where's my husband?"

"He's not here, Tita Alice," Antonio said.

She began to cry. "He hates me. Or he'd be here."

"Of course he doesn't hate you. He..."

Suddenly, her back arched, and she screamed. She grabbed his hand and squeezed so hard that his fingers soon felt numb.

"I've been pushing now, for a while," she said. "But the baby isn't coming. It feels different from my other babies. I need to go to the hospital."

Another spasm racked her body. More straining. Blood seeped on the sheets.

Antonio stumbled out of the bedroom, dazed. "Where are the servants?" he asked Irene.

"They left already," Irene said. "Mama told them to go."

"I should have come earlier!" he murmured, then took a deep breath. "Your mother's very sick," he told the two girls.

The younger one, Christine, started to cry. Irene calmly said, "I know."

"I don't know what I need to do for her," Antonio said. "I can't deliver a child. We'll have to take her to the hospital."

Irene blinked. "Right now?"

"Right now."

"What about the *langbuan*?"

"You and your sister stay here," Antonio instructed. "I will take her."

"No," Irene said. "I want to go with you."

Antonio put both hands on her shoulders. "Irene. It's too dangerous for you to be out there. I don't know how to drive a car, so I have to take your mother in my tricycle. You could get killed. You need to stay here with Christine."

"I need to protect Mama in the tricycle."

Reluctantly, Antonio had to agree.

"When I say so, open the door and run to the tricycle," Antonio instructed Irene. "Don't wait for me, alright? But I'll be there right behind you with your Mama." He glanced at the metal oars they held. "Use this if needed! And the flashlights."

He hoped he was doing the right thing. Tita Alice was too delirious to answer him when he asked if he could take Irene and Christine with them. They would not only help protect their mother, they would protect Antonio so that he could drive the tricycle.

As Antonio carried his aunt in his arms, she moaned her husband's name. He hoped it wasn't too late to save the baby, let alone Tita Alice.

The memory of the last Ghost Moon Night returned to Antonio. Why did these medical emergencies always happen on this accursed day? At first, his uncle's request for his help flattered him. Now he wished his uncle hadn't left and could take care of his wife in a proper car.

Just do your best, Antonio.

Nodding towards Irene, Antonio hung back for just a step while she opened the door. The girls ran out into the black night. He ran out with Tita Alice, keeping his eyes glued to the gate which Irene had left open. Just a few more steps and he'd be outside, where the tricycle waited.

Suddenly, the dog whimpered. And just as suddenly, it became quiet. Antonio thought he heard a noise behind him – a whisper, a flapping of wings, a footstep – and turned.

He saw nothing, so he looked back to the parking lot.

Where was the tricycle?

Screened from his view by a langbuan!

Its wings were massive, a dirty-gray, flapping in jerky motions. They muffled the girls' screams as they fought it away from the sidecar, holding up flashlights. Antonio muscled past, shouldering the *langbuan* away, putting Tita Alice in the sidecar between the girls. Then he ran to the motorcycle.

One kick-start, please God. One kick-start.

One kick and the engine revved into life. "*Salamat po,*" he whispered his thanks. He then wheeled the tricycle around, straight into three *langbuan* who had converged, but now scattered like bowling pins.

Antonio leaned forward and careened out to the road. He kept his focus forward, even though in his peripheral vision, he could see legions of *langbuan* descending from the sky to flank them, like an infernal army.

"Antonio!" Irene screamed into the wind. "Mama is bleeding more!"

"I'm going as fast as I can!" he shouted back, turning his head just enough to so she could hear. When he turned back to the road ahead, he swerved to avoid the *langbuan* who stood on the road, but it was too late. The impact sent them spinning into a shallow ditch. Next thing he knew, he lay on the ground and the world kept spinning.

"Let me help you," a female voice said.

Antonio's eyes fluttered open. A woman sat next to him. She had high cheekbones, full lips, and hair that cascaded down to the waist.

"Yes," he said, "please help me."

She smiled, baring fang-like teeth. Her eyes turned into dark sockets and a snake slithered out of one nostril. Her wings fanned out and flapped.

Heaven have mercy on us!

He kicked and sent her scrambling back like a giant crab, then ran back to the upturned sidecar.

It was empty.

A few feet away, he saw the girls and their mother, lying on the ground. Two *langbuan* hovered over them. One was stroking Tita Alice's belly. Antonio grabbed the oars and slashed at the creatures. They shrieked and flew backwards.

Irene opened her eyes and smiled. "I just had the nicest dream."

"Irene," Antonio said. "You have to get up and help me. Let's go, now!"

Fear crept back into her eyes as she looked around, blinked a few times, and realization dawned. She got up and shivered, then coaxed a thumb-sucking Christine from a curled up position. Antonio picked up Tita Alice. She felt hot on her arms, but her belly, where the creature had touched her, felt icy cold.

As they ran to the tricycle, *langbuan* massed overhead. Antonio righted the sidecar and got moving again. The creatures flew alongside, reaching and pulling. Christine was doing a good job of jabbing each attacker when suddenly, he felt the tricycle rise from the road. The *langbuan* were carrying it.

Irene and Christine screamed. Below them, the village looked smaller and smaller.

Antonio killed the engine, got in the sidecar, and held the oar at ready, his stomach churning. One *langbuan* pulled at little Christine. She cried out and reached for Antonio, who grabbed her. With the other hand, he swung the oar at the *langbuan*, shattering its spine. It tumbled from the sky, screaming.

One of the creatures dove into the sidecar, right where the girls and Antonio were sitting. It tried to embrace Irene, but she fought back, kicking and shoved it out. It fell into another *langbuan*, who punched it in the face.

Antonio looked at the landscape below and at the *langbuan*. He needed to take a chance, even if it meant they might fall to their death. He started hitting the monsters with the oar until he drove some of them away. A few returned, but more and more, they stayed away. The cloud thinned to just a half-dozen creatures until the tricycle hovered neared the ground. He kept hitting them, until he pried the last one's claws off the metal, sending the tricycle hurtling down.

Bracing himself for the impact, the tricycle hit the ground, sending Antonio flipping out of the sidecar into something

GHOST MOON NIGHT

wet. Sinky. Muddy. When he opened his eyes in amazement, the tricycle was sitting in the middle of a rice paddy. The girls and their mother lay sprawled in the mud. A water buffalo in a nearby pen snorted.

"Cupid!" he said. They were at Antonio's house. Here was safety!

The *langbuan* flew overhead in a dark circular mass. Antonio jumped onto the motorcycle, waited for the girls to climb in with their mother, and revved the engine. The wheels only spun in the mud. A *langbuan* flew down at full speed. Its yellow eyes glimmered and its tongue hung out to the side. Antonio lifted the handlebars and revved the engine until the motorcycle leaped out of the paddy and bumped back onto the dryer ground. The *langbuan* flew right where the tricycle would have been had it kept going.

The creature circled to attack again.

Antonio felt something nudge his arm. It was the oar, offered by Christine, whose eyes were huge and round on her tiny face.

Crack!

Antonio stuck the oar into the *langbuan*'s ribcage. It hissed and flew back. Then it descended again, only to be hit on the face. Screaming, it circled up and back down, its tail lashing at Antonio's head. His temple throbbed. Antonio revved the engine and threw the oar into the sidecar.

The tricycle raced down the yard, pursued by *langbuan*. Antonio felt a warm wetness trickling from his forehead, stinging his eye. When he wiped it off, blood covered his hand.

He drove the tricycle right up to the back door. Skidding to a stop, he pounded on the door. "Mama! Papa!" he said. "Let us in!"

The girls screamed as *langbuan* swooped down upon Antonio and grabbed his mid-riff, his arms. The door opened and Mama exclaimed, "*Dios mio!*" Antonio dropped Tita Alice on the threshold, his arms still in the *langbuan*'s icy grip.

Papa appeared with a lantern, shoving it into the creatures' faces. "Get out!" he said. "Get out!" while Mama pulled Tita Alice into the house. The girls followed.

Antonio twisted out of the monsters' loosened grip, stumbled into the house, and heard the door slam shut behind him. He slumped to the ground, stabbing pain radiating *everywhere*. Mama touched his head and he flinched.

"Don't worry…'bout me," Antonio said, as Mama's face became blurred and everything went black.

45

NTONIO OPENED HIS eyes and tried to sit up. A sharp pain erupted on his temple, and he lay down again.

"There, there," a voice soothed. "Lie still like a good boy."

A woman in a white nurse uniform held a huge syringe in her hand. He looked over her shoulder and saw white walls, cabinets, and an open window which framed a shade tree and dappled sunlight. White cotton curtains moved in the slight breeze.

He licked his lips, which were cracked and dry. "Where am I?" he asked.

"The hospital," the woman said.

"Why?"

"Why?" She laughed like he'd said a funny joke. "You nearly died last night."

"Where's Tita Alice? The girls?"

"If you mean the lady who had the baby, she's two rooms down. The girls are fine. No one else has been hospitalized. Just you and your Tita Alice. Rest now. The doctor will be here soon."

"Wait. How long have I been here?"

"A day." Then she left.

He lay there with a worrisome thought forming in his mind. *I'm supposed to be at work.*

He sat up, too fast. His body shook and his skin felt chilled, but he swung one leg, then the other over the edge of the bed. *Breathe. Breathe.*

"Antonio, what are you doing?" Trining bustled in front of him and gestured for him to move back to the bed.

"I need to get out of here. My tricycle…"

"Has been destroyed."

"What?" Antonio cried.

"The tricycle got broken up pretty good," Trining said.

"What do you mean 'broken'?" Antonio asked.

"Well, between the tires exploding, the mud coating everything, and the *langbuan* picking up your tricycle and dropping it on the front *veranda,* I'd say it's pretty broken."

Antonio groaned again. "What will I tell Mr. Mijares?"

"Oh, don't worry, he knows. His man, Bubuy, came by today and took your tricycle. He said something about squaring up with you sometime."

"Yes, he will," Antonio said.

"So just lie back and relax. You don't have a tricycle to drive right now, anyway."

As he lay back down, he asked, "What happened to the baby?"

"Here are your parents now," Trining said, looking anxious to leave. "They can tell you."

"Are you alright?" Mama asked Antonio, her eyes searching his face.

"Yes, I'm fine. Is Tita Alice alright? What happened to the baby?"

"Alice is recovering, but the baby didn't make it. He came out stillborn. Do you know what it means?"

"He was already dead?"

"Yes."

"That's too bad."

Mama smoothed his bangs. "Last night, I had a feeling you were in trouble. I prayed for you."

"Thank you, Mama."

"I don't think my heart can take any more of these episodes,"

Mama said. "We have a rule of staying inside on Ghost Moon Night. Follow it."

"I know." He tried to smile but his mouth hurt.

Papa traded places with Mama. "I'm sorry, Antonio."

Antonio couldn't believe it. Papa was apologizing.

Expelling a deep breath, Papa said, "Life's too short for fights." He patted Antonio's hand awkwardly. "You're a good son and I've been hard on you."

"Thanks, Papa." Antonio knew how hard that was for Papa to say those words. His eyes fluttered shut. They felt so heavy. "You're...a good...father, too."

"Shh. Rest now," Mama said.

"Antonio?"

He opened his eyes. His uncle, Tito Oscar stood at his bedside. "My dear nephew," he said.

"Hello, Tito Oscar." Smiling didn't hurt as much.

Tito Oscar's eyes brimmed with tears. "Your Tita Alice and I are very grateful to you for what you did last night. You saved her life."

"But not your son's. I'm so sorry."

Tito Oscar's eyes darkened with anger. "No, he died in the hands of the *langbuan*."

"Mama said he was stillborn."

"We'll never know if he had a chance outside the womb. Maybe he did." He smiled wistfully. "I would have taken him fishing, taught him everything I know."

Silence descended upon the room. Tito Oscar rubbed his stubbled chin. He looked tired, like he hadn't slept.

There was a knock, and Yolly stood in the hospital room door. Tito Oscar turned and said, "Come in, Antonio's friend."

"I'll go and check on your Tita Alice," Tito Oscar said, and left them alone.

"You should have learned from the last Ghost Moon Night," she said, "and not make trips to the hospital."

He smiled. "I had no choice."

"Well, you had a choice. You just chose to be a crazy hero."

"Is that what I am," he teased. "A hero?"

"To some," she said.

"And to you?"

"Just crazy."

She sat on a chair and took out the newspaper. "I thought maybe you'd be starved for entertainment," she said. "Do you want me to read you the news?"

He smiled to himself. He never read the news. Papa did. But he decided to humor her. "Alright."

Antonio listened, not so much to the stories, but the sound of her voice. When she finished a story, she looked at him. "More?"

"More." Being an invalid wasn't too bad, he decided.

46

BACK AT HOME, after being discharged from the hospital, Antonio noticed something different right away. Lolo and Lola's portrait was still there, as well as Lolo's medal, but the Vicks Vaporub was missing from the *salas* side table. The flip flops weren't by the *sala* set. He limped into the house and asked, "Where's Lolo Sonny?"

Mama and Papa exchanged glances. "He's not here," Mama said.

Antonio looked from one to the other. "I can see that. Where is he?"

"At the hospital."

"What? What happened? Why didn't you tell me? I was just there. I could have seen him!"

"He's not at *that* hospital."

"It's getting too hard to help him," Papa said. "One day while you were working, he climbed a tree. It took forever to help him down. One of these times, he'll get himself seriously hurt."

Antonio said, "So, he's not hurt? Why is he in the hospital?"

Mama gave him a steely glance. "The doctor said we should

confine him at the hospital in Nagat."

"For the *loko-loko*!" Antonio said, slamming his hand on the wood *sala*. "For crazy people like Mad Juana!"

Mama looked out the window, then back at Antonio. "The night you rescued Tita Alice, Lolo slipped out of the house. We found him the next day, incoherent and confused, in Cupid's water trough."

"Out with the *langbuan* all night!"

"Luckily, Cupid protected him. We can't take chances any more. The regular hospital can't keep a wandering patient like him."

"Why don't you or Papa just tend him all day?"

"His situation is more than we can handle," Mama said. "You need to accept the fact that Lolo needs medical care."

"If only he had music," Antonio murmured.

"Music!" Papa gestured impatiently.

"You don't understand."

"No," Papa said, "*you* don't understand. Things have gone from bad to worse for this town. I've noticed a pattern. Lolo Sonny's not himself. You're not yourself. Even the harvest has not been as good. Our seedlings are diseased. All this happened since that priest came to town."

Antonio frowned. "What does Father Sebastian have to do with this?"

"He's been encouraging the village to abandon tradition. And even actively rid this town of *langbuan*. Change things."

"He's the one voice of reason in this town," Antonio countered.

"I know the priest's been talking to you," Papa said. "Mama and I think you should avoid him. Just let him mind his own business."

"And you call yourselves Christian!"

"Antonio!" Mama said.

"I'm sorry," he muttered, then stood up.

"Where are you going?" Papa asked.

"I'm going to see Lolo Sonny."

The bus stopped just outside a fenced compound in Nagat. The town looked bigger than Dasalin, with houses closer to each other and streets more congested with tricycles. And jeepneys, long passenger vehicles patterned after American military jeeps. Antonio followed two other passengers out to what looked, at first glance, like a wasteland of barren dirt, scrawny trees, and stray cats everywhere. The fence rose to about ten feet tall, topped with barbed wire.

Was this a mental hospital or a prison?

A security guard patted him down, then sent him to the two-story building. A row of bushes lined the driveway. Thorny and twisted. Inhospitable.

Inside the building, there were no pictures on the white walls. A receptionist sat behind a small, cramped desk. Antonio asked to see Lolo Sonny and she gave him a room number.

A nurse led him down a hallway, a flight of stairs and another hallway. The door opened into a small, cell-like room, about fifteen feet by fifteen feet. Lolo Sonny sat on a bench in a soiled hospital dressing gown. As Antonio came up to him, he noticed bolts held the bench and bed to the floor. The mattress didn't have a sheet or pillow.

"Lolo," Antonio said, coming up to put his hand to his forehead in a *mano*.

Lolo Sonny cringed and pulled his arm back.

"It's alright, Mr. Pulido," the nurse said. "It's your grandson."

Shaking his head, Lolo Sonny refused to look at Antonio.

"Lolo."

Lolo Sonny kept his head averted.

Antonio turned to the nurse. "Why won't he look at me?"

"That's how he is," she said, shrugging. "Your grandfather is old and sick. He's in the early stages of dementia."

"He loves music," Antonio said. "Can you put on music for him? That'll calm him."

"Music isn't allowed," she said. "It can agitate other patients."

"What if the doctor prescribes it?"

"Well, then, we would play music for them. But only if the doctor says so."

Antonio looked at his grandfather's averted face and felt his heart break. "I'll talk to him in private now."

"Just pretend I'm not in the room," she said.

So he talked to Lolo Sonny self-consciously. He rambled about Cupid, about Jose leaving for college, about the price of eggs. Anything to keep the conversation going. The nurse stared at Antonio like *he* should be the one incarcerated.

Antonio looked at his watch. Just fifteen minutes and it felt like a lifetime. Meanwhile, Lolo Sonny refused to turn his head or respond in any way. Admitting defeat, Antonio told the nurse, "I'm done now."

Another nurse had to come and lead him through the maze of hallways and stairs. Antonio walked through the empty lobby and past the thorny bushes. It wasn't until he was in the bus, on the way back to Dasalin that Antonio, alone on the back seat, pressed his fists to his eyes and cried.

Before sunset, Antonio and his family hitched Cupid to the cart and drove to Tito Oscar's house for the baby's wake. Antonio kept to himself, even with Papa's pointed stares as though Antonio had done something wrong.

All Antonio could think of was Lolo Sonny.

Along the beach, beyond the house, the funeral procession had already started. At the head of the procession, Tito Oscar carried the little white coffin on his shoulder.

Antonio and his family got out of the cart and fell in step with the mourners. Someone began singing "The Lord's Prayer" in their Tagalog language, accompanied by a guitar, and many joined in.

Like a white serpent, the procession slithered into one of the doors of the house. After Tito Oscar lay the coffin on a table, a swarm of mourners gave their condolences. Antonio waited for the crowd to thin and queued up. When Tito Oscar saw him, he put an arm over Antonio's shoulder.

"I'm so sorry, Tito Oscar, for the baby," Antonio said.

"Ah, Antonio." Tito Oscar sighed. "My heart breaks, but I don't argue with God's will."

Tita Alice sipped a glass of water, her expression icy.

"Sorry Tita," Antonio said.

"You'd better be!" Her lip curled. "You were supposed to come earlier. I'd have been in the hospital sooner."

Taken by surprise, he stammered another apology.

"Alice," Tito Oscar said. "Why take out your grief on this young man when he helped you?"

Tita Alice flung her glass on the floor, breaking it into a million glittering pieces, then ran crying upstairs.

That night, Antonio dreamed that he was dead. He lay in a coffin, and one by one, mourners came to pay their last respects.

Papa and Mama came forward. Mama wore the black blouse she wore to funerals and her hair was pinned up. Papa wore a shirt still dirty from farm work. "How could you be so disrespectful?" Mama admonished him.

"If you'd just give me more money, I could buy myself a new shirt," Papa said. "Anyway, he's dead, what does it matter?"

"Romy, he's in a place between the living and the dead," Mama said. "I wouldn't be surprised if he's in this room with us right now."

Papa sighed. "Even in death, Antonio cannot make up his mind!" When Mama drifted away, Papa stayed behind and whispered, "Antonio, now that you're in the spirit world, can you please tell me who'll win the cockfight?"

Father Sebastian came up next. He held up an empty jar. "I couldn't resist it, but seeing all these people, I am collecting more donations for my altar. I hope you don't mind." His eyes twinkled.

After the priest left his side, Tandang Lino came by. "I wouldn't believe anything Father Sebastian tells you. He's full of coffee beans!"

Tito Oscar followed. "I wanted to take you fishing. We missed our chance, didn't we?"

No, Antonio wanted to say. *I can still go fishing. I can hear you and see you; why can't I fish with you?* He tried to grab his uncle's arm, but he couldn't move.

The door burst open and a strong gust of wind blew in.

"Thank you for coming," Mama said to an unseen guest. "And thank you for treating my son so well while he worked for you."

Antonio couldn't see over his coffin, but he knew that voice. It was Bubuy saying, "I'm sorry about your son. He was one of my best apprentices." Now he came forward, his head bowed. His eyes darted right to left, slowly grinning. "I warned you this would happen if you told anyone our little secret."

The priest came forward and Bubuy, bowing his head reverently, backed up. "It's time to shut the coffin," Father Sebastian said.

Now Antonio watched from above his coffin and looked at his dead self. What horrible orange make-up! He never slicked his hair back with pomade like that while alive. And what a dirty, rumpled shirt! The shirt twitched, stretched, tore at the shoulders. Gray wings popped through the cloth and unfurled.

The image changed. Antonio lay on his back in the coffin once again. Father Sebastian tried to shut the lid, but Antonio's wings got in the way.

No! he said, but it seemed Father Sebastian couldn't hear him. The priest pressed down harder until the wings snapped and darkness smothered Antonio.

47

A WEEK LATER, ANTONIO sat across from Mr. Mijares and put a canvas bag on the table.

"This is the money I owe you, Mr. Mijares, for the tricycle repairs," he said.

Mr. Mijares looked in the bag for a long moment. "This is a lot of money."

"Yes, it is," Antonio said.

Mr. Mijares leaned back and studied him. "You are an interesting young man. You could have just walked away from the tricycle and told Bubuy it was his problem."

"That's not how my parents raised me."

"Well, your parents are to be commended. So what now? Are you ready to go back to work for me?"

Antonio stared. "I thought for sure you wouldn't hire me back."

"Why ever not?"

"I just ruined your tricycle."

Mr. Mijares shrugged. "It's just a machine. A tricycle without a good, dependable driver, is worthless."

Antonio smiled, then reached over to shake Mr. Mijares'

hand. "Thank you! But the repairs aren't done yet, are they?"

"No. I'll have Bubuy give you a loaner for now."

"That would be wonderful!" He shook his boss's hand once again.

Mr. Mijares had Bubuy come in and had Antonio step out. The two men were closeted together for a few minutes. When Bubuy came out, his face was more dour than usual. He asked Antonio to meet him in his office.

"I don't know why the boss has taken a liking to you," Bubuy said. "But he has. Alright, I admit I can see why. You have a brain in that head of yours. And gumption. That's why I chose you for the job I did."

Bubuy handed Antonio a piece of paper. It was the day's late fee list. Immediately, Antonio's glance fell on a name towards the bottom. Nando Nakpil. "Mang Nando's been good about paying, hasn't he?" Antonio asked.

"Not lately. Plus, I don't like his attitude. We have to rein in that man. We don't want him planting seeds of discontent among the other drivers." Bubuy leaned back and studied Antonio. "I've heard that some squabbles are breaking out between drivers over parking. Some of the older drivers are claiming seniority. The younger drivers are jumping the lines."

"I've seen a few times where this has happened," Antonio said, "but it's not that common."

"Well, I wanted it curbed completely. From now on, to protect your spot on the line, a driver has to pay a protection fee."

"More fees?" Antonio said.

Bubuy's gaze hardened. "We need to keep everyone in line. I want you to collect this protection money." He turned his head and pointedly glanced at the record player.

Antonio thought of Lolo Sonny. And how this monster was capitalizing on an old man's need.

"Alright," he said, trying to keep his anger under a mask.

Bubuy examined his nails. "Now, if you'll work for me, you'd better zip your mouth. No more talking back or disrespecting. Understand?"

"I understand."

"This just might be the start of a fine partnership. Go and hunt down our late fees and come back for further instructions."

Antonio got up and walked to the door.

"Oh, and Pulido," Bubuy said. "I hate that shirt. Don't ever wear it again."

Clenching his jaw, Antonio nodded. "Yes, Bubuy."

Bubuy grinned, and Antonio hated himself.

Yolly sat in Mang Nando's sidecar when Antonio came around. She smiled at him in greeting, and he nodded back coolly. Confusion washed over her features, and then she turned cool as well.

If I'm to do this, Antonio thought, *I can't be friends with any of the other drivers. Or their families.*

"I've come for your late fee," Antonio told the old man.

Mang Nando frowned. "I paid my boundary fee when I first got in this morning."

"Which makes it late still."

"We've had this discussion before, remember?" Mang Nando said. "And you've let it go, young man."

"I can't. Not this time." Antonio held out his hand and waited.

Surprise filled Mang Nando's eyes. "I don't understand."

"Then let me explain," Antonio said. "You pay the late fee, and I will leave. You don't pay the late fee, and Bubuy will take your tricycle from you."

Mang Nando swallowed. Blinked. He felt in his back pocket and produced a beat-up wallet.

"Antonio," Yolly cried, "why are you doing this?"

Antonio refused to look at her. "This is between me and your grandfather, Yolly."

Mang Nando nodded. "He's right. I've been amiss. I should pay." His hand shook as he counted out the change. "I don't have enough here. Do you think I can pay tomorrow?"

"I have enough!" Yolly thrust some peso bills under Antonio's nose. "Now take your dirty money and leave us alone!"

Mang Nando's eyes held no apology on behalf of his granddaughter. But then, Antonio didn't expect one. Calmly, he picked up the money and moved on to the next driver. And the next, until he completed his list. Then he walked over to Bubuy's office and gave him the money.

Bubuy held up the peso bills to his face and kissed them. "Well done."

In the hallway, Antonio leaned against the wall and closed his eyes. He relived Yolly's horrified expression. Her loathing glance.

I can't do this.

But then he thought of his grandfather, alone and without music in a stark hospital room. He forced himself to walk on, get his loaner tricycle and start another day.

"*Hoy!*" Trining called out to Antonio as he crossed the backyard after feeding Cupid. She was cutting vegetables for dinner in the outside kitchen and set the knife down with a clatter. "What's wrong with your tough *kukote*?"

Antonio raised his hands as though to ward off a blow. "What?"

"What?" Trining mimicked. "You're not stupid. You know what I'm talking about."

"I have no idea what you're talking about," Antonio lied.

"It's all over town that you're working for that vermin Bubuy. Why, you're worse than his henchmen, they say."

Antonio bristled and walked off. "I don't have time for this gossip."

"Also, they say you broke the heart of Mang Nando's granddaughter. That's the worst."

Antonio paused and turned back at the doorway. "I didn't break Yolly's heart."

"Ah, my heavens. Is that her name? What a sweet name. She probably cries in her pillow every night, that angel."

"I doubt that very much. She's probably turned her pillow into my image and pokes pins in it, is more like it. Who told you about her?"

"You'll be amazed at what you can learn from washing clothes at the river."

"Well, you have your news mixed up. Yolly would never cry over a jerk like me."

"Oh, so you admit you are one."

"I don't have to explain myself to you. You wouldn't understand."

"You're right, I don't understand," she shook the kitchen knife at him. "There's no excuse great enough to break the law."

"Bubuy says it's legal."

"It sounds like extortion to me."

Antonio made an impatient noise.

"*Ay*, don't you be clucking at me," Trining said. "I'm just getting started. Why haven't you helped at the church? Father Sebastian has asked about you a few times. He thinks you're turning heathen."

"Maybe I am."

"Some people think you've lost your senses over a record player. A record player!" She scoffed. "Of all things! Your mother is worried about you."

"I can see why she worries, if you feed her all sorts of lies."

"But are they, Antonio? Are they *lies*?"

She stared at him. He tried to avert his eyes, but she grabbed his face in her hands. He could smell garlic on her hands.

"I've known you since you were a little boy," she said. "Why are you selling your soul? Have you thought of what will happen to you when you die? Aren't you scared you'll turn into a *langbuan*, too?"

Antonio pushed her hands away and ran into the house. He kept running until he was in his bedroom and slammed the door shut.

Did I make a mistake? My reason is good, isn't it?

He lay on his bed and stared at the ceiling for a long time. Bubuy said Antonio was doing great. He might even earn the record player sooner than planned.

Shouldn't Antonio be elated?

Instead, he felt like the lowest of the lowest of creatures.

Three months later

ARE YOU READY?" Bubuy asked Antonio.

Asim and Ngungot stood behind Bubuy in Bubuy's office, and Antonio sat across from them. "I think so," Antonio said.

"You 'think' so!" Bubuy laughed. "Did you hear that men? There's enthusiasm for you!" Asim and Ngungot dutifully laughed along.

Bubuy lifted the record player from the floor and put it on the desk.

Antonio just stared. He had dreamed about his moment for so long. So why did his smile feel forced?

"Go on," Bubuy said, "touch it. All your hard work, wrapped up in a tidy little package."

Antonio touched it and opened the lid.

"A deal's a deal," Bubuy said. "Enjoy!"

Antonio staggered out with the record player. It felt like a boulder attached to his neck. He put it on his tricycle passenger seat and sped home.

It's mine now. I'll give it to Lolo. That'll make it all right.

With that thought, he felt a little better. But once he got

home – avoiding Trining's prying eyes – and went to his room, the heavy feeling returned.

What had he done?

He set the record player on the floor and just stared at it for a long time. Then he got up, opened his chest of drawers and pulled out a square envelope. Jose had sent it to him from Manila. He turned the machine on and set the stylus on the record. Moments later, Doris Day's husky, mesmerizing voice filled his bedroom.

When the song ended, Antonio lifted the stylus off the record and replaced it carefully. The player sounded better than he'd imagined.

But a voice in his head persisted. *What about honor? The poor tricycle drivers? And Yolly?*

Antonio covered his ears with his hands as he muttered, "Shut up! Shut up!"

49

September
Thirty-three minutes before Ghost Moon Night

ANTONIO'S HEAD ACHED, after the day's usual craziness. Earlier in the day, a fight broke out in the market over a measly kilo of fatty pork. His route slowed down midday, then picked up again starting at four, with passengers asking – no, demanding – that he drive faster.

As he revved his tricycle to pull out of the station, he saw Yolly coming out of Sandoval's. She glanced at him coldly and looked away. The past three months, they acted like complete strangers around each other. Once, he found her praying alone at the church and almost told her why he was working for Bubuy, but he chickened out. She probably wouldn't understand anyway. She'd say it was a poor excuse.

His motorcycle tires squealed as he tore out of the dirt lot.

Halfway home, Antonio's motorbike sputtered. He looked down at the gas gauge and slapped it. Nearly empty! He had been so distracted by Yolly, he'd forgotten to buy gasoline. He double-backed to the town pump near the expressway. Its gray-haired owner came out, wiping his hands on his rag.

"Can I buy some petrol?" Antonio asked.

"I don't have any."

"Even just a little?"

"I don't have any. Sorry." He didn't sound sorry at all. "Why don't you try the one by the station?"

"Can you please check?"

"No." His lip curled. "My brother worked for Mr. Mijares. Until you made him pay money he couldn't afford. I hope you get stranded out there."

"Wait!" Antonio said, but the owner went inside the little station shack and slammed the door shut.

Antonio expelled a deep breath and went to the bus station. By the time he got there, the pumps were closed for the night. Mang Nando's tricycle came abreast of his and he glimpsed Yolly's rigid posture and averted face. For one moment, Antonio thought about flagging them down, but surely Yolly would just reject him. He glanced at the gas gauge and decided he had enough petrol to get home.

At fifteen minutes to sunset, the tricycle died. Right beside the graveyard.

Like jagged teeth, tombstones and vaults stood between him and the Lady of Miracles Church. Between him and safety. He tried to revive his tricycle. It started once, but died again.

Three minutes until sunset.

He took off running towards the church, through the graveyard. At first, he kept to the ground, squeezing between vaults. After he got caught on a vine and nearly tripped, he climbed a vault and started jumping from one to another. Mama's voice echoed in his head.

Don't climb the vaults, Antonio. That's disrespectful.

"*Pasensya po!*" he apologized, as he stepped on another vault. "Sorry!"

Running across each vault, he made good time. And then he faltered. Stopped and stared. The miniature city of what had been white vaults glowed orange-red, reflecting the setting sun behind him.

Ignore the sunset. Just make it past the graveyard.

Too late.

Dozens of *langbuan* floated down from the sky like wisps of fabric. Over his shoulder, the sun clung to its last breath. Then the mountains devoured the last rays, plunging the graveyard into darkness.

As his eyes adjusted, he saw the vague outlines of the vaults and the church beyond. Closer now, but not close enough.

It took just a moment, of him raising his head to assess how much of the graveyard was left to cross, but it was enough to distract him from the next vault. He thought it was closer than it was. The next step jarred his leg as his foot landed. A sharp pain radiated from his shin. He sucked in his breath.

Don't stop! Keep moving!

For one second, he tried to stand on that leg, but he just buckled under.

Stay calm. Just let your leg recover. Then move on! The church is just right there.

His breath came in ragged spurts and his heart hammered in his chest. He tested his leg. It hurt still, but not as much. Landing on it, he cried out. The sensation felt like a hot poker had been wedged between his joints.

He glanced at the church.

Just get yourself there.

Each step brought agony to Antonio, but still, he went from vault to vault until all that was left were two rows. He stepped out, but there wasn't anything in place, just air and vines. He fell in a narrow space between vaults. He lay there for a moment, winded.

Then his heart pounded like a hundred drums.

Above him, a *langbuan* hovered, the wings fanning a familiar scent. The smell of rotting mabolo fruit.

Mang Fermin's mouth slit open into a toothless grin. The flesh on his hands and arms had begun to decompose, leaving a thin veneer of flesh on bone. Cotton plugged his nostrils. He was wearing his burial clothes, now dingy with dirt.

He held up a mabolo. "Want one?" he asked, his *langbuan* wings unfurling behind him.

50

ANTONIO GOT UP and ran, ignoring the pain on his leg. He skimmed the top of vaults, scrambled over and past crosses and statues, then hurtled himself into the church courtyard. Wings slashed the air behind him in hot pursuit.

The church looked like a pale fortress against the monstrous night.

A gust of wind swirled around Antonio as Mang Fermin planted himself between the parish house and Antonio.

"Too bad I don't have a shotgun," Mang Fermin said.

Too bad *I* don't have a shotgun, Antonio thought. In the corner of his eye, he saw Father Sebastian's old, rusty sedan, parked just a half-dozen car lengths away. He ran to it, his body slamming to a stop against the front passenger door as he yanked the handle.

The door was locked.

He ran to the back passenger door and pulled on the handle so hard, when it did open, it bounced back on its hinges. Just as Mang Fermin dove for him, Antonio got in the car. Mang Fermin's hand snapped off with a crunch as Antonio slammed the door shut on it and pounded down on the lock. Mang

Fermin's enraged howl echoed in the night.

Moments later, Mang Fermin watched him closely, his uninjured hand clawing at the windows, which were fogging up from Antonio's breath.

Thud!

A mabolo hit the window and slid down in its slime.

Thud! Thud!

Mang Fermin kept throwing fruit at the windows, each time making a dull, thudding noise.

Antonio dove for the glove compartment. With shaking fingers he went through its contents: papers, coins, sunglasses. A big silver flashlight. Pulling it out, he slid the switch to the "on" position but nothing happened.

He shook it again.

Nothing.

He shook it a third time, *please please please,* and the marvelous light came on. He listened for the thudding of fruit and trained the beam of the flashlight towards that direction. Mang Fermin shrieked, launching himself backwards. Antonio kept the beam of light moving while his eyes scoured the darkness.

Smash!

A rock broke through the front windshield, showering Antonio with broken glass. Through the jagged opening, Mang Fermin's remaining hand reached for Antonio's throat.

Antonio swung the flashlight and clubbed the hand with all his strength. Mang Fermin pulled back then lunged again, his hand knocking the flashlight to the floor. Antonio kicked, but Mang Fermin got hold of his right foot, his grip tightening until that foot felt numb with cold.

While kicking repeatedly with the other foot, Antonio reached for the flashlight, feeling the ribbed metal at his fingertips. Antonio trained the light onto Mang Fermin's face. Mang Fermin hissed and let him go.

Plink!

The bulb in the flashlight gave out, leaving Antonio in darkness. Mang Fermin laughed.

Antonio gauged the distance of the church from the car. He wouldn't make it, he knew, not with Mang Fermin and those wings. They would bring about his death.

Or, since they wouldn't fit *under* the car, his salvation.

Antonio turned on the headlights, sending Mang Fermin reeling backwards. Then Antonio dove into the backseat, opened the right rear door, and slid under the car. In the glow of the headlamps, Antonio could see a shadowy figure moving around the car. He lay as still as he could on his side.

Mang Fermin's grinning face appeared. He reached for Antonio, grazing his leg and clawing at his chest, but he couldn't stretch that far. Those huge wings kept him from fitting under the car.

Every time he tried, Antonio kicked at his hand. Mang Fermin kept following him around the car, but Antonio just scooting away. Then Mang Fermin disappeared.

Antonio strained to hear, hoping Mang Fermin had lost interest.

Ding! Clang!

Mang Fermin was hitting or throwing something at the body of the car. After that barrage, the car rose up a little in the air, falling down on Antonio, filling his mouth, ears and nose with pieces of rusted metal.

The car rose and fell on him. Again and again.

Antonio curled up into a ball and protected his head with his arms, praying for dawn.

51

Mang Fermin's bony finger poked at Antonio. Snarling, Antonio slapped it away.

"*Dios mio!*" a woman's voice said. "He's still alive!"

Antonio opened his eyes. He shook off a thick layer of metal and dust from his head. All around him were car parts, muffler, tailpipe, a wheel.

And glorious light from the morning sun. It was the day after Ghost Moon Night.

What he thought was Mang Fermin's finger was the end of a walking cane beside a pair of feet encased in a woven slippers connected to scrawny legs in a skirt.

He touched his face, his arm, his legs. Tender to the touch, scraped, bloody. "I'm alive!" he shouted.

"He's gone insane," a woman said. "I wouldn't stand too close if I were you."

Antonio crawled out to the sunlight. His "regulars," Aling Rosal and Aling Kamia gaped at him. Aling Rosal limped forward and whacked him on the leg with her cane.

"There you are, you irresponsible young man," she said. "We waited for our ride but you never came!"

GHOST MOON NIGHT

After the old ladies berated him, Antonio went to Mass, sitting on the last pew. People turned to stare. Father Sebastian paused in the middle of Mass and stammered, as though taken aback by his appearance. When Mass was over, Father Sebastian walked over to Antonio.

"Well," Father Sebastian said. "What happened to you?"

"I ran out of gasoline last night and...and had a little bit of trouble." Antonio bit his lip. "Can I just *show* you what happened?"

When Father Sebastian nodded, Antonio led him to the courtyard, where car parts were scattered about.

"Oh my," the priest said.

"I know. I'm sorry."

"I don't understand. *You* did this?"

Antonio said, "The *langbuan* did. I was fine in the car for a little while, until Mang Fermin – who is a *langbuan* now, by the way – broke the window. I got under the car and he couldn't get to me, but he sure destroyed it. I'm so sorry."

"Ah well, I can always flag down a tricycle." He smiled wryly. "Have you had breakfast?"

"No. In fact, I haven't had dinner yet."

"Come join me." The priest went to look for Henry. Henry brought a plate of *tocino* and eggs, then left them alone at the kitchen table. Antonio's eyes grew big as he looked at the food and dug in.

"This is delicious," Antonio said, his mouth full of food. "Thank you."

"You're making a habit of *langbuan* encounters," Father Sebastian said.

"It appears so, doesn't it?" Antonio laughed.

"Some might say you have an *anting-anting*."

"I wish I had an amulet." Antonio cocked his head. "I thought as Christians, we shouldn't believe in those things."

Father Sebastian sipped his coffee. "Oh I think such powers exist. But they aren't necessarily from God."

"Father Sebastian, if your desire is righteous, but the means you use isn't as...righteous...can you be forgiven?"

"You mean does the end justify the means?"

Antonio nodded.

"What do you think?" Father Sebastian said.

"You're like my mother." Antonio grinned. "She never comes right out to say what I should do, but always makes me think about it."

"A wise mother."

"And an unwise son." He looked at Father Sebastian, whose kind eyes seemed to promise safety and understanding.

Antonio cleared his throat. "Since a little after graduation, I've been involved in a shady scheme with Bubuy Alvarez. He makes life hell – let me correct that – *I* make life hell for other drivers unless they cooperate. He takes their tricycles if they don't. So the next day, they pay their fees, just to stay on Bubuy's good side. I get a cut of the money."

Father Sebastian's eyes stayed gentle. "You said you did this for a righteous reason?"

"My Lolo is sick and he needs a record player."

"Sorry," Father Sebastian said, setting down his cup. "I don't understand."

"Certain songs calm him. Some agitate him. He had a transistor radio once, and it broke. The record player would be so much better. He likes certain songs over others. I did consider another radio once, but, let's just say that option soon disappeared."

"And how does Bubuy factor in?"

"Bubuy knows something about my grandfather that looks very bad. He said he'd tell everyone unless I worked for him this way. And he'd also give me the record player after a short time. I got so desperate for my grandfather, I agreed to do it. I wanted my grandfather to have a record player. To save his life. Music is as important to him as breathing." Antonio's fork clattered onto his plate. "I made a mistake and I want to make it right."

Father Sebastian leaned back in his chair. "What do you think your grandfather would want you to do then?"

Antonio pushed off from the table and stood up, shaky and grim, but resolved. "Clean myself up first," he said.

52

ANTONIO PARKED HIS tricycle by the Mijares building just as Bubuy came out.

"Well, well, well," Bubuy said, planting himself in Antonio's path. He took out a cigarette and lit it. "We're late today, are we? I thought about sending Ngungot for your tricycle."

"I need to talk to Mr. Mijares," Antonio said. "Let me pass, please."

Bubuy didn't budge. "Did you hear that, Ngungot? Asim? A disrespectful tone, wouldn't you say?"

"Yes, boss," the two goons said.

"What's with you, Pulido?" Bubuy asked, blowing smoke at Antonio. "The *langbuan* ate your brain?"

"I'm seeing clearly, for once," Antonio said.

Bubuy slapped his thigh and laughed. "You mean you got a conscience all of a sudden?"

"I've always had a conscience. I'm just going to follow it now."

Bubuy's smile faded. "What about your grandfather's... pristine war record?"

"You can do what you want with it. Nobody would believe

you."

"Oh, you think so?" But Bubuy sounded less cocky.

"Also, if I'm going to continue working here," Antonio said, "I will do it on my own terms."

Bubuy threw his cigarette on the ground. "Anyone who wants to work here only does so on my terms."

The door to Mr. Mijares' building opened. A man came out. Bubuy had his back turned to him, but Antonio could see who it was.

"And what terms are those?" Antonio asked Bubuy.

Bubuy smiled. "That if you don't do as Bubuy Alvarez says, you will be out of a job."

Antonio's glance flickered over Bubuy's shoulder. "What about Mr. Mijares?"

Bubuy scoffed. "Mr. Mijares is nothing without me."

The man who had just come out of the building cleared his throat and Bubuy turned around. "Mr. Mijares!" He hid his cigarette behind him and flicked it to the ground.

"I'm nothing without you, Bubuy?" Mr. Mijares said.

"I just meant...I was not..." Bubuy stammered.

A piece of ash floated onto Mr. Mijares' shirt, and he flicked it off. "I guess we'll see, won't we? Because you're fired."

Bubuy's mouth gaped open.

"Oh, and Bubuy," Mr. Mijares said, glancing at the cigarette smoldering on the dirt lot, then at Asim and Ngungot. "On your way out, pick up your trash."

"And that's the whole truth." Antonio took a deep breath and watched Mr. Mijares' reaction. Antonio had just recounted Bubuy's scheme and his role, in Mr. Mijares' office. Mr. Mijares' small eyes in that huge head assessed him.

"Do you realize you've just implicated yourself in a crime?" Mr. Mijares said.

Antonio swallowed. *A crime.* Coming from Mr. Mijares, it sounded like he was due for an execution. "Yes, sir."

"I had high hopes for you, Antonio."

"I'm so very sorry to disappoint you, sir."

"Sorry isn't enough. I'm going to have to fire you, you know that?"

Antonio closed his eyes, then opened them again. "Yes, sir."

"I should have you jailed for this."

Antonio gripped the chair.

"But I won't," Mr. Mijares continued.

"You…you won't?"

Mr. Mijares nodded. "I do expect you to give back the money to my drivers."

At first Antonio saw his hopes dashed to the ground. Then he brightened. "I have a record player, sir. If you'd like…I could sell it to you, and you can keep the money."

Mr. Mijares asked, "What am I to do with a record player?"

"It's valuable, sir."

"Listen. I am in the business of hiring out tricycles, not pawning off musical instruments." Mr. Mijares stood up. "I rescind my offer. Get off my property."

Antonio walked back to his tricycle. With trembling fingers, he took off the little statue of baby Jesus and the rosary. Other drivers watched him, whispering among themselves.

Efren walked up to Antonio and spit in his face. "That's for my daughter, who couldn't take her final exam because she couldn't pay her tuition." He spat again. "And for my son, who got sick from skipping too many meals!"

With the back of his hand, Antonio wiped his face but said nothing. News sure traveled fast.

Someone else came up and spat at his feet. "That's for my wife."

And another. "For my sister!"

And yet another. "For my dog. Who's even more of a man than you!"

Antonio walked past the church, where the priest's car was draped with makeshift stage curtains, and where Mrs. Silva had set up a jar for the Lady of Miracles' altar fund. For a donation of a peso, one could look at the car attacked by the *langbuan*. He walked past Yolly's house, where the window shut tightly at his approach. He stopped by the paddy at his house and watched Papa and Cupid plow the fallow hectares for the next planting. He walked through the forest and up the trail to the top of Mount Dasalin, where the hot wind blew fierce, making his eyes sting and he looked over the ocean and the islands dotting the far horizon. How he wished a ship could take him away from Dasalin.

Raising his eyes to the heavens, he watched the clouds scuttle across.

"I'm sorry," he said, low and soft. Then louder: "I'm sorry!" Over and over, until he fell to his knees and, with his hands, hid his shame.

53

B Y THE TIME Antonio got home, it was nearly midnight. Lamplight spilled out to the yard, where the constable had parked his *karitela*. Antonio took a deep breath, then walked into the open doorway. His parents and Constable Martillo looked up from the *sala*. Antonio glanced at the handcuffs and baton at the constable's hip.

Papa stood up. Antonio flinched at the anger in his eyes. *"Walang-hiya ka talaga!"* he said. *Have you no shame!* He rushed towards Antonio, but Mama ran after him and grabbed his arm. "Don't make the situation worse, Romy," she said.

Papa glared at Antonio, jerked his arm away from Mama and sat back down.

"Antonio," Constable Martillo said. "Do you know why I'm here?"

Antonio nodded.

The constable patted his handcuffs. "This time, this isn't some game young man."

"I know," Antonio said.

"But today you get a reprieve."

Antonio didn't dare hope.

"What do you mean, Constable Martillo?" Mama asked.

"It's customary for me to tell the *baranggay* captain about any criminal activity. Your Tito Oscar intervened on your behalf to keep you out of bars until you are tried by the council."

Papa cursed. "Why does he always have to throw his weight around?"

"Hush Romy," Mama said. "Just be grateful."

Antonio stood there, dazed. "You mean I don't have to go to jail right now?"

When the constable nodded, Mama cried.

Antonio went to his bedroom and closed the door. He sat on his bed and put his head in his hands. "Thank you, Lord," he whispered, "for another chance. I promise not to squander it this time."

A few minutes later, he got up and pulled out the record player.

What next?

He could sell the machine back to Timo but knew Timo wouldn't give him the time of day.

He could destroy it, but that would be a stupid waste.

He could give it to Lolo Sonny. But he still hadn't figured out what to do about the music restrictions at the hospital. What if, once Lolo Sonny had the record player, the staff took it away from him?

And then the solution came to him: keep the player and bring his grandfather home so Antonio could prove once and for all that music made a difference in the old man's behavior. He just needed someone to dress up as a doctor and pretend to discharge Lolo Sonny. Jose, maybe?

No.

No more lies.

He would give the record player to Lolo Sonny. As for paying the other drivers, well, he'd just have to deal with that some other way.

GHOST MOON NIGHT

Antonio pushed the record player back under the bed. Hunger gnawed at his insides, but he decided he would just crawl to bed and skip supper.

A deserved penance.

THE NEXT MORNING, Antonio woke in a panic to the rooster's crow. *I need to go to the station now! Before the bus arrives!* Then he remembered that there was no job for him at the station.

He joined his parents at breakfast. Papa grunted and hid behind the newspaper. Mama had bags under her eyes.

"I'm happy to help you on the farm these next few days, Papa," Antonio said.

Papa looked over the paper. "What did you say?"

"I can help you on the farm."

Papa gave him a searching glance, then nodded. "Meet me at the paddy, then, after breakfast. I want to start early. We're in for a hot day."

"Alright."

The aroma of fried galunggong fish and vinegar with *sili* pepper tantalized Antonio's senses, but he couldn't eat. Not until he cleared something up. His set his fork down. "Mama, Papa, I have to tell you something," he said.

His parents waited for him to speak. Taking a deep breath, he told them about the record player, about how Bubuy offered the "extra" job, and how he'd refused. "Then Bubuy said he knew something about Lolo Sonny," Antonio said. "Something that would ruin his reputation. I couldn't let Bubuy do that. He also promised the record player. So I did it."

Papa looked unimpressed. "What could Bubuy possibly know about Lolo that is worth committing a crime over?"

"He knows about Lolo Sonny's work with the Japanese," Antonio said. "He checked out Lolo Sonny's war record when you pawned off his sword."

Papa's mouth drooped. He glanced quickly at Mama, who sighed and shook her head.

When Mama turned to Antonio, her expression had softened. "Some tough choices," she said. "I'm glad you owned up to your mistake. Many of us never do."

"You coddle him too much," Papa told Mama. "Why, you almost sound as though you approve!"

Mama frowned. "What would *you* have done, Romy?"

Papa didn't answer for a long moment. "It doesn't matter what I would have done…"

"Tell me," Mama persisted.

"I would have said no."

"And left your father to his defenses?"

"If he deserves it, yes."

Mama looked away. "I don't know what's more disappointing, that you answered that way, or that I knew you would."

"What?" Papa asked.

"Never mind."

They ate in silence. Occasionally, Antonio glanced at his scowling father and sad mother. Then he excused himself. He changed into a pair of old, calf-length pants. He grabbed his *salakot* hat and wrapped a torn shirt over his neck and the sides of his face. In the mirror, he saw his reflection. He looked like his father.

To Antonio's surprise, Papa had re-hired Arnell, who was able to work only with his one good hand. He and two other workers his father must have hired, too, nodded to Antonio as he joined them on the fields.

The bright green rice seedlings, about half a foot tall and ready to be thinned, grew thickly in sections of the water-filled paddies. Antonio started working on one corner, pulling up clumps of seedlings, careful not to damage the root. Barefoot, he waded into the waterlogged rice paddy, the mud slipping thickly between his toes. The adjacent paddy had been cleared. The surface reflected the dullish gray morning sky.

Antonio took a handful of seedlings and walked a straight line backwards, planting one at a time into the watery mud. There was a rhythm involved: you bend, you plant, you straighten up, then start over. It was a mindless routine. Under the cloudy sky, he could bear the work.

Then the sun came out.

At first, Antonio kept working, even with his back aching from the repetitive motion. Soon, the heat bore down, merciless and indifferent, upon him.

I promised not to be complain.

For several hours, Antonio kept working until the seedlings covered the paddies in neat rows. He paused, straightened his back and stretched. My, did that hurt.

At Papa's signal, they stopped to eat a simple lunch of rice and fish delivered by Trining.

"Thank you," Antonio said as she handed him a plate.

"I gave you extra fish," she said.

He shielded his eyes from the sun. "Why?"

She sniffed. "To fatten you up before they throw you in jail."

55

FTER A COUPLE more days of helping Papa at the farm, Antonio finally could get away to see Lolo Sonny and deliver the record player.

But when he got to the bus terminal, the clerk was closing out the till. "Sorry, there aren't any tickets left for Nagat," she said.

"I need to bring this to my grandfather," Antonio said, showing the clerk the box containing the record player. "*Please.* He needs it."

"Sorry," she said.

Antonio nodded, and began to turn away.

"Wait," she said. "Are you the young man who gave me a ride one Ghost Moon Night? When no one would stop for me?"

She *did* look very familiar, Antonio thought. "Oh, right!" he said.

"Well, then! Come with me and let's talk to the bus driver."

Antonio followed her to the bus, crossing his fingers. She poked her head into the bus and pointed at Antonio.

"That man is a menace to society!" the bus driver said. "I heard what he did to the tricycle drivers. Will he short me the passage money, too?"

Antonio felt his cheeks burn as the other passengers stared at him.

"*Naku naman,* Kulas," the ticket clerk said. "You are quick to judge. He's not even been brought to the council yet. And already, you are thinking the worst of him."

"They know he's guilty. It's just a matter of assigning a punishment."

"Come on, now. I wouldn't be sticking a limb out for someone if I didn't think they deserved it. He wants to see his grandfather, who is very sick."

A pause. "Very well. Tell him to hurry."

The clerk turned to him, beaming and waving him in. Antonio couldn't help notice the irony that his one good deed of the year paid off.

"Lolo Sonny, it's me, Antonio." He knelt at his grandfather's feet in the hospital room, feeling sick to his stomach.

Lolo Sonny sat hunched over, unresponsive in a rattan wheelchair, his skin sallow. Antonio could smell his soiled pants and body odor.

Antonio turned to the nurse. "How long has he been this way?"

The nurse frowned. "He's not able to care for himself. Had we known you were coming, we could have cleaned him up a bit first."

Yes, you probably would have.

"Lolo Sonny," Antonio said, "we're leaving this place."

"I'm sorry," the nurse said, rushing forward, "what did you say?"

"Don't worry, we're not escaping. I just need to get him outside…please. He needs fresh air." He looked around at the thin mattress, the dark curtains, the faded sheet that had fallen to the floor. "I don't think a plant could even survive here."

The nurse frowned and took her post behind the wheelchair. "We can take him out to the balcony."

"Alright," Antonio said. Carrying the record player in his

arms, he followed the nurse and Lolo Sonny down the hall to a set of double doors. Antonio shielded his eyes to the sunlight when the doors opened. Lolo Sonny, whose eyes were closed, didn't flinch.

The balcony had little puddles of standing water but was otherwise clean. The nurse wheeled the chair to a lone rattan bench and left them.

Antonio set the record player on the bench, on the side nearest to Lolo Sonny. He held up three small records. "Do you want me to pick, Lolo Sonny?"

Lolo Sonny's eyelids moved, but that was all.

"*Kundiman*, Doris Day, or Elvis Presley."

No response.

"Well, I'll put on Elvis then. Jose sent it to me as a joke. He knows I can't stand him. But we'll play it, why not?"

Antonio turned on the player, and Elvis launched into a fast song about a hound dog.

Lolo Sonny's head moved. Left, then right. Eyes still closed. Antonio held his breath, then smiled. "You don't like it, Lolo? Is that what you're trying to tell me?"

Antonio picked up another record, grateful the nurse wasn't interfering. "What about Doris Day?"

This time, Lolo Sonny didn't shake his head. He opened his eyes and looked at Antonio, before closing his eyes again.

Antonio didn't move. He just let Doris Day's playful song run through the chorus twice, and fade out. Lolo Sonny's eyes stayed open longer. His lips formed a smile.

Finally, Antonio put on the traditional *kundiman* song. As guitar music filled the air, Lolo Sonny made noises from the back of his throat.

Antonio lifted the stylus and Lolo Sonny erupted in distressed sounds. "What is it, Lolo Sonny? You don't want to hear it?"

Lolo Sonny moved his hand close to the stylus and knocked it off.

"You want it off?"

Lolo Sonny shook his head.

"Oh," Antonio said. "You want it? You *love* it?"

Lolo Sonny nodded.

Antonio smiled. Over and over, they played the song. He

alternated it with Doris Day but Lolo Sonny kept reaching for the *kundiman.*

"Play…it…" he said. When Antonio did, Lolo Sonny's head bobbed gently to the music. "I…love…this…song."

Behind him, Antonio heard footsteps. The nurse and a doctor walked around them so they were facing each other. "I'm afraid we'll have to ask you to leave," the nurse told Antonio.

"Why?" the doctor asked.

"But Dr. Montoya, he's agitating the patient!"

"The patient looks to be in the best spirits he's been since he arrived." Dr. Montoya smiled at Antonio. "So your grandfather likes music, does he?"

"He loves it."

"Can you leave this player for him? We don't have much in the way of musical appliances."

"I bought this record player for him but was told they're not allowed. Without your permission, that is."

Turning to the nurse, the doctor said, "I see no harm in letting him use the record player."

The nurse blustered. "It would agitate the other patients."

The doctor raised his brows. "Most of them are hard of hearing. It's fine."

After an hour, Antonio left the hospital, feeling like a lot of weight had been lifted off his shoulders. Lolo Sonny not only hummed to the music, he also tapped his foot, a development which the doctor noted.

He turned to catch one last glimpse of the hospital. Some of the patients stood at the window watching him. One window caught his eye. A woman watched him. He recognized those eyes and that wild hair.

Mad Juana's mouth widened into a rotten smile.

Antonio woke with a start to someone shaking his shoulder. "*Dong,*" the bus driver said, calling him by the informal term used for a young man. "*Gising na.*" Wake up.

"Thank you," Antonio said, yawning. He stretched and got off the bus. Along the street, he flagged down a tricycle.

240

It sped on. He flagged another. But it sped on as well. A third tricycle came by, and Antonio just looked at the driver without flagging him. Mang Nando slowed down, then stopped several feet away so Antonio had to run after it.

Mang Nando wasn't smiling. "Need a ride?"

Yolly sat in the sidecar, her expression solemn as well.

"If there's room," Antonio said.

"You can make room, can't you, Yolly?" Mang Nando asked.

Yolly moved over to one side. Antonio took that as a yes and climbed in. He thanked her but she just kept her body turned away from him.

"Where to?" Mang Nando asked.

"My house please," Antonio said.

The tricycle zipped along the expressway. As they passed Mang Fermin's old place, Antonio noticed that the work of clearing the trees was going remarkably fast. The land didn't look dark and forbidding anymore.

He glanced at Yolly's profile. The wind blew her loose hair back. For a change, she didn't have it in a ponytail. "I like your hair that way," he shouted over the roar of the motorcycle and the wind.

She pressed her lips together. But she still wouldn't look at him.

As the tricycle rounded the corner towards Antonio's street, the force of the movement sent him sliding towards Yolly, squishing her against the side of the tricycle. She gave him a dirty look and he held up both hands as he slid back.

"I don't expect you to forgive me," he said, "but I need to tell you I'm really, really sorry. I made a huge mistake."

"Yes, you did," she said. This time, she looked at him and snapped, "My grandfather trusted you. He took you in and taught you what he knew. Yet you repaid him with cruelty and disrespect."

"If you'll give me a chance, I can explain," Antonio said.

She folded her arms. "You have until your house."

So he told her. At first, she sat stiffly, but then her arms dropped. Then she shook her head slowly, and wrapped her arms around herself again.

"I don't expect you to continue being my friend," he said,

"but if you can forgive me…"

She held up a hand. "Just…stop."

"But…"

"I said, stop!" She pointed at something in front of the tricycle. Antonio looked and gasped.

Mang Nando slowed down and stopped at the edge of a crowd who blocked their way on Antonio's street. Flames engulfed his house, and smoke billowed out of it.

56

A BUCKET BRIGADE WORKED to save the hut but even Antonio could tell it was a lost cause. Flames reached out like tentacles while black smoke billowed from the windows. He searched for Mama and found her with some neighbors. His relief turned to terror when he heard her scream Papa's name.

"Mama," he said, when he reached her side.

Mama was weeping. She clutched Antonio's shirt and started to say, "Your father…" but he couldn't make out the rest of the words.

Arnell explained, "Mang Romy went in to get something."

"In our bedroom," Mama sobbed. "I told him…it wasn't worth it…"

Where they stood, Antonio could feel the heat of the flames. He could hardly see the contours of the house.

He heard Mama cry, "Antonio!" as he ran into the hut. He ran into a wall of smoke in the *salas*. His lungs burned. Stripping off his shirt, he held it to his mouth and nose. He staggered to the kitchen, through more smoke and flames, and somehow found his way around the corner to his parents' bedroom.

"Papa!" he shouted, lowering the shirt from his mouth.

Acrid smoke burned into his throat, making him cough as he thrust the shirt over his face again.

He crouched down and could make out furniture – the bed, the dresser, slippers. And there, on the floor, was Papa. Antonio fell to his knees beside his father, smoke billowing in hot, black clouds around them. Antonio dropped his shirt and grabbed Papa's arm, dragging his father's leaden body toward the window. Suddenly, the floor caved under them. He ignored the burning pain on the soles of his feet and shoved at the burning timbers. Grabbing Papa, he hauled him from the hut while people screamed outside. Someone doused him with water, causing him to stagger backwards onto the ground.

He opened his eyes and tried to focus. The sky. Worried faces. Mama, crying. Yolly, too.

His throat hurt as he said, "Papa…?"

Beside him, Papa hadn't moved.

Arnell hauled Antonio up the steps of the hospital. Antonio's legs didn't seem to be working right. It was hard to focus. Ahead of him, neighbors carried Papa through the entrance and down the hall. Antonio didn't know where Mama was, or Yolly. A nurse met him in the small lobby and took him into a room.

"Good luck," Arnell said.

"Thanks," Antonio whispered, his throat raw.

As the nurse helped Antonio onto a hospital bed, he cried out in pain.

"Is my father alive?" he asked.

"He's in bad shape," the nurse said, "but a miracle could still happen." Then she left him.

He looked down the length of his body and shuddered. His clothes were tattered, his skin raw. The soles of his feet were tender to the touch. He had a huge red gash on his leg where a floor beam fell on him.

But he was alive.

A few minutes passed. Where was everyone? Why wasn't anyone telling him anything? He got off the bed and walked gingerly until he reached the door. Yolly was walking down the hall and ran over to him. She covered her mouth, her eyes filling with tears.

"I look terrible, don't I?' Antonio said.

"Your hair looks funny," she said. "You really shouldn't be walking around."

"I need to see my father," he said. "Will you help me find him?"

She gestured down the hall. "I saw your mother down here."

He took a step, and another, then sucked in his breath as pain shot up his foot. Yolly came to his side and let him put an arm over her shoulders.

"I don't need help," he said.

"Don't be stubborn."

He smiled to himself despite the pain. Finally, they made it to a doorway, through which a doctor was leaving. Yolly stood off to the side. Mama saw Antonio and cried out. She put out a hand, stopped short of touching him, and covered her mouth with trembling hands. "Son," she said, choking back a sob.

"How is he?" Antonio asked.

She shook her head.

Antonio made his way to his father's bedside and flinched. With one glance at the horrific ruin of Papa's body, Antonio quickly brought his focus to his father's unrecognizable face.

Papa's lips moved. Antonio placed his ear close to Papa's lips only to hear him moan.

Antonio turned to Mama. "What did he go back for?"

"I don't know," she said.

There was a knock on the door. Father Sebastian stood at the doorway. "I hope I'm not intruding," he said.

"Of course not, Father," Mama said, her voice catching. "Please come in."

Father Sebastian walked to Papa's bedside. "I came as soon as I heard."

"Thank you for coming," Mama said.

Everyone but Father Sebastian left the room to give Papa privacy for his confession. Antonio waited on the floor, outside the room. When the priest came out, his face looked pale. "He's asking for you and your family," he told Antonio.

245

Papa died near midnight. Mama looked like a small child, huddled up on a chair beside Papa, her head bent tight against her chest, her shoulders shaking. She shook her head violently when Antonio touched her arm. Unable to control his own emotions, Antonio staggered into the hall, dropping the weight of his own stinging body against a wall. He felt a gentle touch on his face and opened his eyes.

Yolly whispered, "I'm so sorry."

Yolly's hand moved, carefully avoiding his wounds. It circled behind his neck, gently pulling his head down to her shoulder. She leaned her cheek against his hair, as his breath shuddered and gasped against the pain inside.

When he heard footsteps, he straightened, blinking at a nurse, who looked away as she passed.

As he looked back at Yolly, he noticed her smudged blouse and tired eyes. He sniffed, straightening. "I'm alright. It's late. You should go home."

She stood there a moment, then nodded slowly. "I'll see you again soon," she said, giving him a backward glance as she walked down the hall.

57

ANTONIO STAYED IN the hospital for two days. As they left the hospital, with Mama driving the cart, she told him that Bubuy Alvarez had been arrested for burning their house down. Antonio's entire body tightened and he gripped the seat with aching hands.

"How did they know he did it?" Antonio asked.

"After he boasted his crime over a few beers, someone told Constable Martillo. The *baranggay tanod* searched his house and found gas cans."

Antonio sputtered. "That...that spawn of the devil!" He blinked at the sky, then bowed his head. "The thing is, it's all my fault!"

"You aren't responsible for Bubuy's crime," Mama said.

"I know. But still."

"Here," Mama said, handing him something. "Your father was wearing this when he died. Would you like to have it?"

It was a shell pendant on a chain, like Mang Fermin's. Antonio thanked her and slipped it over his head. For all their disagreements, he loved Papa. He touched the pendant, suddenly overcome with the thought that his father loved him too, in his own gruff way.

The family held a three-day wake, after which they held Papa's burial. Henry, the parish caretaker, orchestrated the lowering of Papa's coffin into a vault paid for by Tito Oscar, and lowered the concrete lid over it. Antonio wondered if Papa was turning over in his grave, being indebted to Tito Oscar until the end.

"I hope you know that you can count on me for help," Tito Oscar told Mama.

"I know," she said. "And I appreciate it."

With their house burned to the ground, Tito Oscar opened his house to them. Mama and Antonio each had a room and the servants didn't treat them any differently. However, their presence seemed to put a strain on his uncle's marriage. Many nights, he heard Tito Oscar and Tita Alice arguing in their bedroom.

Lolo Sonny came to the burial. How much better he looked! Gone was the vague expression. He smiled sweetly when spoken to. He even seemed to understand who the burial was for and wiped away tears from his face with a trembling hand. He was doing so well, the family was able to convince the doctor to discharge him on a probationary status. Trining offered to listen from the kitchen and change the records when they were done playing. Tito Oscar slipped Antonio money for more records.

Mang Nando and Yolly came to the burial. Yolly came to him, giving him a hug that was a second longer than normal. She withdrew slowly, watching his face, giving him the tiniest, compressed smile, before moving away.

"I'll take Lolo Sonny home," Tito Oscar offered. "Would you like a ride, Margarita? Antonio?"

"Go ahead," Antonio told Mama. "I'll walk home."

"Can I stay with you?" Tito Oscar's daughter Irene asked Antonio.

"No, but thanks," Antonio said. When he saw his cousin's

248

mouth droop, he said, more gently, "I just want to be alone for a little bit, alright?"

Irene nodded. "Alright."

Antonio heard the sound of car doors opening and closing, the engine rumbling and the car pulling away.

Finally, he was alone. There had been too many people crowding him lately, people who claimed to know Papa.

"I talked to him once," a man said. "We were both lined up at the cockfight."

"He would always wave at me on the way to the cockfight," a woman said. "What a friendly man."

A man recalled, "He and I were friends in school. But it's been years since I talked to him."

Sometimes, Antonio wondered if he ever got to know Papa beyond being a farmer, beyond his gambling vice. He wished he could have asked him what life was like for him as a boy.

But now he would never know.

A gust of wind stirred the acacia leaves above him. Antonio heard someone whisper his name. If this was a message from the afterlife, he wanted to hear it. He wanted to pass a message of his own.

"Papa?" he called out.

No answer. Just a mournful wind that swept across the deserted graveyard. He climbed on Papa's vault and lay on it, facing the canopy of tree limbs that swayed in the wind.

"Papa, here I am," he said, gripping the sides of Papa's vault. "Forgive me."

The whisper came again, this time sounding more desperate. *Antonio! Save me!*

"Where are you?" Antonio sat up and looked wildly around.

Somewhere deep, hideous...Lord forgive me!

Silence thrummed through the graveyard, sudden and intense. No other whispers came, even though Antonio called Papa's name and waited for a reply. He kept calling out until his voice got hoarse. Until the dark of night descended upon him and upon the cemetery's city of souls.

58

TWO WEEKS LATER, in the gathering room at the *baranggay* hall, the Dasalin council called a meeting to decide Antonio's fate.

Bubuy had already been tried, convicted and sentenced. Antonio attended Bubuy's hearing, where the man was unrepentant to the last.

Antonio's uncle, Tito Oscar, who headed the council, had to excuse himself from discussing and voting on Antonio's case. He sat beside Mama in the audience as people filed into two rows of benches. The rest had to stand where they could.

As Antonio came in, he saw Mr. Mijares and recognized many tricycle drivers in the audience. They all had grim expressions, except for Mang Nando, who gave him a reassuring nod. Yolly and Father Sebastian did, too. He nodded, grateful to see friendly faces. Antonio sat on a chair and faced the rest of the council members, who included Tandang Lino and Mr. Sandoval, the store owner.

Mr. Sandoval started the meeting. "Antonio Pulido, a charge of extortion and theft has been leveled against you. We have several villagers willing to testify today."

One by one, tricycle drivers came up, telling of Antonio's "heartlessness and greed."

"What do you have to say for yourself?" Mr. Sandoval said.

"I did commit that crime, sir," Antonio said. "Out of love for my Lolo Sonny."

The room erupted into whispers. Mr. Sandoval pounded the table with his fist. "Explain yourself."

"Bubuy blackmailed me," Antonio said.

The room erupted into whispers and guffaws.

"What do you mean?" Mr. Sandoval said.

Antonio glanced at the people behind him, at the faces with so many different expressions. He drew a breath and said, "May I tell you in private?"

Mr. Sandoval frowned, but motioned the council over. They stepped into the corner, where Antonio told them everything.

At last it was done. The council sent him back and huddled, talking in low tones, frowning in Antonio's direction. Then they moved back.

Mr. Sandoval's expression was pensive. He asked, "Does anyone wish to vouch for Antonio's character? Anyone but his family, that is."

"I will."

Everyone turned to see Father Sebastian stand. Antonio smiled at him.

"I first met Antonio when I arrived in Dasalin," Father Sebastian said. "He picked me up and was friendly and respectful. Ever since, he has impressed me with his goodness. As he himself explained, he had a compelling reason to deviate from his honorable character."

"Honorable!" someone scoffed.

"Yes." Father Sebastian swiveled towards the voice. "Honorable. I've seen him perform acts of service for others. I've known him to rescue a girl from *langbuan*. He nearly got killed saving his father from a fire. Those acts are a mark of a strong character, someone who puts others above himself!"

Silence descended on the council. They tapped their fingers on the table and rubbed their chins. They asked a few more questions. Antonio answered them as truthfully as he could.

Mr. Sandoval surveyed the room. "Any other comments before the council votes on this?"

Tandang Lino said, "May I make an observation?"

Mr. Sandoval gestured towards the older man. "Of course."

"The fruit doesn't fall far from the tree," Tandang Lino said.

Antonio's heart sank.

Tandang Lino, his mouth quivering, continued. "In life, Romy Pulido gambled. He left debts unpaid. If his bad habits had only been curbed early on in life, he wouldn't have descended into a lifestyle of deceit and avarice." He pointed a shaking finger at Antonio. "Let this young man off easily, and you won't have taught him a lesson. He will carry this bad behavior through the rest of his life."

"Thank you, Tandang Lino," Mr. Sandoval said. "Anyone else?"

When no one raised their hand, the council followed Tandang Lino to another room. Antonio heard conversation swirl around and about him. He looked over his shoulder and made eye contact with Yolly. She smiled, and he felt better.

However this turns out, everything will be okay.

After a half hour, the council returned with hard-to-read expressions. Antonio clenched his fists so hard, his nails dug into his flesh.

Mang Sandoval cleared his throat and faced the audience. "By a vote of 3-2, the council has sentenced Antonio Pulido to two years of debtors' prison unless he is able to pay back all of the money he owes the other drivers."

Pandemonium erupted once again.

All of the money! How could he even earn the money when he would be behind bars? And Mama! What will happen to her? Who will help her with the farm?

These thoughts bombarded Antonio's mind as Constable Martillo led him away in handcuffs.

59

THE STENCH OF urine made Antonio's eyes water. He had a prison cell with just enough room for a bunk bed, about the same width of two people abreast on the side, and a smelly latrine in the corner. No one else shared the cell with him. Three times a day, a guard marched out the dozen or so inmates to a mess hall to eat the same unappetizing food. Every other day, the prisoners bathed in a communal area with *tabo* cans and big barrels of water.

On the third day, a visitor came to see Antonio. After a clanging and opening of locks, Father Sebastian appeared outside his jail cell. The guard unlocked the door, letting the priest step in.

"Do you like my accommodations?" Antonio said, bowing and making a sweeping gesture with his hand.

Father Sebastian smiled and sat on the edge of the woven mat that covered the lower bunk bed. "This is luxurious indeed. Are you well?"

"Under the circumstances, yes."

"I saw your mother at church. She asked me to offer a Mass for you, and I did."

"That's very kind of you, Father Sebastian. Is she alright?"
The priest nodded. "She strikes me as a strong woman, but
I think all her recent losses have brought her down."

"I know," Antonio whispered, guilt washing over him.

"I've been mulling things over," Father Sebastian said. "It
will take some doing, getting the parish approval, for instance.
But I will propose that you get the altar fund to pay your debts."

"The altar fund! That's very generous, Father, but no one
will agree. Besides everything else, they think I stole the altar
fund before."

"You and I know you didn't steal it," the priest said quietly.
"It will hinge upon one condition, of course."

"And that is...?"

"That you destroy the *langbuan*."

For a long moment, Antonio stared. "Father Sebastian, with
due respect, that sounds like a joke."

"About the altar fund? I'm serious."

"But getting rid of the *langbuan*!" Antonio shook his head.
"That's impossible."

"Only because no one's ever succeeded before."

"I have no idea how to even go about that."

In the dim cell light, the priest's eyes glimmered. "You've
encountered them enough. You know their weaknesses and
strengths. You can figure something out." Father Sebastian
put a hand on his shoulder. "Last Ghost Moon Night, as I shut
the church door, I saw the *langbuan*. They looked like a legion
of soldiers going to battle. Everyone says they're growing in
numbers and I think they're right. We cannot let them win."

Slowly, Antonio nodded, realizing that even when he
finished his jail term, unless he did something to change
people's minds about him, there would be no life for him in
Dasalin. For all the times he'd wished otherwise, he now knew.
He wanted to go home, to be with his mother, to at least attempt
to set things right. Perhaps he could give her a reason to lift her
chin.

"You're right, Father," he said. "If the parish will give me
another chance, I will do my best to destroy the *langbuan*. Not
just to pay off my debts. Not just to gain my freedom. I'll do it
for my mother and for other families. For Yolly."

Father Sebastian smiled. "Thank you. I'll help you in

whatever way I can."

When the priest left, Antonio stood by the cell window, looked at the quarter moon through the bars. Like clockwork, this town ate, worked, played, and worshipped around Ghost Moon Night. What would life be like without *langbuan*?

He remembered receiving a letter from Jose in Manila. "On Ghost Moon Night," Jose wrote, "I huddled inside my apartment, shutting my window. Some guys came over, inviting me to a party and I looked at them like they lost their minds. Until I realized there were no *langbuan* in Manila. I could open my windows and doors and only the mosquitoes could come in. I walked out of my apartment like a free man, making *tambay* at the sidewalk until dawn and the police told us to go home."

At least Antonio could die trying to make a difference. He lay down, folding his arms behind his head.

60

AFTER SUNDAY'S MASS, Father Sebastian asked Mrs. Silva to gather everyone in the parish commons.

"How much money do we have in the altar fund, Mrs. Silva?" Father Sebastian asked.

She told him a number and then asked, "Why, Father Sebastian?"

"I shall explain it shortly." To the crowd, he said, "I have been thinking and praying about the altar fund. Although I truly have appreciated all that Mrs. Silva has done to raise the amount, I don't think we should use it for a new altar."

"What?" Mrs. Silva said, sitting up straight.

"I'd like to propose that the funds be used to get rid of the *langbuan* instead."

A frenzied murmur rippled through the room, with Mrs. Silva being the loudest. "When we collected that money, Father Sebastian, we told everyone that it would go towards a new altar. We can't change the designation now!"

"It was allotted for the altar." Father Sebastian nodded. "But I have since realized that protecting the lives of our villagers is far more important than a marble altar."

GHOST MOON NIGHT

Mrs. Silva fanned herself vigorously. "I respectfully disagree. Besides, how do you propose we use the altar fund money to get rid of the *langbuan*?"

"Use it as a reward for the person who successfully does it," the priest said. "As a reward. An incentive."

Mrs. Silva scowled, but said nothing.

Nando Nakpil raised his hand. "I know how nice it would be to have a new altar, Mrs. Silva. But my daughter-in-law would still be alive were it not for those monsters."

Beside him, Yolly's expression was grim.

Mrs. Mijares raised her hand. "My sister died because of them."

Margarita Pulido, Antonio's mother, turned at her seat. "Mine did, too."

"Who here hasn't been touched by this curse in some way or another?" Father Sebastian asked. "Who's lost a loved one on Ghost Moon Night?"

Hands shot up. They mentioned a brother, a child, a grandfather. Mrs. Silva's rigid posture softened, like a plant drooping from lack of water.

"Timo will do it!" Mr. Sandoval said.

"No, I won't!" his son said, to laughter.

"But think of the reward money!" his father said.

"Killing the *langbuan*?" Timo made a face. "No, thanks!"

A few other people volunteered, but the offers were quickly rescinded when their loved ones protested.

Tandang Lino lifted his cane. "It's impossible. Can you blame these people for not coming forward?"

"I have someone in mind," the priest announced. "Someone who has already said they would do it."

"Who?" Tandang Lino asked.

"Antonio Pulido."

Mrs. Pulido and Father Sebastian exchanged glances. Right after visiting Antonio, Father Sebastian told her of his plan. At first she looked sick at the thought. But then she went to see Antonio, and gave her blessing.

"Absolutely not!" Mrs. Silva said. "He's a thief and a crook!"

"He didn't steal it. I received a confession from the true thief." Father Sebastian glanced down, remembering Romy Pulido's deathbed confession.

257

"Even if he didn't," Mrs. Silva said, "he stole money from the tricycle drivers."

"So he did. If you'll just give him another chance..."

"After he serves his time," Tandang Lino said.

"And after the rest of our village is wiped out by these monsters?" Father Sebastian asked. "By then it will be too late."

The parishioners looked at each other. Many murmured in agreement. Tandang Lino looked old, all of a sudden, and Father Sebastian felt sorry for him.

"I won't live much longer," Tandang Lino said. "I agree with Father Sebastian. It's time to band together to destroy the *langbuan*."

Their glances locked. Father Sebastian nodded gratefully.

"Justice must be served," Tandang Lino said. "Antonio Pulido must pay for his crime. What better way than to break our curse?"

The audience murmured their agreement. Father Sebastian said a silent prayer of thanks.

61

CONSTABLE MARTILLO UNLOCKED Antonio's handcuffs and gave him a few centavos for tricycle fare.

"Thank you," Antonio said.

"You can enjoy your freedom if you abide by the following conditions," the constable said. "You are free until Ghost Moon Night. If you destroy the *langbuan*, you will be a rich man. If you don't, you'll either be dead or back in prison."

How bright his future was, Antonio decided.

Using the centavos the constable gave him, Antonio took a tricycle down to Tito Oscar's house. Along the way, he saw that Mang Fermin's orchard had almost entirely been cleared, save for just a clump of trees. Beyond the clearing, Antonio could see the ocean and the dusky blue outline of mountains on distant islands.

The tricycle dropped him off and he passed through Tito Oscar's gate. Cupid bellowed his greeting loudly from his pen. Antonio walked over and scratched him on his head.

Mama came out of the house and embraced Antonio tightly. "I knew as soon as I heard Cupid that you were home. Welcome back, son."

As they walked back to the house, Mama told him that she was starting to earn money by sewing again. A neighbor gave her an old sewing machine that was just gathering dust.

"Good. And how about Lolo? How is he?"

"Much, much better." Mama led him to a room near the kitchen, where Lolo Sonny listened to the record player, his foot tapping to *kundiman* guitar music. Antonio knelt on the floor beside Lolo Sonny and pressed the old man's hand to his forehead.

"Hello, Lolo," Antonio said, his voice catching in his throat.

Lolo Sonny beamed. Then he went back to tapping.

"The music makes a huge difference," Mama said.

"I know."

Then she warned him to be respectful of Tito Oscar's house and to always pick up after himself. "Alice is unhappy with us being here," she said. "It's hard sharing a kitchen when you're a woman. I've learned to just bite my tongue. I wish...ah, but I don't want to be ungrateful."

"What do you wish?"

"That I could earn enough money to buy another house," she said.

"When I destroy the *langbuan*," Antonio vowed, "I'll build you another house, Mama. I'll work and save and do everything I can until you have a home again."

Mama touched his cheek. "Worry about the *langbuan* first."

Then she added, "Mang Nando, Tandang Lino and Tito Oscar offered to support you in whatever way they can. And Yolly, too."

Antonio cocked his head. *Mama, matchmaking!* But Mama only looked at him innocently.

And so it was that two hours later, Antonio found himself standing on the road in front of Tandang Lino's fence. The bench under the shade tree was empty.

He approached the door and said, "*Tao po!*" but no one answered. He tried it three more times.

Maybe he isn't home.

As he turned to leave, a crotchety voice said, "What do you want?"

"I came to bring you some *malagkit*," Antonio said, glad for the ruse. His mother said it would break the ice, but looking at

GHOST MOON NIGHT

Tandang Lino, he knew he would be thawing an iceberg.

Tandang Lino glared at him, then shuffled out through the dirt courtyard and to his bench under the shade tree. He ate two pieces of the sticky rice dessert, his dentures clacking together, then said, "Well?"

"Well what, Tandang Lino?" Antonio said.

"Aren't you going to ask me how to get rid of the *langbuan*?"

Antonio nodded. "How?"

"I don't know." He cackled, then took another bite of *malagkit*. He chewed for so long that Antonio wanted to scream.

"But I know someone who might," the old man said, finally. "Juana Abad."

"Mad Juana? But she's insane!"

"She very well may be, but her brother used to boast that he held a secret to fighting off the *langbuan*. Unfortunately, he took that secret to his grave. For years, people tried to pry that information from him. He was as stingy with the secret as he was with his mabolos."

"Tell your mother her *malagkit* was very good," Tandang Lino said in parting. "And go visit Mad Juana!"

"Thank you," Antonio said, knowing that that was a very long shot. He'd have to think about it.

He next went to Tito Oscar. Antonio asked him if he knew of any attempts in the past to break the curse, but Tito Oscar merely shook his head. "You can see for yourself, Antonio, but the archives at the town plaza don't contain any helpful information. I've already looked, when I was a new *baranggay captain*, wet behind the ears."

"Just the same," Antonio said, "I'd like to look."

"Be my guest."

Antonio pored over the dusty tomes and, like his uncle said, found nothing.

Finally, Antonio went to Mang Nando, who was parked at the depot, waiting for passengers. "I don't have any information," he said, "but if I can give you a ride on my tricycle, just let me know."

"Thank you!"

Antonio hesitated, before asking after Yolly. Mang Nando smiled. "Working at the bank, as usual."

261

62

ANTONIO POSTED A letter to Jose in the mail about getting Mang Isidro's journal, then headed out to find Yolly. The small bank sat on a quiet corner near the depot. He recognized the two tellers. They had gone to his school a few years before.

"I'm looking for Yolly Nakpil," he said.

"She's not here," one teller said, crossing her arms in front of her chest.

"Yes, she is," the other one said, smiling.

"Well, she's not in the bank," the curt one said.

"Walk outside and go around to the back," the friendly one said. As he walked out the door, he heard the curt teller say, "Wasn't that Antonio Pulido, the one who stole from the tricycle drivers?"

"Yes," the friendly one said, "but he did it for his grandfather…"

Following their directions, he wondered what Yolly did for work in the back lot. And then he saw her. She stood on a step stool, a rag in her hand, washing windows. She frowned in concentration and tendrils escaped a rubber band that held her hair back. Suddenly, she became aware of his presence.

Turning her head, her eyes widened. She pushed a lock of hair from her forehead.

"So this is where you work," he said.

She nodded. "Yes, and isn't it glamorous?"

"It's honest work," he said.

She smiled, then jumped off the step stool, rag in hand. "You're out of jail."

"Speaking of dishonest work, yes."

"I hear you have a big job ahead of you."

"That's why I came, to ask you if you could help me."

She raised an eyebrow. "Help you do what?"

"I need to go to the hospital at Nagat and ask Mad Juana some questions. Can you come with me? I was planning on taking the bus."

"Why are you asking me?"

"I thought maybe you could help make her feel comfortable, since you're a girl."

She cocked her head and looked at him. "Is that the only reason?"

"What other reason is there?"

"Could it be you're scared?"

"Of course not!"

"I agree on one condition," Yolly said.

"What?"

"I want the window seat."

She got her window seat. The following Friday, Antonio sat beside her, feeling like every bone in his body rattled on the thinly padded benches. Every few minutes, he caught a whiff of exhaust and a blast of hot air from the window which didn't want to open all the way.

"Did you ever think of going to college?" Antonio asked. "You were the smartest girl in school."

She shrugged. "Sure. But I can't just leave my grandfather. I'm all he has. Maybe someday..."

"I don't know if I could leave my mother, too."

A sampaguita flower garland vendor boarded the bus and

held a garland of tiny, delicate –looking yellow-white flowers to Antonio's nose, making him sneeze. "For your *novia*," the vendor said.

"I'm not his girlfriend," Yolly corrected him.

Antonio felt in his pocket for change leftover from bus fare Mama gave him. He took a coin out, bought a garland and handed it to Yolly. "Here. You can have one anyway."

She took the garland from him and hung it from a hook above her window. "Thanks," she said, smiling.

As the bus ride continued, Yolly's eyelids drooped, and she fell asleep. Her cheek leaned precariously towards his shoulder, and when it made contact, she sat up as though scalded.

After a few minutes, she fell asleep again. This time, when her head settled against his shoulder, she didn't wake up. Her face in repose looked vulnerable and soft. If he leaned forward just a little, his lips could touch hers.

Antonio swallowed and looked away.

An hour later, the bus jolted to a stop at Nagat. Yolly woke up and pushed away from him. "Sorry," she said.

"You had better be," he teased. "You said you wanted the window seat. A pillow is extra."

She got up to leave, and he pointed at the garland. "Don't you want your flower?"

"I was just going to leave it."

"Why?" He took the garland and gently put it over her head like a necklace. "It's pretty." She raised her eyes to his, and they stepped away from each other self-consciously.

At the hospital, Antonio asked to see Mad Juana. The nurse asked, "Are you family?"

Antonio said no and Yolly said yes at the same time.

The nurse frowned. "Well, which is it?"

"I'm her niece," Yolly said. The nurse pointed to a line in a ledger. "Please sign," she said, and Yolly signed with a flourish.

"I thought you were against dishonesty," Antonio whispered as they followed the nurse down the hall.

"Do you really think she'd have let us see Mad Juana if we

weren't family?"

"Probably not," Antonio conceded.

"That's what I thought."

"Still."

"Oh, stop fussing. Just ask her what you need and let's leave this place."

The nurse unlocked a door, went through a hallway, and unlocked another door. Finally, she stopped in front of a room and unlocked it, the sound of the turning lock echoing in the hallway.

"I'll leave the door locked but I'll just be out here, if you need me," the nurse said.

63

ANTONIO'S EYES WERE immediately drawn to the seashell pendant hanging from Mad Juana's neck. When he looked in her eyes, recognition glimmered in them.

"You have a necklace," she said, "just like mine." She held up her pendant, and, true enough, they were exactly the same.

Mad Juana peered past a cloud of snarled hair, her gaze shifting from him to Yolly and back. "Who are you?"

"I'm Antonio Pulido, and this is Yolly Nakpil."

"Don't you know to take off your hat in the presence of royalty?" Mad Juana said.

He began to say, "But I'm not wearing…"

Yolly jabbed him in the ribs. "Alright," she said, taking off an imaginary hat. He followed suit.

"That's better," Mad Juana said. "Have you seen my husband?"

"Who's your husband?" Yolly asked.

"Prince Rainier of Monaco."

Yolly shook her head. "Not yet."

"He's always late." Mad Juana folded her arms and brooded.

"He said for you to go ahead and tell us about the *langbuan*,"

Antonio prompted her.

"Do you have to be so brash?" Yolly whispered to him.

"We haven't the whole day to visit about royalty," he whispered back. Loudly, he asked Mad Juana: "Do you remember that day when you saw the *langbuan*?"

In reply, Mad Juana slammed her hands down on her metal bed. The clanging sound echoed throughout the room.

"There," Yolly muttered, "you've upset her."

The nurse rushed in. "What's wrong?"

"Nothing," Antonio assured her. Fortunately, Mad Juana sat there, calm as can be, twirling her hair.

When the nurse left, Yolly asked, "Describe the day you saw the *langbuan*."

"Brash," he whispered.

"It's so dark here," Mad Juana whimpered.

"Where are you?" Yolly asked.

"In a cave. The others have left me."

"Who are the others?"

"Fermin and Romy," she said.

"Romy?" Antonio asked, surprised.

"It's their idea of a funny joke. But it's not funny." She moaned.

"What do you see?" Antonio asked.

For a long moment, Mad Juana didn't speak. When she did, her voice sounded strangled. "They're coming, the *langbuan* are coming. I can hear their wings. There are so many of them. They haven't seen me yet. I see the devil himself. I have a good hiding place, but will they see me? Fermin says they wouldn't, not with the amulet."

"What amulet?"

Mad Juana raised her head and pulled at the necklace around her neck. "This."

Yolly and Antonio exchanged glances. "What does it do?" Yolly asked.

"It protects you from the *langbuan*."

Antonio remembered the pendant, hanging around his neck

under his shirt. "What about destroying the *langbuan*?"

"Fermin knows, but he won't tell me."

"We need to get that amulet," Antonio whispered to Yolly. "It won't do her any good here."

Yolly looked around, then curtseyed to Mad Juana. "Princess, I have a gift for you."

Mad Juana flashed her rotten teeth. "You do?"

"Yes, a garland." Yolly took off the sampaguita garland from her neck. "Would you like a trade? Your necklace for this one."

"No," Mad Juana said, her eyes widening as Yolly approached her.

Yolly froze.

"*I* will take it off," Mad Juana said. "Princesses cannot have commoners touch them."

"Of course," Yolly said. The exchange was done and Yolly gave Antonio the amulet. He slipped it in his pocket.

Mad Juana cowered to the corner and covered her head with her arms. "They're all over me, flying, clawing. Help, oh please help!"

"Who are? The *langbuan*?" He wanted to quiet her down before the nurse noticed. "It's alright. You're out of the cave now."

Mad Juana shrank back. "You!" she spat out. "Do you want to murder me too, like you did my brother? Get your hands off me."

"What is she talking about?" Yolly said.

"I don't know," Antonio said.

"Fermin let you into the orchard, all these years," Mad Juana said. "Why did you have to kill him, *Romy*? And now, you've come for me?"

Yolly gasped while Antonio felt like he'd just been punched in the gut.

Without warning, Mad Juana lunged forward, slapping at him. He warded her off with his arms, then kicked when he felt her teeth bite his flesh. Yolly screamed for her to get off and pulled Mad Juana by the hair.

Mad Juana fell backwards in a heap, taking Yolly with her. The nurse ran in and skidded to a stop but not soon enough, as she tripped over Antonio.

"I need to talk to her some more," he said, but the nurse began to push them out the door.

"The only talking you'll do is to the police, if you don't get out," she said.

"Juana bit you good," Yolly said on the bus, looking at Antonio's arm that was turning an ugly shade of purple.

"With my luck, she's rabid."

"I don't think you could be more insane than you already are." Yolly looked out the window, then back at him. "I'm sorry about what she said about your father." She paused and then said, "You don't think it's true, do you?"

He shook his head, then muttered, "I don't know anymore. The scary thing is, the signs were there that he might have. But why? Did he do it for me? Because Mang Fermin got mad at me earlier that week and shot at me? Oh, this is so confusing."

"Juana *is* mad," Yolly said. "She could be wrong..."

"I hope so."

"Can I see the amulet?" she asked. He handed it to her. She inspected it and gave it back.

"What did she mean when she said she 'let him in the orchard'?"

"Probably just being friends, all these years," Antonio guessed.

"Did you get the answers you were hoping for?"

"We have amulets. That switch was brilliant, by the way. That's a start. But I still don't know what Mang Fermin knew. Unless..."

"Unless what?"

"Unless he wrote something in his journal." He paused. "I wrote to Jose asking him if he could help me. I need him to get the journal from Mang Fermin's cousin and bring it to me."

"Why don't you just fetch it from Manila?"

"I don't have money for the bus fare. Anything I earn from the farm will go to the drivers. Including your grandfather."

Yolly arched an eyebrow. "You sound...noble."

"After Papa died," he said, "I decided that money isn't

269

everything. Papa thought it was, and look what happened to him."

"Yes," Yolly said. "Just ask Grace if she can live without money."

"Are you jealous of Grace?" he teased.

"Of course not!" she said.

"You know," he said softly, "I'm glad *you* came with me on this adventure instead of Grace."

Yolly blushed a lovely shade of pink.

64

WITH EACH NEW day, Antonio savored his freedom. In the evenings after farming, he sat in Tito Oscar's *salas* listening to music with Lolo Sonny. The old man's eyes sparkled again and he could say more complete sentences.

Even though there were tense moments with Tita Alice, mostly over the use of the kitchen, life at Tito Oscar's followed a predictable routine. As Tito Oscar got ready to leave for work, Irene followed Antonio around. They'd wave to her father at the driveway, and Irene would ask, "What are you doing today, Antonio?"

"First thing," Trining interrupted one day, "is breakfast." They helped Lolo Sonny into the kitchen and sat down to a breakfast of *longganisa* sausage and fried rice. Mama, Tita Alice and Christine were already seated. Trining came in with one of Tita Alice's servants and served the food.

"I hear you're probing around for something to defeat the *langbuan*," Trining said. "I know something."

"Why didn't you say so in the first place?" Antonio said.

"You didn't ask!" Trining retorted

"Please, Trining," Tita Alice said, "do we have to talk about

JEWEL ALLEN

those monsters at the table?"

"Sorry, *Ate*." Then she whispered to Antonio, "I'll talk to you later."

Antonio found Trining later, in the *batalan*, helping Tito Oscar's maids grate coconut into a basin.

"You know something about the *langbuan*?" Antonio said.

"I was a little girl," Trining said, "I had just moved to Dasalin. My aunt and uncle took me in because my mother was too sick to care for me. One day, my aunt told me to stay inside from dusk until dawn."

"On Ghost Moon Night?" Antonio asked.

"Yes." Trining nodded. "And so I did. I waited until dawn to open my window. Well, maybe a few minutes too early, as it was still dark. My uncle's house faced Mount Dasalin. There was enough light I could make out the mountainside. When I opened the window, I thought there was a mudslide on the mountain. The dirt looked like it was moving. But it wasn't dirt."

"What was it?" he asked.

"I saw a horde of *langbuan* turn into monkeys and disappear into the trees right by the house," Trining said.

"Monkeys." Antonio stared. "But that is absurd. Why would they go into the monkeys' bodies?"

"My uncle explained that the *langbuan* need hosts so they can keep their souls safe until the next Ghost Moon Night." She paused. "What was very strange about this whole thing was that, the following year, an epidemic wiped out the monkeys on Mount Dasalin. So the question is, where do they dwell now? That, no one has been able to figure out. Ever since, I've tried to catch a glimpse of *langbuan* on the mountains, but I haven't seen anything."

After this conversation, Antonio took stock of what he knew:

1. The *langbuan* needed an animal host so that their souls could come to life again the following Ghost Moon Night.
2. His shell amulet would protect him from the *langbuan*.
3. He just needed to know how to destroy them once he found their home.

Mang Fermin knew how. If only Jose could get his journal

to him soon!

Antonio had been calling a lot from the telephone at Aling Dona's restaurant. Sometimes, he couldn't understand Jose, the connection was so poor. Finally, he extracted Jose's promise that he would deliver it in person because there wasn't time to mail it.

"Luckily for you," Jose said, "One of my frat brothers here is going home to his province, and he'll give me a ride partway."

"What, and leave you along the expressway?" Antonio teased.

"I *could* walk, our drills are keeping me in good shape. But I'll take the bus home, thank you."

Antonio's cousin Irene patted his shoulder. "You'll destroy the *langbuan*," she said. "I know you can."

"I sure hope so," Antonio said. He liked being a free man.

65

October
Six hours before Ghost Moon Night

I N THE HIGHLY unlikely chance that he could have forgotten, everyone reminded Antonio it was Ghost Moon Night. From Trining telling him to eat a good breakfast so he could fight, to Irene offering to wash Cupid so he could dazzle the monsters, and to Tito Oscar asking if Antonio wanted to borrow his car (which Antonio declined because he only knew how to drive a tricycle, not a car).

Today was the day!

His stomach clenched. All he had in his favor were two amulets and the knowledge that the *langbuan* liked to inhabit animals during their off-times.

A little before noon, he stopped by the parish to talk to Father Sebastian. The priest had sent a message for Antonio to see him before the noonday Mass.

Antonio tried to be upbeat describing what he knew about the *langbuan.* "But honestly," he admitted, "until I see Mang Fermin's journal, I am not sure I have enough information."

Father Sebastian's eyes twinkled. "What if I tell you I know where the *langbuan* lair is?"

"You do?" Antonio said, almost falling off his chair.

"Do you know Dennis Ursua?"

Antonio nodded. He was one of the parishioners.

"He dug holes in a cave to earn money," Father Sebastian said. "He overheard the man who hired him talking to someone about how the cave was expressly being prepared so the *langbuan* could stay in it."

Antonio felt a prickle of excitement. "Who hired him?"

"It is a strange name, one I've never heard before."

"Do you believe Mang Dennis?"

"He's one of my most faithful parishioners. So yes, I do."

Energy surged through Antonio's body. "I need to know where this cave is."

"I believe he's waiting for Mass at the chapel," Father Sebastian said. "Let me call him in."

Antonio drove Cupid and the cart to the bus depot and waited for Jose. When the bus arrived, Antonio met Jose at the door. Jose descended the bus steps in a pair of rubber shoes, knee-high socks, pants as wide as a tent, and a shirt in a bright shade of orange. He looked the same, only slightly taller. And ready to join the circus.

The first thing Jose said was, "I'm sorry about your father." The second was, "Your hair looks like spiky durian," referring to the green, smelly fruit. "Are you out of pomade?"

It was good to have Jose back.

On the cart-ride home, Antonio listened politely as Jose told him about college, Grace, cafeteria food, fraternities, Grace, basketball, Grace, and roommates. It was a good thing Antonio was over Grace or he might have pounded his friend a bit.

"But enough of that," Jose said. "Did you want this?" He held up Mang Fermin's journal.

Jose drove the cart while Antonio flipped through the journal. The entries were sparse enough that by the time they reached Jose's house, he had read them all. It was hard to believe that Mang Fermin wrote them. Some were quotes to live by.

Some were observations on life and how to deal with problems.

Antonio sighed and closed the book. As he did so, a piece of paper fluttered from the back. He picked it up and read it, his eyes widening.

"Jose," he said. "I think I've got something here!"

"What?"

"Instructions for Ghost Moon Night," Antonio read. "Wear the amulet at all times. Don't share it with anyone. They are most vulnerable during the last few minutes before dawn. Keep the lair unobstructed so that the *langbuan* can return safely. Establish a habitat for the animal host to ensure their long life."

"The bats!" Antonio and Jose said in unison.

"But without the mabolo trees," Jose wondered aloud, "where are the bats – and the *langbuan* – roosting?"

"As it happens, Father Sebastian's caretaker knows where the lair is." Antonio told Jose about Dennis Ursua.

"Good!" Then Jose scratched his head. "But why did Mang Fermin want to protect the *langbuan*?"

"Because he's a mean man with nothing better to do?"

"Well, besides that. What did he get out of them?"

Antonio shrugged. "I can't even begin to guess. The journal doesn't say why."

Jose pulled up in front of his house and handed the reins back to Antonio.

"Are you coming with me tonight?" Antonio asked.

"I'm kind of busy," Jose said.

"Jose."

"I don't know..."

"I'll give you an amulet to wear. You'll be protected."

They went back and forth for a while until, finally, Jose threw his hands in the air. "Oh. Alright. But I think it's a bad idea."

"You're amazing! Bring a lantern. I'll come by for you at 4:30."

"In the morning?" Jose groaned. "Tell me, how will we destroy this *langbuan* lair?"

"I'll talk to Arnell. He'll get me some dynamite."

"What?" Jose said. "The fool who blew his hand up will help us? And isn't dynamite illegal?"

"I already cleared it with Constable Martillo. Do you have

any other ideas?" When Jose shook his head, Antonio said, "I didn't think so."

"I'll see you at 4:30," Jose said. "No earlier. And bring the amulets."

66

4:20 a.m., same Ghost Moon Night

AFTER A SLEEPLESS night, Antonio opened Tito Oscar's front door and stepped over the threshold. Patting the shell amulet dangling from his neck, he shut the door. He went to Cupid's pen, calling him over. His faithful old water buffalo lumbered to him and snorted into his outstretched hand. "Ready, Cupid?" Antonio asked. Cupid snorted again and he took it as a yes. "Good. At least one of us is." Stringing a rope through Cupid's nose ring, he led him to the cart.

"Good old Cupid, your ignorance is your saving grace," Antonio said. "Do you realize you're braver than many residents of this town? You're so easy to handle once a rope is put through your nose ring, everyone assumes you are a weakling. But who's the one cowering in their pen this dawn? Not you. If you do your part, I'll do mine. Deal?"

Antonio nudged Cupid with the whip and his water buffalo lurched forward. The cart wheels clattered on the uneven dirt road, making a loud racket. Windows opened ever so slightly, letting out light from within huts. Neighbors watched his progress. Antonio waved, but no one waved back. They shut their windows, even more tightly, it seemed. After all, ghosts were out that night.

Ghosts. All of a sudden, Antonio's knees felt as soft as sticky rice.

He reminded himself of his mission: to find the home of the *langbuan*, so he could destroy it and help the town get rid of *langbuan* forever. And then he could win the reward and pay off his debts. If there was some prize money left over, he could get himself his own record player.

Get a grip on yourself. You still owe the tricycle drivers money.

Antonio hummed his favorite Perry Como songs until he thought even Cupid seemed to join in. His water buffalo made little grunting noises which meant he was happy. Antonio was glad. He certainly did not want a grumpy water buffalo for a sidekick if he had to launch a defense against evil creatures. The thought caused him to stop humming abruptly. Maybe he *did* want a grumpy water buffalo after all.

Once in a while, Antonio thought he saw movement above him, but when he looked, whatever it was, was gone. He tapped the amulet in his hand and smiled.

At Jose's house, Antonio knocked on the window. Jose opened it an inch and motioned for Antonio to come closer. "I changed my mind," Jose said.

"Too late."

"I really don't want to die. I have a math test next week."

"Just think, if you die, you won't ever have to take a math test." Antonio held up one of the shell amulets. "But this will protect you from the *langbuan*."

"That's the amulet? A shell necklace? What, you poke their eyes with it?"

"Stop joking and come out now. Or don't. Just make up your mind!"

"I'm coming," Jose grumbled. Carrying a lantern, he climbed out of his window and put on the necklace. "Do you think the *langbuan* would attack me first because I'm taller?"

Antonio flicked the reins. "I hope so."

Moths danced around the lantern light, which illuminated the ruts in the dirt road. Jose caught a moth in his hands, then let it go. "Did I tell you that Grace and I happened to be in the same dance together?" he asked. "And that we danced and I walked her home?"

"As in Grace Mijares?"

"I really didn't want to dance with her," Jose said. "She practically *forced* me. I told her, 'You know, my friend Antonio is a better dancer.'"

Antonio chuckled. "I don't like Grace anymore."

"Really?" Jose grinned. "You mean I can actually ask her out and not have to feel guilty?"

"Yes."

"Wait. Did you change your mind because of Yolly? I thought she was trouble. Isn't she the one that has a rabid dog?"

"That's all true. But it's different now."

"Good! That simplifies things. Now I only have to sneak around Grace's father!"

They moved quickly through the empty streets to the road that led up to the mountain trail. To the cave which Mang Dennis, the grave-digging parishioner, described. Antonio had gone up earlier in the day to see where and how far the cave was.

Destroy the graves, destroy the lair.

Cupid pulled the cart up the mountainside slowly but surely. When they reached the top of the mountain, the horizon began to welcome dawn. First-light seeped through like fizzy soda escaping from a shaken bottle of Royal Tru Orange, its bottle cap pried open so very slowly.

That meant they had precious little time to chase after the *langbuan*. It meant they had to work fast. Antonio was thinking these very important thoughts when he saw the man standing in the middle of the road. He reined Cupid to a stop.

"Why are we stopping?" Jose asked.

"This man might need our help."

"What if he's a *langbuan*?"

"Do you see any wings?" Antonio greeted the man: "Good morning!"

The man raised his arm slowly, as though he was weak from exhaustion. Meanwhile, Cupid snorted and stomped.

"By chance sir," Antonio said as Cupid lurched about,

"have you seen any *langbuan*?"

The man pointed behind him.

"Thank you!" he said. "Can we repay your kindness by offering you a ride?"

"Let's take care of the *langbuan* before we do service projects, shall we?" Jose said.

Suddenly, Cupid shook his head so wildly that the reins got caught around one of his horns. Antonio took his eyes off the man for just a second to see to the snarled reins. When he looked up again, the man had disappeared.

"Where did he go?" he asked Jose.

"He was just right there," Jose said.

Antonio felt a strong breeze. Something caught his eye, to the right, just above his head. Slowly, he looked up. A *langbuan*, his wings unfurled and his rotting face oozing disgusting liquid, hovered above.

Antonio could only think of one thing. *Retreat!*

"I WON'T BE NEEDING a ride, thank you, son," the *langbuan* said.

Antonio couldn't breathe, couldn't think, couldn't move. There was Papa, hovering, his burnt shreds of skin peeling down his exposed arms. The wind wafted the smell of smoldered rot.

Antonio felt Jose elbow him hard in the ribs, and he blinked, gasping. Papa grinned, his brows lowering, a snarl escaping. This was his father no longer, but a demon.

"Remember our plan," Antonio whispered to Jose.

"We have one?" Jose whispered back.

"Go!" He shoved Jose out of the cart, still whispering. "Blow up the cave!"

Jose scampered away.

Shaking hard, Antonio gripped Cupid's rope. "Are you cursed for killing Mang Fermin?" Antonio asked Papa.

"No one welcomed me at the pearly gates, so to speak," Papa said, "to show me my record of misdeeds."

"But did you kill him?" Antonio persisted. "I have to know."

"Yes."

"Why, Papa?"

GHOST MOON NIGHT

"Why did you work for Bubuy?" Papa countered.

"That's not even the same thing!" Antonio cried.

"It's still a sin. I've seen other *langbuan*. People I thought had lived good lives. Few will escape the fate of the *langbuan*. Not even you son, so why even be righteous and try?"

"That's not what they teach us at church."

"Religion won't prevail," Papa said. "You have my blessing to sin as much as you want. As a *langbuan*, you still get hungry and thirsty, but you grow in strength each time you draw warmth from a human. You have special powers." He flapped his wings slowly. "Flying is ecstasy, my son."

"And misery!" Antonio countered. "You will never be free. On Ghost Moon Night, you will always be a *langbuan*. Out to destroy others."

"Just think," Papa said, "no farm chores. One night a month, we just fly around and visit villagers. Or talk to our children, like we're talking right now."

"And maim, kill, and steal souls! I'd rather be a farmer any day than be a slave to Satan."

Papa flew lower. Closer. "How I'd have loved for you to say you love to farm when I was alive. As it is, I don't want you to be a farmer. Join me, Antonio."

Antonio raised the lantern. "No, Papa. I won't."

Papa flapped his wing and knocked the lantern out of Antonio's hand. The lantern fell on the ground and shattered. The flame spread quickly. Papa scooped dirt from the ground and smothered the fire.

"That light won't do you any good now," Papa said, grinning.

Antonio held up his arms to ward off Papa's attack. At the very last second, Papa bounced off, repelled.

"What?" Papa sputtered. "You have my amulet?"

"You had it around your neck when you died," Antonio said. "That's what you went into the fire to save, right? How ironic that it's what you died for."

"Antonio!" Jose shouted. "Help!"

Papa kept a respectful distance as Antonio drove Cupid towards Jose's voice. Dozens of *langbuan*, their wings flapping briskly, hovered over Jose, who stood at the mouth of a cave, a lantern throwing an arc of light at his feet. Antonio jumped out

283

of the cart and joined him.

"It works," Jose said, holding up the pendant, "but I don't like having them gather 'round like this."

"I'll ward them off while you throw the dynamite in," Antonio whispered. "You're sure there are graves in there?"

"I looked, yes! I stopped counting at fifty!"

Papa joined the hovering *langbuan*. "You silly boys. You think a small amulet and a measly lantern can save you from all of us?"

The *langbuan* pressed in on them. Antonio turned every which way, holding up the pendant.

Jose said, "He has a good point."

"Don't let them intimidate you," Antonio said.

"*Hoy!*" Jose cried. Antonio turned. A *langbuan* held a bundle of dynamite in her hands. Jose lunged for it.

"Jose," Antonio said. "Hand me that lantern."

When Jose did so, Antonio raised it and Papa laughed. "Pathetic child. That might stop us if your fuel wasn't running out..."

The flame *had* grown dim. Suddenly, Antonio threw the lantern onto the ground. This time, the flames set the grasses on fire quickly. The *langbuan* shrank back.

"Let's go, Jose!" Antonio said, running towards Cupid and the cart.

"But the dynamite?"

"Leave it!"

Antonio turned. Some of *langbuan*'s clothes had caught on fire, and they flapped around like panicked birds. The one *langbuan* who had taken the dynamite from Jose dropped the bundle.

"Quick, Cupid," Antonio said, whipping his water buffalo. "Get off the mountain! Get off..."

A series of deafening booms made the mountain shudder. The reins slipped from Antonio's hands as the force launched him into the air and sent him tumbling, tumbling down a ravine. Jose followed shortly after, landing next to Antonio.

"Well," Jose groaned. "I'll admit, that was more exciting than math class."

The ravine wasn't too deep but it had a sheer drop, so the two couldn't climb up easily. Antonio whistled and Cupid peered over the edge. *Langbuan* weren't flying around.

"Lower your reins, Cupid!" Antonio said.

"Like Rapunzel, except smellier," Jose said, as they each took a rein and climbed out of the ravine.

Antonio patted his water buffalo on the head. "Good boy," he said. Then he stood still, taking stock of their surroundings. A crater now stood in place of the cave. Bits and pieces of the *langbuan* lay scattered about.

Papa...? He looked closely, but couldn't really tell. They were all pretty decimated.

And then Jose pulled him up and hugged him until he almost couldn't breathe.

68

November
Five hours after sunset, 11:00 p.m., Ghost Moon Night

A MONTH PASSED AFTER the massive explosion on Mount Dasalin.

The following Ghost Moon Night, at eleven o'clock, all the village windows and doors in Dasalin remained bolted. Except for one.

Antonio stood by his bedroom window and watched the horizon with his window slightly open. This bedroom window was in a house in the middle of town. Mama had managed to scrounge up enough money so she and Antonio could rent their own place.

Minutes ticked by. A half hour. Another hour. The night sky had no moon. Neither did it have *langbuan*. Antonio kept the amulet in his pocket but didn't put it on. Then he left his room, unbolted the front door and stepped outside.

He stood there for several minutes. Watching. Waiting. Confirming. And, when he was sure, smiling.

Slowly, windows and doors opened. Someone came out, one with a lantern, turning this way and that. Someone else, and another, came out, without lanterns. By the time an hour had passed, families streamed into the street to witness the miracle, hugging each other, crying and laughing.

"The curse is broken!" someone shouted.

Villagers swarmed around Antonio and bore him on their shoulders while cheering his name.

People lined the streets, waving handkerchiefs in an impromptu parade that featured Antonio and Jose in a cart pulled by Cupid. Jose had come home and stayed overnight to make sure the curse was broken.

"Aren't you missing a math test for this?" Antonio asked Jose.

"Yes," Jose said, looking glum.

Tito Oscar hugged both boys, while Tita Alice and the girls embraced them, too. Aling Mila handed them ice-cold bottles of Sarsi. Nando Nakpil sat in his tricycle and honked his horn. Father Sebastian smiled and waved, while nearby, Mrs. Silva collected money for a new altar fund. Mr. Mijares almost smiled, while his wife patted Antonio's shoulder like he was her favorite nephew. Yolly's eyes shone as she waved at him.

Timo, on the other hand, looked like he had severe indigestion. "Jose helped him," Timo grudgingly pointed out, but people heckled and drowned out his words. Tandang Lino had a partial scowl, too. Or maybe that was how he looked like normally. Which could be forgiven on that day. Antonio was too happy to allow anyone to spoil it for him.

The *langbuan*, gone forever!

The crowd got rowdier as they neared the church. The constable had to repeatedly tell people to please back off and give the heroes room. Children showered Cupid with flowers. Their parents darted forward just to touch Antonio's hand or arm with their handkerchief.

Finally, Antonio reined Cupid to a stop at the church courtyard. Here, the applause, the shouts, were deafening. Father Sebastian came forward with a jar of money. "Thank you," he said. "You can split the money however you want."

Jose grabbed and held it away from Antonio's reach. "Why should I share?"

"Because if you don't, the tricycle drivers won't get their money and you'll have to answer to Mrs. Silva."

Jose saw her just then, and quickly shoved the jar back at Antonio.

Mama and Antonio left their house to catch the midnight Mass just as the bells tolled. Normally, Midnight Mass was held around Christmas, but Father Sebastian decided to hold one this Ghost Moon Night as a gesture of thanks to God.

Paputok, fireworks, rivaled New Year's Eve's. In the main plaza, smoke clouded the air. Someone lit a *sinturon ni* Judas, or Judas belt, setting off a rapid gunfire sound. Children twirled *lusis,* and the sparkler left mesmerizing, circular trails. Some blew into brightly-colored *turotot.*

Mrs. Sandoval and Timo sold fireworks in a booth on the street. She beckoned for Antonio to come over. "Here are some fireworks," she said, handing him a bagful of little *redentador.*

"Thanks, Mrs. Sandoval," Antonio said, "but I don't have money."

Timo said, "He's right, Ma, he can't afford it."

"Hush, Timo." To Antonio, she said, "it's free. Just as a thank you for all the business you've sent my way this Ghost Moon Night. Were it not for you, I wouldn't be selling this much merchandise."

"Alright," Antonio said, stuffing the bag in his pocket. "Thanks."

"*Hoy.*" Timo barked. "Tell Jose …if he breaks Grace's heart, I'll beat him up."

Yolly, dressed in a yellow skirt and matching blouse, met Antonio and his mother at the church entrance.

"You look pretty," Antonio said, squeezing her hand. She smiled and squeezed his hand right back.

"And you look…dirty." She wrinkled her nose.

"Sorry," he said, glancing at the pants he forgot to change. "I live a farmer's life now."

Father Sebastian smiled at Antonio from the pulpit. How Antonio admired the priest. Had it not been for him, their town would still be cowering on Ghost Moon Night. Antonio covered Yolly's hand with his and there it stayed throughout Mass.

Ah, life couldn't be more perfect.

After Mass, Antonio, Mama and Yolly found Tito Oscar and Irene waiting at Antonio's house with a mouth-watering roasted *litson*, or suckling pig. Ridding the village of the curse was reason for celebration, Tito Oscar decided. Mama brought out a plank of wood, wiped it down and set it on the dining table. The pig fit perfectly on it. Lolo Sonny stayed up late to join in the festivities. Mama gave him the first slice of *litson*. And the first pick of music on the record player.

"Have you seen your handiwork?" Tito Oscar asked Antonio. "I haven't seen this town come alive like this in a long time on such a dark night! Thanks to you!"

"Mind you, Oscar," Mama said, "you're going to make his head swell."

"Margarita, let him enjoy it while it lasts," Tito Oscar said. "It's not every day that a young man helps his town get rid of ghosts. Anyway, Antonio, I was wondering if you'd like to fish tonight. Just you and me. It's so dark the fish will bite all the quicker."

Antonio looked at Yolly, a question in his eyes.

"Go ahead," she said. "Catch me a big one."

After their curse-breaking feast, Tito Oscar took Antonio to his house to pick up fishing gear. A sleepy Irene tagged along and begged to come, but Tito Oscar said it was 3:00 *in the morning* and well past her bedtime. She pouted a little, then hugged Antonio good night. Tito Oscar and Antonio went to the dock and boarded an outrigger boat. Then they launched out to sea.

For an hour, they fished in contented silence. In the distance, Antonio could see the village still lighting up the sky with fireworks. What pretty formations they made, going on for several minutes, then dwindling.

"Antonio," Tito Oscar said.

Antonio turned.

Tito Oscar smiled. "I'm so proud of you. You've proven yourself a man. I've hesitated offering this, out of respect to your father, but I wanted to offer you something...something I've been thinking about for a long time."

69

"I WANT TO OFFER you a partnership in my business," Tito Oscar said.

Antonio stared. "Me, Tito Oscar?"

Tito Oscar nodded. "I'm not getting any younger, and I need to partner with an intelligent young man who can carry on my legacy."

"I...I don't know what to say."

"Say that you're honored. That you'll do it."

"Of course," Antonio said, his heart leaping with joy. "I'd be crazy not to."

"Then let's shake on it. By so doing, you give me your word to give your best to this partnership."

They shook hands. With a fishing pole in hand, and a business partnership with his uncle, life was looking good, indeed.

"Antonio," Tito Oscar said, "do you have any idea what I do for my business?"

"Catch fish?"

"Not just fish, but *lots* of fish."

"I know. I think it's amazing. Every time I stop by your fish stand at the market, I notice that you have twice as many as the other vendors. What's your secret?"

"Do you really want to know?"

Something in Tito Oscar's voice made Antonio stare, but his uncle was only his usual, smiling self.

"Sure," Antonio said. "If I'm going to be a partner, I might as well start learning all there is to know."

"Well, first, I fish in waters that don't have a lot of competition. Second, I fish efficiently. I use the best equipment I can lay my hands on. And third, I employ a good crew."

"Should I be taking notes?" Antonio joked.

"No, there's no need for that. You'll soon learn it by heart." Again, that odd-sounding voice. Tito Oscar set down his pole and crouched down by a pile under a tarp. "What do you think is under this, Antonio?"

"Fish?" he guessed.

"No. Guess again." Tito Oscar flicked back the tarp and held up a bottle full of what looked like granules, and a long piece of string.

Antonio stared at it. "A firework?"

Tito Oscar grinned. "Dynamite."

Antonio's fishing pole fell on the boat floor in a clatter. "What?"

"One can lose a hand over this. Like your neighbor Arnell did."

Antonio looked at the bottle, then at Tito Oscar.

"Your neighbor Arnell didn't know it, but he worked for me," Tito Oscar said. "I have very loyal men who do my recruiting. And training. Arnell didn't follow instructions."

"I don't understand," Antonio said, backing up slowly."Why?"

"I gave you my reasons." Tito Oscar picked up Antonio's fishing pole. Antonio accepted it with cold, clammy hands.

"Do you know when the best way is to fish efficiently without competition and with a loyal crew?" Tito Oscar asked.

Antonio shook his head.

"On Ghost Moon Night."

"But what about the *langbuan*? How did you manage to fish outside?"

"I have an amulet." Tito Oscar pulled out a seashell pendant from behind his shirt. "Does this not look familiar?"

Antonio instinctively touched his shirt, feeling for the pendant. Then he remembered, it was in his pocket. "Papa had one, and you had one, too!" he murmured.

"As did Fermin and Mad Juana." Tito Oscar smiled. "There are four of these, crafted from a spell given to your Lolo Sonny by the pirates who cursed our town seventy-five years ago. As a young boy, he tried to save the pirates and earned their eternal gratitude.

"That same gentleness allowed me freedom. I got away with a lot of misdeeds as a child and teen, mainly because your Lolo Sonny wouldn't discipline me. He sent me away to other relatives a few times, but finally, I was old enough he just let me return and live my life.

"I studied the *langbuan*. Their habits and powers. I realized that I could very well harness those powers for a lucrative fishing business. Papa's always been protected. But I took it one step further. Built my wealth. I asked my father for the amulets on the pretext of protecting my family."

Antonio trembled. "I wasn't surprised to find Mang Fermin's journal and see he knew something about Ghost Moon Night. But you, Tito Oscar?"

"Oh, so you saw *my* journal?"

"It was yours?"

"I gave it to Fermin so he could read the instructions. He never could remember. Nor was he dependable. He wanted to do his own thing. Selling that mabolo orchard was the biggest mistake of his life. I couldn't convince him otherwise, and he even threatened to expose me. He got greedy and wanted more money. By framing Mad Juana, we got rid of both liabilities. The fool was so anxious to sell the orchard to the lumber plant. Now look where that brought us. A denuded forest and no more roosting places the *langbuan* hosts – the bats.

"Papa knew, and yet he didn't say anything about it."

Tito Oscar nodded. "He helped me get my dynamite materials, like the fertilizer."

"He always set aside bags for you at the start of planting season," Antonio said, remembering.

"Yes, it was more discreet that way. No one questions why a farmer has to buy fertilizer bags by the dozens."

GHOST MOON NIGHT

Antonio's world felt topsy-turvy, like he didn't know which way was up. "So now that the *langbuan* are gone, what are you going to do?"

Tito Oscar smiled. "That's the thing. They aren't gone."

Antonio felt his blood freeze. "What do you mean? I destroyed the cave!"

"My dear gullible Antonio. That parishioner blabbed about the cave and the graves for the *langbuan*, he works for me."

"He lied to the priest!"

"Sometimes, people aren't as they seem. I would never have guessed, for example, that you'd work for someone like Bubuy. At any rate, you blew up the wrong cave." Tito Oscar turned his face towards the village. "The *langbuan* will now possess the *kuding*. Clever, don't you think? No one would dare hurt these sacred birds. Tandang Lino would never allow it. Which allows me to expand the curse in this region."

"Region?" Antonio echoed.

Tito Oscar nodded. "I want to expand my empire outside Dasalin into the bigger cities. Can you imagine hosts of rats? Or schools of fish? As a businessman, I'm always looking for ways to grow my business. Why stop at dynamite fishing? I figured I could make more amulets and send out a trusted circle of associates to break into warehouses while their wealthy owners are safely in their houses."

Antonio stood there in shock, but forced a smile on his face.

Tito Oscar turned his face towards the village. "Would you look at that? I do believe our neighbors' stash of fireworks is dwindling. That's too bad. How will they protect themselves now from *langbuan*?"

In Ghost Moon Night's feeble light, Antonio saw a flock emerge from the *kuding* cliffs and move in a thick cloud. *Langbuan*, dozens and dozens of them, headed inland.

70

MAMA. YOLLY. LOLO *Sonny!* Antonio lunged for the edge of the boat.

A hard blow knocked him backwards, making him see double as he landed next to the tarp. "What are you doing?" Tito Oscar growled.

"My family and friends," Antonio gasped, looking for a way around his uncle. "What have you done? Why didn't the *langbuan* come out until now? How do you control them?"

"I protect them and their habitat and they protect me. Tonight, they followed my bidding. I told them to wait, to lull the village into thinking you're all safe."

"Then for the love of all things holy, stop them, Tito Oscar, please! They'll kill Mama. They'll kill your father!"

"Your mother is smarter than most in this village. She'll get inside and she'll get my father inside. But either way, he won't be in this world much longer, and he has his own demons. He'd make an interesting *langbuan*, don't you think? When that happens, will you even want to destroy him?"

Antonio got up on his feet. "*Halimaw!*" Monster! He threw himself at Tito Oscar, knocking him to the boat deck. Antonio pounced, grabbing his uncle by the neck. Tito Oscar swung hard, hitting Antonio's ribs. Antonio held on for dear life, knowing to let go was death – to him and all the villagers. Tito Oscar hit and hit, but Antonio was desperate. Only when Tito Oscar weakened, did Antonio begin breathing. But that's when Tito Oscar's leg flew up, throwing Antonio against the side of the boat, half in and half out. He grasped at his uncle a moment before he felt himself being thrown overboard.

Sputtering to the surface, he started to swim to shore. He needed to warn the village.

"Funny," he heard Tito Oscar say. "You remind me of fish." Antonio looked back. In Tito Oscar's right hand, he held one of the bottles.

Antonio swam faster. And then he heard him say, "Stay back!"

Above Tito Oscar, *langbuan* swirled. A dozen landed on the boat deck, their wings clicking shut. "I have an amulet," Tito Oscar said, patting frantically at his neck. "Stay back!"

But Tito Oscar wouldn't find his amulet. It was in Antonio's hand. He'd yanked it off as he went over.

The creatures pressed in closer and closer.

"Wait," Tito Oscar said. "Wait!"

The *langbuan* waited a minute, then converged upon him, smothering his cries.

Wearing two amulets, galloped to the village on one of Tito Oscar's carriage horses. *Langbuan* watched his progress, but left him alone.

Hurry!

The streets that had pulsed with life earlier now sat eerily empty. *Was* he too late? Along the way, he passed corpses, their faces twisted in fear, fireworks scattered around their bodies.

And then he glimpsed a beautiful sight: the Lady of Miracles Church lit up from within as though from hundreds of candles. He got off the horse, pounded on the door while shouting, "Let me in! It's me, Antonio!"

The door opened to let him in. He entered and shut the door

quickly. He faced a chapel-full of angry parishioners.

Timo ran up to him and shoved Antonio to the floor. "Some hero you are!" Villagers crowded Antonio and threw questions at him.

Why are they back? How come you're alive? What are you going to do about them?

"I know you are all angry, as you should be," Antonio said, standing up. "I have answers. And we have another chance to *truly* destroy them forever."

"We did this once already," Jose said, detaching himself from the crowd. He looked upset. "Everyone's mad at me. For once, I don't have any brilliant answers."

Antonio clasped his hands and begged for another chance. "I know who is behind this. And I know now how we can destroy them!"

Someone said, "Don't …harm…the *langbuan*."

Antonio looked into Lolo Sonny's beseeching eyes and moved so he could stand over the pew where the old man sat.

"They need to be destroyed," he told his grandfather.

"Just spirits…who made mistakes…"

"They kill people, Lolo Sonny. Tito Oscar had an arrangement with them. Now, they're on their own, and who knows what they will do? When the curse is gone, their spirits will be free."

"I… know," Lolo Sonny whispered. Tears welled in his eyes. "It's… time. Guitar music…*kundiman*…play it and they… will stop."

"Wait," Antonio said. "You mean music will destroy them, Lolo Sonny?"

"*Kundiman*. I played it…they left me alone. Didn't hurt… me."

Antonio hugged his grandfather. "Thank you!"

Turning to the crowd, he said, "We need to fight them, once and for all. Doesn't *anyone* believe me?"

There was silence, and then Mama stepped forward. "I believe you."

Father Sebastian and Yolly said, "Me, too."

Antonio's chest swelled, grateful. Then he turned to Jose. "And you, Jose?"

Jose sighed. "Yes, I do." Then he pulled out his amulet.

"Aren't you glad I kept this? I will help you. But this is it, alright?"

"Thank you!" Antonio said. He embraced Mama, shook the priest's hand and put Tito Oscar's amulet around Yolly's neck, his finger lingering on her cheek. Then he scanned the chapel. "Is Jopet Mijares here?"

When Grace's brother raised his hand, Antonio asked, "Can you drive your jeep? We need it to go up to the cliffs."

Jopet handed Antonio the keys. "Here, take it."

Tandang Lino stood in the back. "Why do you need to go up to the cliffs?"

"We want to destroy the actual *langbuan* lair," was all Antonio said.

On his way out, Antonio glanced towards the stained glass windows, relieved to see that metal reinforced them. And then he left the chapel, followed by Jose.

The pair mounted the horse and galloped towards the river.

"Where are we going?" Jose asked.

"We'll get Jopet's jeep, the record player, and some fishing nets from Tito Oscar's."

"And the plan is?"

"We'll block their little nests on the upper cliff, and that main nest. Play some music. Let's hope dawn comes soon."

At the Mijares estate, they found some unused fireworks and lighters at an abandoned picnic and loaded them in the back of the jeep.

"Fireworks and jeeps," Jose said. "Just think, someday, I will be marrying into this fun family."

Antonio thought of Mrs. Mijares. "Good luck with that." He threw the record player in the back seat beside a box of super-rockets that Jopet had stashed.

"We'll never make it up to the *kuding* cave in time," Jose said, gazing up at the lightening sky.

"Yes, we will," Antonio said, mostly to convince himself.

Once in the jeep, Jose began fiddling with the instruments. "Now which one makes this thing go?" he wondered out loud. He tried a gear, killing the engine. Starting the ignition again, he tried a couple more gears until they finally moved. He also found the radio button and played some Elvis.

"We're going backwards," Antonio pointed out.

"Shh. I can't concentrate."

"Just please don't ruin the jeep before the *langbuan*'s had a try at it."

"You mean at the lair?"

"No, the one bearing down on us!"

Antonio was ready to kick at the *langbuan* who tried to swipe at him, but the *langbuan* just reared back, hissing. Jose revved the engine and gunned the gas pedal, making the jeep lurch and careen wildly onto the road.

"Can't you go faster?" Antonio shouted.

"I'm going as fast as I can!" Jose shouted back.

Somewhere along the way, they lost the *langbuan*. They sped to Tito Oscar's house, stopped for just a second and grabbed all the fishing nets they could find. Several minutes later, the jeep roared on, bumping and jostling its way up the mountain until they reached the *kuding* cliff.

"Stop, right here!" Antonio said.

Jose slammed on the brakes, throwing both of them against the dashboard. They scrambled out, hauling the fish nets and covering the rock face. They placed large rocks on the net's edge to hold it firmly in place.

"There's another cave, on top of this cliff. If we cover that, they won't be able to hide anywhere else."

They reached the cave and draped the last net over it.

"Look," Jose said.

Above them, *langbuan* hovered, at least a hundred-strong, men and women dressed in burial clothes, the whiteness of their clothes contrasting terribly with their decaying faces. Antonio recognized many: *Mang* Baby, from down the street, whose nightly beatings of his wife were fodder for gossip;

298

Captain Guttierrez, the former *baranggay* captain who allegedly murdered a campaign opponent. Even the young woman who clerked at the bank.

They glared, teeth bared. Behind the creatures, the edge of the horizon was changing to a pinker tinge. Antonio's heart leaped. He could see dawn approaching, but they couldn't. Maybe, just maybe, he could trick them into defeat.

He grabbed the smaller fireworks they'd taken from the Mijares estate and gave some to Jose. "Light and toss!" he said. They lobbed lit fireworks at the monsters, slowing them down, until they ran out of ammunition. Then it was just the two of them between a legion of undead and their cave of safety.

The *langbuan* advanced, just as the horizon began to lighten. In a low voice, Antonio whispered instructions to Jose who ran to do as he was bid, disappearing behind the rocks near the cave. One of the *langbuan* detached himself from the group. Papa was more decomposed than the last time Antonio saw him.

"You keep disappointing me, son," he said.

"Can you blame me, Papa?" When his father came closer, Antonio brandished his pendant. "I have an amulet. You can't hurt me."

The pendant broke free from the necklace and fell to the ground, crumbling into dust. His father laughed as he stood right in Antonio's face.

"Fortunately," Antonio said, "I have another amulet." He took out the super rocket and lighter that he found in Jopet's jeep, jammed it into Papa's waistband and lit the fuse. Papa's smile faded and he tried to grab it, but he wasn't quick enough. The firework launched in the air, taking him with it. It exploded into a spectacular light show. A moment later, tufts of Papa's hair and a shred of his pants settled on the ground at Antonio's feet.

Antonio choked back tears as he realized what he had just done.

Papa! he screamed in anguish, inside. *Papa, forgive me!* He fell to his knees and sobbed.

"Antonio," Jose said.

"What?" Antonio raised his head.

"The fight's not over."

"Yes." Antonio took a deep breath and stood up. "Let's

finish it."

He ran to the jeep, turned the record player on, and put on the *kundiman* record. A half-dozen *langbuan* howled and chased them.

"It's not working!" Antonio said.

Jose looked at the *langbuan*. "I see that."

Some *langbuan* were now trying to remove the net covering the main cave.

"Jam this jeep down that cave," Antonio told Jose.

"The jeep won't fit on the ridge," Jose said. "We won't even make it to the cave."

"Yes, we will," Antonio yelled, hoping he was right. "And we'll keep the *langbuan* from re-entering. Just get it in!"

"You are crazy! We're going to die!"

"No, I'm brilliant," Antonio cried, jerking his door closed. "The jeep will catch on the walls of the cave where it narrows."

Still looking skeptical, Jose shifted into gear.

Antonio checked the horizon. It was turning a lighter shade of pink. "We haven't much time."

Jose took a deep breath. "Here goes nothing!"

They bounced toward the cave, the tires knocking rocks off the narrow ridge, the headlights making crazy arcs ahead. The two exchanged glances, and Antonio nodded. Jose closed his eyes and stepped on the gas pedal, the tires making a squealing noise. Then, there was a crash as the jeep tore through the fish nets and fell in the cave. With a horrible screeching sound, the jeep hit and got wedged into the entrance. It slipped once, raining rocks onto Antonio and Jose, who cringed in their seats. But then it held.

Antonio wasn't sure where up and down was. He slurred his next words: "I don't know how Jopet will get this jeep out."

Jose chuckled. "He likes fixing his jeep more than driving it."

Suddenly, the jeep rose, then fell.

"Tell me that's an earthquake," Jose said.

Angry hisses came from above, and a clawed hand tried to squeeze past the narrow opening between the cave lip and the jeep window. "I wish it *were* an earthquake," Antonio said.

Suddenly, swarms of *langbuan* attacked them. Arms, claws, like squid tentacles curling around Antonio's head and limbs.

GHOST MOON NIGHT

Each touch numbed his skin. Until he could hardly move.

"Jose! Use your amulet!"

"I lost it. It must have fallen when we tipped over."

Again, the jeep rocked back and forth. Antonio fell forward and hit the dashboard of the jeep, bumping the radio knob.

At the first notes of the familiar tune, a *kundiman* from his grandfather's childhood, Antonio felt a warmth come back into his body, his skin. The *langbuan* still touched and grabbed him, but he felt no pain. He kicked at the *langbuan* arms until some bones cracked and shattered.

"The music," he told Jose. "It's helping. Healing."

"You better believe it," Jose said. "For a while, I thought I was turning into a popsicle."

Suddenly, the jeep turned sideways. "Uh-oh," Jose said. "This doesn't feel right." The jeep creaked, shifted, and then creaked again.

Antonio held tight to the back of his seat. But it wasn't enough. As he started to slip down, he stretched out his leg and jammed it into a crack in the rock. He gritted his teeth as a sharp pain radiated from his shin.

"They're trying to tilt us in!" Jose said. "We'll die!"

"I'm sorry for getting you mixed up in this," Antonio said.

The jeep tilted some more. Antonio closed his eyes, bracing himself for the fall. Then, the *langbuan* shoved away from the jeep, flew up and away.

"What happened?" Jose said, craning his neck.

Light and warmth washed over them. Antonio grinned. "Dawn, my friend." Sunrise had arrived, yellow rays stretching forth to the heavens, like angel wings.

Above them, there was a terrible cacophony of screaming and screeching, a gust of wind from desperate battering of wings and a horrible, sickening odor of seared rotting flesh. Then a great sucking noise. One by one, the *langbuan* disappeared, their shreds of clothing falling empty, like angel wings. Interspersed with the sweet *kundiman* song on the radio.

Jose shimmied out of the jeep first, clinging onto the rocks with his long, lanky arms, and helped Antonio out of the cave.

"I never thought I'd love *kundiman* more than Elvis," Jose said.

"We did it!" Antonio whooped and yelled at the top of his

301

voice at the rising, glorious sun.

"We really did it this time!" Jose paused. "Didn't we?"

Antonio surveyed their little village below, scoured it for any sign of *langbuan* or their animal hosts. "I think so," he said.

Just as the jeep fell and crashed onto the cave floor below.

A FTER THE DESTRUCTION of the *langbuan*, Jopet's jeep stayed broken inside the cave. A monument to Antonio and Jose's heroism, the constable said, as news photographers took photos of the pair.

A monument to their insanity, Yolly begged to differ, as she leaned over Antonio, his leg stretched out in a cast on a hospital bed.

"Cripple," she said, smiling. She looked like she wanted to kiss him, but between Jose wiggling his eyebrows at them from the next bed over and a grim-looking Mr. Mijares standing behind her, it wasn't a good time. But he grabbed and kissed her anyway.

"You owe my family a jeep," Mr. Mijares told Antonio.

"I'll pay you back, sir," Antonio promised. "It'll take a while, of course."

"How about if you help me with my tricycle business instead? I need a new supervisor."

"I've actually thought about going to school in Manila.

Someone read about me in the newspaper and offered me a scholarship."

"But what about your farm?"

"Arnell will take care of it for Mama." Antonio looked at Yolly. "I have other reasons for going to Manila. My *girlfriend* is going to study there, too."

Yolly scrunched her face comically.

"*Uy*," Jose teased.

"My offer stands when you are done with school," Mr. Mijares said.

"Thank you, sir," Antonio said. "I really appreciate it."

"I didn't know you two were thinking of going to Manila!" Jose said. "That's great! It's going to be fun, you and Yolly, me and..." He glanced at Mr. Mijares and cleared his throat. "... anyway. Antonio and I can live at this boarding house I've heard about." He lowered his voice. "It's haunted."

"Haunted?" Yolly rolled her eyes.

Antonio smiled. "We'll see," he said. "We'll see."

While Father Sebastian sprinkled the cave with holy water, "just in case," Mrs. Silva collected altar donations. The *langbuan* didn't return, but the effort to collect money paid off. Within a year, Mrs. Silva got Father Sebastian a marble altar from Romblon. It promptly broke after he hit it during one impassioned sermon.

Tandang Lino died, revered like the *kuding* by many. Unlike the *kuding*, Tandang Lino did not get a *fiesta* named after him.

Mama opened the first ready-to-wear clothing store in Dasalin. It became so successful, she soon leased space in her store to the Sandovals.

Tita Alice and the girls sold their house and moved away. But Irene kept in touch. She eventually joined the Coast Guard, breaking up smuggling rings. Turns out Tito Oscar kept another journal, listing all his loyal men. They were all arrested.

Henry got married and opened a funeral parlor.

304

GHOST MOON NIGHT

Lolo Sonny lived another ten years and breathed his last breath while the record player played his favorite song.

As for Antonio, Yolly, Jose and Cupid, well, that's a wonderful story for another day.

THE END

GLOSSARY

Aling – Miss
Aray! – Ouch!
aswang – vampire
baranggay – basic form of government, equivalent to a village
Barong Tagalog – native dress of Filipino males
bibingka – sticky rice dessert
Dios mio – My God
Dong – an informal name to call a boy or young man
hay naku – Oh dear.
Gising na – Wake up
Hoy! – Hey!
kamiso de china – a shirt made of lightweight material
karitela – horse-drawn carriage
kukote – head
la panciteria – the noddle shop
litson – roasted pig, usually on a spit
lolo – grandfather
lola - grandmother
makikisuyo po – May I ask your help with…?
Mang – Mr.
mano – a gesture of respect that involves pressing the hand of an elderly against one's forehead
novia – girlfriend
paputok – firework
patintero – a street game similar to Red Rover
po – a respectful form of address for elderly or superiors
redentador – a type of firework
sabungan - cockfight
salakot – woven hat
sari-sari store – variety store

siesta – midday nap
sinturon – belt
Tao po! – a greeting shouted when a guest approaches someone's house
Tatay - father
turotot – trumpet
veranda – front porch
walis tingting – stiff broom made of twigs and bound together, usually for outdoor use

SPECIAL THANKS TO

My Heavenly Father, who blesses me with opportunities, blessings, ideas and energy every day.

Alauna Cowdell, Pamela Keller and Cristian Erickson, my very first critique buddies, for encouraging me to write about zombies by reading that first *Ghost Moon Night* draft. Your friendship has meant a lot to me over the years. A special mention to Cristian's husband, Jeff, who asked her to go to critique group so he could read the rest of the story. My phenomenal writer's group: Karen Hoover, Shanna Tull, Wendy Elliott and Michelle Jefferies, for introducing me to the wonderful wacky world of writers and LDStorymakers. Shirley Bahlmann, for telling me after that LDStorymakers First Chapter Contest to write the rest of the book and for doggedly asking me, "When are you publishing Ghost Moon Night?"

Jonene Ficklin, Editor Extraordinaire, for your friendship since that fateful writers retreat. Your brilliant edits asked all the questions I knew I should ask but didn't want to (to avoid more rewrites). You kept me going (at five a.m.!) when I thought I didn't have it in me to keep going and polished Antonio from stone to valuable gem. My cover artist, Mikey Brooks, and my formatter, E.M. Tippetts, for catching my vision and translating this novel into a beautiful work of art. Also Julie Bellon for the dead-on, killer-blurb!

Carol Buhler, who gave me my first detailed critique, without which this novel would not be what it is today. You taught me about revision just like you taught me horseback riding - through tough love!

My talented friends in Tooele Writers, who make me laugh as we've learned together. Amy Sandbak, for your generous friendship and for being such a good beta reader; Jennie Bennett, for the blurbage genius; and Laura Bastian, for the word count wars and advice. The generous authors on the Facebook page Author's Think Tank. My other beta readers, Joy Brady, Leslie Jenkins and Malu Norton for adding your perspective.

My parents, Carmelo and Celestina Punzalan, for introducing me to books and music, as well as for being my biggest fans. My siblings Joy and Lizor, for all those hours we spent making wax sculptures during black-outs and scaring each other silly with ghost stories.

My children - Sierra, Wesley and Sabrina - who inspire me to be a better person and mother through their Christ-like examples and putting family first. And for all the times that they've cooked dinner or hung laundry because "Mom is under deadline."

And last but not least, my sweet, amazing, incredible husband Drew, for letting me write, encouraging me to say "no" to even yet another "brilliant" project, and for saving us thousands of dollars in therapy bills.

Q&A
WITH *GHOST MOON NIGHT* AUTHOR
JEWEL ALLEN

Q. What inspired you to write *Ghost Moon Night*?

A. In 2008, I wanted to enter a first chapter contest at LDStorymakers Writer's Conference. I had just bought an electric typewriter and relished that exciting feeling of putting on a fresh sheet of paper. I knew I wanted the novel to be scary because I'm a sucker for creepy ghost stories. After I thought for a minute, this is what came out: "There's a ghost moon tonight."

I pictured a grandfather telling his grandson about the time when he was growing up and there was one night of the month without a moon, and ghosts came out. That first sentence didn't stay in the final manuscript. In fact, the point of view changed altogether, to the narrator's younger 17-year-old self, but I still like that first chapter. It takes me back to the nights in the Philippines when I would listen, wide-eyed, to elderly relatives telling a ghost story.

That first chapter won first place in the suspense division. As the prizes were being handed out, one of the judges said, "I want to know what happens next!" Well, as it was, there weren't any other pages to the story. I had to write on, thanks to that encouraging response, and just so I knew for myself what happened. Incidentally, I soon replaced the typewriter with a computer. I ran out of typewriter ribbon as the story grew.

Q. Is this autobiographical?

A. Um, no. For one thing, I'm not a boy. However, I drew

a lot from my experiences traveling to the rural provinces and visiting my relatives. One particular experience I remember was going to my best friend's province in Ilocos Sur and witnessing the funeral of a baby. It was a fishing village, and we watched the villagers carry the little coffin into the house from the beach under the moonlight. That image always stayed with me, and it played an important part in *Ghost Moon Night*. I do include a lot of references to the Philippine culture because I spent the first 15 years of my life there. I got homesick writing this novel.

Q. Are there really *langbuan* in the Philippines? A *kuding* festival?

A. *Langbuan*, as I imagined them, no. The word is a combination of the Tagalog words *walang* which means "none" and *buwan* which means "moon". But vampires and the undead are very much a part of the Philippine mythology. As for *kuding*, that's a made up name, but swallows do live in Philippine cliffs.

Q. I don't like gory horror novels. Is this gory?

A. Although there are some scary scenes in the book, this is not a slasher-type novel. You might want to check and make sure the house doors and windows are all shut tightly before reading *Ghost Moon Night*, however.

For more book trivia and Philippine goodies, visit
www.JewelAllen.com.

ABOUT THE AUTHOR

PHOTO CREDIT: TIFFANY HAWKE

Jewel Allen is an award-winning journalist, author and ghostwriter. Growing up in the Philippines, she lived through a lot of typhoons and power outages which led to her love of ghost stories told in candlelight. At 16, she came to Utah, roomed with her mom at Utah State University and earned a bachelor's degree in English. For the next two decades, she worked as a freelance journalist. Today she lives in Utah and runs a memoir publishing company, Treasured Stories, helping clients from start to published. She's been a lead singer for a rock band, loves sardines and anything that reminds her of the Philippines, and is happiest when she cooks Filipino food for her family and friends. For fun extras and updates, visit

www.JewelAllen.com.

This paperback interior was designed and formatted by

www.emtippettsbookdesigns.com

Artisan interiors for discerning authors and publishers.